PRAISE FOR *UNDER COLOR OF LAW*

"Harrowing evidence for Spike Lee's famous claim that everything that happens in America is about race."

—*Kirkus Reviews*

"Clark's ripped-from-the-headlines police procedural should make readers uncomfortable. It's a frightening, tragic tale."

—*Library Journal* (starred review)

"This is a smart, suspenseful police procedural with a timely plot."

—*Publishers Weekly*

"An absolutely riveting book that belongs in the pantheon of LA crime novels alongside Connelly's *The Black Echo*, Mosley's *Devil in a Blue Dress*, and Ellroy's *The Black Dahlia*. *Under Color of Law* is a landmine placed at the intersection of law enforcement, race, media, and politics by an author who clearly knows the volatile territory. I cannot wait to read the next Trevor Finnegan book."

—Jason Pinter, bestselling author of *Hide Away*

"Aaron Philip Clark's *Under Color of Law* is extraordinary. It's a police procedural with a conscience, as invested in examining how and why American law enforcement so often fails to uphold its mandate to protect and serve all people equally as it is in telling a compelling story. You'll read on for the mystery at its core, but you'll remember *Under Color of Law* long after the read for the things it will teach you about the challenges of being a good cop of color in the age of George Floyd and Breonna Taylor."

—Gar Anthony Haywood, Sh̶a̶m̶u̶s̶ a̶n̶d̶ A̶n̶t̶h̶o̶n̶y̶ A̶w̶a̶r̶d̶–̶w̶i̶n̶ning

seen

"Echoes of Richard Wright reverberate in Aaron Philip Clark's poignant and powerful series debut. *Under Color of Law* is a fearless and candid novel about the moral complexities of modern American law enforcement. Fans of Walter Mosley will gravitate to Clark's razor-sharp prose as he tells the story of a Black detective trying to solve the murder of one of the LAPD's own and, in the process, pursuing his own redemption."

—Brian Andrews, *Wall Street Journal* and international bestselling author

BLUE
LIKE
ME

Also by
Aaron Philip Clark

Trevor Finnegan series

Under Color of Law

Paul Little series

The Science of Paul
A Healthy Fear of Man

Stand-Alone Novels

The Furious Way

BLUE LIKE ME

AARON PHILIP CLARK

THOMAS & MERCER

Published by Thomas & Mercer, Seattle

www.apub.com

Amazon, the Amazon logo, and Thomas & Mercer are trademarks of Amazon.com, Inc., or its affiliates.

ISBN-13: 9781542039697
ISBN-10: 154203969X

Cover design by Rex Bonomelli

Printed in the United States of America

For my family. I'm sustained by your love and support.

CHAPTER ONE

Venice, California—not everything's a victim. Some places around here still cling to life: classic diners, coffee shops, dive bars, and timeworn lodges like the Surfside Motel, which hearkens back to the 1950s, when road-tripping families occupied rooms. Then came the free-loving bohemians and, now, dope-sick junkies selling sex for money and drugs. It's how the motel survives, kept afloat by a steady stream of sex workers and johns who rent rooms by the hour. Located north of Lincoln, blocks away from million-dollar homes, the motel is dismally kept, with white paint chipping from stucco and a decrepit sign advertising free cable TV.

I sit parked on Rose Court in front of a quick-change oil shop. The street is a sprawling graveyard of failed businesses. A neighborhood that's gone under. Ground zero for what could have been.

I surveil two LAPD officers from the driver's seat of my '68 Ford Falcon Futura. The Falcon doesn't raise suspicion. It's forgettable. Primer gray with speckled rust, or what gearheads call "cancer." It's the type of car that blends in on any street. If I park in a blue-collar neighborhood, the Falcon is rarely the only classic on the block needing a paint job. In wealthier neighborhoods, it's easily a restoration project for a collector. In Venice, it fits in either category.

Through my camera's Zeiss lens, I watch Officers Chris Garvey and Brian Yoshida sit inside their parked black-and-white outside Room Sixteen. Garvey gets out of the unit. He's a tall white man with a physique that says he prefers weightlifting over cardio. Yoshida, a dark-haired man, swings the passenger-side door open and vomits. Scoping the parking lot, Garvey doesn't look put off by his partner's nasty showing. He reaches into the back seat and pulls out a cuffed redheaded girl who looks barely old enough to buy cigarettes. He spins her to face the car, presses his pelvis against her backside, and grins. He moves her hair to the side and speaks into her ear. I don't need to be a lip reader to know his words repulse her. He pulls out another girl in cuffs; her hair is streaked hot pink and blue. He leans her against the car as well. Both girls look cold. One's shivering. The days run hot, but the nights can chill to the bone, especially for girls wearing tight-fitting bikini tops, denim shorts cut high above their thighs, and slip-on gum-soled sneakers made famous by skateboarding Z-Boys. I focus the lens on their legs, which are covered in sores and bruises. The girls look spent, sickly.

I snap three medium shots, adjust the lens for a close-up on the cops' faces, and take three more pictures. If I didn't know any better, I'd say the girls are everyday surfers, not an uncommon sight in an area known as the Ghetto by the Sea. Girls who spend their days lying on the beach, occasionally riding the waves and scoring coke. The thought of them turning tricks in bathrooms and motels wouldn't enter my mind.

Garvey uncuffs the girls and slips money into the redhead's back pocket. The girls walk into the motel's lobby. The officers get back into their patrol car, Garvey behind the wheel. When the girls return, they pass the black-and-white and walk upstairs to Room Eighteen. Garvey drives to the side of the building. I start the Falcon, pull out, and enter the motel's parking lot. The patrol car is parked near a dumpster, where someone has discarded a stained mattress and a mini fridge. I watch the officers get out, climb the stairs, and ready themselves for what awaits them in the room. They knock on the door, it opens. I snap pictures, a few dozen. They enter the room, the redhead shuts the door, and I know what comes next.

The shots aren't enough. Every private eye knows the casket doesn't close without the money shot.

I note two security cameras: one near the lobby's door, the other mounted on a wall and pointing toward the stairs. There's no way to be sure if they're functioning, but I always presume they are.

I adjust my hat's brim so it draws a heavy shadow over my face, lift the collar of my jacket to shield my neck and cheeks, and get out of the car, camera in hand. Walking upstairs, I can hear voices, giggles, and sensual moans. As I approach Room Eighteen, I reach for the door handle, hoping the redhead kept it unlocked. I turn it slowly and push. The door creaks, but I'm confident it's gone unheard, given the increasingly loud moans. The room feels like a humid morning, and there's a distinct smell. Unpleasant, ripe. Bodies are contorted, folded like origami on two queen-size mattresses. I squeeze my camera lens through the cracked doorway and gently press the red button. The light meter alerts me that the indigo glow from the TV isn't enough for full exposure.

Dammit. If only the girls had turned on the vanity light over the sink, I'd have something to work with. I set the camera to auto, aware the next shot will produce a flash. I've got two minutes, maybe three, once the pictures have been taken, before Garvey and Yoshida suspend their coitus and come after me. I push the button. There's a blinding white flare. The shutter rapidly opens and closes, taking several pictures a second. "What the hell?" Garvey says, pushing the naked girl off him. She shrieks, bouncing from the mattress to the floor. "Son of a bitch!" he yells, searching for his underwear buried in the sheets.

I take another picture of Garvey's ruddy face, slam the door, and run downstairs to the Falcon. Before getting in, I look back to see Yoshida with his gun drawn, making his way downstairs with Garvey close behind. Yoshida's agile in a way Garvey isn't and seems to slide down the steps as if they were greased with bacon drippings.

I steady my hand enough to turn the key in the ignition, gassing the Falcon and whipping through the parking lot toward Lincoln. The lifeblood of the Falcon is speed, and when I drive above ninety-five miles per hour, it feels like I'm teetering on a cliff's edge, dancing on a high mountain . . .

Garvey and Yoshida pick up speed in my rearview—no lightbar or sirens, just the headlights of their Crown Vic. I've seen many desperate men in my work. I know what they're capable of. The photos on the camera's memory card mean the end of their careers—besmirchment, their names in newspapers and spoken on prime-time news. That alone is worth putting me in a body cast, or worse.

Traffic is up ahead, a sea of brake lights. I'd be a fool to lead the cops on a chase through Venice. I can't give them a reason to shoot me. I turn right down an alley that runs behind a shopping center. I drive the alley until it ends and make a right onto a street leading into a residential community. The road snakes through a quiet, well-lit neighborhood where the streets have names like Maple and Chestnut. Luxury cars sit in driveways. A neighborhood watch sign is posted below a surveillance camera mounted on a streetlamp pole. Clearing a speed bump, I check my rearview.

Nothing. I keep driving north.

I reach a stop sign, check the rearview again, and see headlights hovering a few streets behind. It may be Garvey and Yoshida. It's best to move in darkness. I cut the headlights, ease up on the brake, and gas the car forward. I need to get to Lincoln. I roll down the window and listen for the hard squeal of a braking semitruck, a barrage of car horns, the bass-heavy rattle of a subwoofer. Anything that tells me I'm close to Lincoln, the bustling street that runs through the Westside.

The car's headlights grow brighter in the rearview. I run the stop sign, then another, and another, creating distance between me and the trailing vehicle. As I approach another stop sign, I see the lights of a gas station across the street. Have I meandered my way back to Lincoln? I flick my headlights on and pull into traffic once the way is clear. I check my six, then left and right for Garvey and Yoshida. I bully my way to the left turn lane and drive into the gas station on a stale yellow. I slow the Falcon to a rumble, looking for a place to hunker, anywhere without much light or many people. It's a busy night, so my options are limited. I park inside the car wash bay, turn off the engine and headlights, and wait. The bay has a lemony redolence designed to mask the harsh odor of cleaning agents. I relax my hands on the steering wheel, take a few calming breaths, and listen to the echo of a water drip. I hear the chortle of a motorcycle, the beep of an alarm, but no chirping sirens or bullhorn.

I turn on the police scanner and roll through channels, listening for chatter from Garvey and Yoshida. What if they get impatient and put out an APB for my vehicle? I wouldn't make it six blocks before being pulled over. If I'm brought in, then what? I've got no friends left on the force, but there must be some people who still respect me enough to listen to what I'd have to say. But I wouldn't need to say much, only show their sergeant or captain the candid photos depicting two of LAPD's finest bare-assed with sex workers.

That's why Garvey and Yoshida will want to handle me themselves.

I hear the wail of the police siren. There's no way to know if it's Garvey and Yoshida, but I stand by. I turn on my smartphone's hotspot and switch on my camera. I upload the photos to my data cloud. The siren is getting louder, closer. I dig a finger deeper into my shirt collar, feel a band of sweat around my neck. If it's them, all I can do is hope they aren't canny enough to circle the car wash, because, if they do, they're sure to see the tail of the Falcon jutting out from the dark tomb of the wash bay.

I sit white-knuckled, stewing in sweat for ten minutes until I can't hear the sirens anymore. I start the Falcon, press the gas pedal slowly, and pull out of the wash bay. I round to the front of the gas station, exit onto Lincoln, and drive easy for half a mile. I merge onto the 10 headed east, torpedo into the fast lane, roll down the window, and breathe cool air. The wind sweeps over the car's hood, whistling violently, sounding how I'd imagine a chorus of angels wailing over this savage city would. What happens when God loses patience with us?

My mother said the Good Book speaks of fire next time. Makes sense; fire is a cleansing thing. New life can grow from ashes. If Sarada knew these kinds of thoughts swirled around in my head, she'd worry my depression was returning. But I know what that darkness feels like, and this is something different.

The Falcon pushes through the city of thirteen million souls, rumbling along the freeway's pummeled pavement. Some call LA a hopeless gutter, but I'm anchored to it. I tune the radio to an alternative station. Nirvana's "Lithium" plays loud. I think about Kurt Cobain—his poetry and how he died. He conquered death. Circumvented it by making music that lives forever. And I wonder if I'll do something so exceptional, so indelible, that when I'm gone, people will think of me as something other than a disgraced ex-cop, another failed son of the city.

———

It's after midnight when I park the Falcon in the garage of the two-bedroom townhouse that Sarada and I share. It's tucked away in Sierra Madre, a hillside community north of Pasadena. It's quiet, with winding hiking trails leading deep into the San Gabriel Mountains. We probably couldn't afford its tranquil comfort if it weren't for Sarada's successful bakery, Spinners, and my wrongful-termination settlement with the LAPD. Add to that what Bergman pays me for taking pictures of dirty cops, and we're living well. But it doesn't mean I don't worry. As a black man in Sierra Madre, I often think it's only a matter of time before a resident who doesn't think I belong in the neighborhood calls the police out of fear or vindictiveness. Sarada seems less concerned. She tends to keep to herself, never complaining about living in the community. But she harbors little enthusiasm for our neighborhood.

I enter the townhouse, make my way upstairs, and stand in the doorway to the master bedroom. Sarada is buried under the covers. Watching her sleep, snug under the duvet, can be so poignantly beautiful that it isn't until I lie next to her, listening to her heartbeat, her body pressed against mine, that I know I'm not dreaming. It's frightening to love someone so much that words seem moot. But Sarada's love sustains me.

I kick off my boots and undress to shower. The water streams from the rain head. As I look in the mirror, slowly being consumed by steam, I notice that the face looking back at me isn't aging well. It's drawn, worn out. I rub my hand over the long scar running down my lower back, the thick, raised skin. A keloid, a permanent reminder of the day that I nearly died two years ago. My actions as a cop had sent me down a treacherous path, and lately I've felt like my new occupation could mean history is repeating itself.

After my shower, I towel off and throw on a pair of lounge pants and a T-shirt. I enter the room adjacent to our suite that we use as a study and painting studio. The room is large; the walls are adorned with oil and acrylic paintings, some abstract, others still lifes. It's become a gallery of healing, each painting symbolizing a step in my recovery. There are landscapes painted during a health retreat, acrylic renderings of the Ojai Valley and Big Sur, with sweeping strokes of tan and umber that form pristine beaches and sunlit cliffsides. There are portraits of a radiant Sarada, and one of my father as a young LAPD officer that I painted from a photograph. The only things revelatory about his face are his eyes, which showcase a vulnerability and sadness he works to keep hidden.

French doors lead from the study to an enclosed balcony that has been converted into a sunroom, where Sarada and I drink tea and bask in the beauty around us. As lovely as she says my paintings are, they pale compared to the enchanting view of the mountains. I look forward to winter rains because it means the mountains will be snowcapped. Sometimes, high winds blow flurries from the peaks, and I forget for a few early morning hours that we live in Southern California.

I sit in my ergonomic chair, an indulgence after having suffered aches from poor office chairs throughout my entire law enforcement career. My computer is an upgrade as well. Two monitors bookend my laptop screen. Sarada calls it my command center. I must admit it does look official. I take the memory card from my camera and push it into a slot on the laptop, then drag the photos from the night's surveillance into a folder labeled "Garvey_Yoshida_Nov2016." Even though the photos are uploaded to the cloud, I'm old school. I still like to keep them on an external hard drive in case the cloud storage fails. As the photos are copied to the folder, I open the FBI's Most Wanted page in a browser window. Amanda "Boston" Walsh, pictured in her police uniform, sticks out among the civilians in casual clothes and correctional jumpsuits. Her photo is third in the top row of the Ten Most Wanted Fugitives. No expression, not even a hint of a smile. Did she have the heart of a killer then, or was it something she grew into?

Under her photo, there's a litany of charges: Unlawful Flight to Avoid Prosecution, Murder in the First Degree, Conspiracy to Commit Murder in the First Degree, Murder in the Second Degree under Color of Law. Boston has been on the run for two years, and if she's ever caught, it'll mean life in prison or death row. She deserves the latter.

"Rough night?" Sarada asks.

I turn to see her leaning in the doorway and dressed in a pearly silk robe, hair wrapped in a black scarf, plum skin glistening with shea butter. "Sorry if I woke you," I say.

"I could barely keep my eyes closed," she says. "Always too restless when you're out there." She rests her hand on my shoulder. "You OK?"

"Just been thinking . . ."

"About the election?" she asks. "Have to admit, I'm a little worried, too. Might be good that we'll be out of the country."

"No," I say. "About Brandon Soledad."

"Oh," she says, stepping closer to move behind my chair. She works her thumbs into my shoulders. "And that means thinking about Walsh?"

"Unfortunately."

"Should you give Dr. Angell a call? It's been a while." She digs deeper into my traps. "God, you're tense."

"I'll make an appointment," I say, watching the download progress bar on the screen. "Might just be the case I'm working . . ."

"LAPD again?"

"Yes."

"It'll all be a distant memory soon," she says, kneading the knots in my back. "Have you figured out what you'll do while I'm training?"

"Not sure," I say. "Might take a painting course."

Sarada nods enthusiastically. "That would be wonderful, babe."

I know it's what she wants to hear, but the truth is I've got no idea how to spend my time in Rungis, France. I haven't done much to prepare, aside from purchasing a wool coat and the *Idiot's Guide to Speaking French*. "But don't worry about me. I'll figure something out," I say, then kiss Sarada's hand and turn to face her. "I'm proud of you . . . I probably don't say that enough."

"That's sweet of you," she says.

"I don't want anything to ever hold you back."

"OK," she says with a peculiar expression. "Not sure why anything would hold me back."

"I guess I'm saying I just want the best for you."

"I know you do," she says. "I want the same for you, which is why I hope this whole Amanda Walsh thing comes to a close soon."

I face the screen again, looking at Walsh's photo.

Sarada presses her thumbs into the base of my neck and gently traces the curve of my bald head. "Just try to relax in France. Forget about LA for a while."

I sigh, thinking about my father. It's the longest I'll go without seeing him. Even though I don't visit him as often as I should, there's comfort in knowing that if he needs me, I'm twelve miles away.

As if reading my mind, Sarada says, "He'll be fine, you know."

"Pop hasn't been fine for years."

"You know what I mean." She reaches around the chair and kisses me. Her lips are extra soft and taste like peppermint. The tightness in my shoulders seems to lessen. Sarada deepens her kiss, then breaks away. "Don't stay up too late," she says. "The bed's cold without you." She turns to go back to our bedroom. Even if the world goes to hell, I know Sarada's got my six.

The photos finish uploading. Sixty-eight in total. I don't know if I should feel pride or sadness, considering the nature of the work. I shut down my computer and head to bed. I lie down next to Sarada and throw my arm around her. She nudges closer to me. I think about what life will be like in France. As a man who has never lived outside Los Angeles, I'm troubled by a nagging thought.

What if there's no place on God's green earth where I can let my guard down?

CHAPTER TWO

The new home of Bergman and Associates is an office building on Fifth Street in Bunker Hill. It overlooks the public library's communal gardens and fountains. Once dubbed "a blighted community," the historic neighborhood became fertile ground for law offices decades ago. Boutique and global law firms with offices in fifteen countries poured money into decrepit buildings infested with pests, rodents, and asbestos. A modern Bunker Hill meant gutting the 1930s buildings and remodeling them with lustrous flair.

"Good morning, Rusty," I say to the security guard stationed behind a half-circle-shaped desk in the marbled lobby.

"Morning, Mr. Finnegan," he says, adjusting his faded red clip-on tie. The uniform is dated. The starched white shirt, shiny black vest, and matching pants make Rusty look more like a train conductor than security. Not that it matters to David Bergman, the building's owner and occupier of two of its six floors. Even though I advised against it, Bergman contracted with the security company that charged the least and had the most unfavorable reviews. I'm not sure if it's arrogance or dim-wittedness that makes one of the most hated men in Los Angeles believe he can risk his safety with mediocre security. I suppose we got fortunate with Rusty, an Iraq War veteran who has the kind of face that makes you want to look the other way. Rusty has what my father calls "prison stink eye." I don't know if he ever served time, but he's got a tough glower, a short temper, and a tendency to allow the smallest disagreements to simmer to a boil.

"Bergman's already upstairs," Rusty says. "Came in with what looked like a grande latte, so watch yourself."

"Thanks for the warning," I say, noticing a person who isn't dressed like a gardener sweeping in front of the building. I dig in my suit's breast pocket for my key card. "How are the kids?"

"You know, driving my wife and me crazy. You wouldn't believe what my son did last weekend . . . I tell you, if I could ground him for a century, I would."

"Well, you get him to eighteen, then he's out of your hands," I say, pulling the white plastic card out.

"I wish. Kids these days don't leave the house, Mr. Finnegan. I got a neighbor with a twenty-eight-year-old son living in his basement. He makes dance videos and posts them online. Claims to be an influencer. Whatever the hell that is." Rusty presses a few buttons on a keyboard while looking at a security screen. "You thinking of having a few crumb snatchers?"

"No time soon." I take another look at the person sweeping dead leaves and trash scattered by last night's Santa Ana winds. "New gardeners?"

"Mr. Bergman's idea. Says he wants to give back to the community by hiring homeless folks to clean up around here. I told him it was a terrible idea. We can't vet these people. Most of them don't even have ID."

Rusty and Bergman rarely see eye to eye when it comes to the building's security, and though Rusty may come off brash and opinionated, he's usually right. "What's it, like, some kind of outreach program?" I ask.

"Who knows? Just makes me nervous." Rusty glares hard at the person sweeping. They're wearing so many clothes—a hooded sweatshirt under a trench coat, a baseball cap, and cargo pants with military-style boots—that I can't get a good look at them.

The elevator opens. Two men in bargain-basement suits exit. They likely came down from the second floor, which is home to a property insurance company specializing in earthquake and flood protection. They've got the same look as car salesmen, polished and pleasant enough to make the hard sell bearable. Bergman says insurance companies are his favorite tenants; they pay on time and don't leave a mess when they vacate.

Insurance agents work seven days a week, but we've got to be the only law firm pulling the same shift. "I'll catch up with you, Rusty." I get into the elevator before it closes.

"You got it, boss," he says as the doors shut.

I insert my key card into a slot on the control panel. The fifth and sixth floors aren't accessible if the card isn't inserted. I press the button for the sixth floor and check my cell phone during the ride up.

The doors open, and when I step out of the elevator, I can feel a current of tension wafting through the air like the stench of sun-cooked garbage. As usual, Kimber, Bergman's legal assistant, is staffing the front desk, her jadeite eyes locked to her computer's screen as she nurses a diet cola for breakfast.

"Morning," I say. "Anything I should know?" Rusty already gave me the heads-up about Bergman potentially being on a warpath, but Kimber knows him best, and if he's really in a funk, she might be the only one able to get him out of it.

She looks up from the screen. "You're ten minutes late," she says, her french-tipped fingernails pecking away on the keyboard. "He's been looking for you."

I look at my watch. "Traffic on the 110," I say. "What's Bergman's deal?"

Kimber looks toward the hallway leading to Bergman's office and beckons me closer. I lean in. "Wish I knew, but it could be a big case," she says. "Last time I saw him this worked up, you were his client."

Not long ago, Kimber treating me with a modicum of civility was as unlikely as me winning the Powerball. That I've garnered any respect from her is still remarkable, given the hate she harbored for me. After all, I was an LAPD detective—soiled, some might say, beyond forgiveness. I was everything Kimber, Bergman, most defense attorneys, and probably half of LA despised.

Her cell phone vibrates. She opens a text message, reads it, and then sets the phone back on her desk.

I hear hard footsteps. Bergman enters the lobby from the hallway dressed in a dark suit. Wool, maybe houndstooth? A fabric too warm for the day's mild temperature. "Finnegan, you're finally here," he says.

"The 110 was backed up . . ."

"It's fine, it's fine. Let's talk in my office."

"Good luck," Kimber whispers to me, returning to her work.

I follow Bergman down the hallway toward his office. We enter the large sun-drenched room. He slides behind his executive desk, something fit for the Oval Office, and takes a seat in a burgundy high-back chair. On the wall behind him are framed awards and certificates from his time as a volunteer law instructor for a youth enrichment program called California's Future Lawyers of America. What appears to be missing from the wall is anything related to his work as an attorney, which I've always found odd. When I've asked Bergman about his career and his time as a prosecutor, or even how many cases he's worked in his nearly twenty years of practice, he consistently responds, "What's it matter? I work them as I get them." It doesn't take crack detective skills to surmise that Bergman loves the law but hates being a lawyer.

"Have a seat," he says. I unbutton my suit coat and sit in a leather armchair. "How'd it go last night?"

"Uploaded the photos to the server," I say. "You tell me."

"I saw," he says. "Quite the shots." He pulls a handkerchief from his pocket and dabs his perspiring brow. Two naked cops boning sex workers would make most people perspire, or maybe it's the hound-stooth? "The client was pleased," he adds.

"They followed me," I say.

"The officers?"

"Came close to catching me . . . closer than any other time."

Bergman laces his fingers together and props them on his desk. "Clearly, they couldn't keep up," he says with the ease of a man who's never been chased by police.

"I want to know who hired us."

"Not this again. I told you—the less you know, the better."

I heave a sigh of frustration and bring my fist to my chin. "Do you know how many emails I've gotten this month about cops lining their pockets with money taken off grandmothers? And the woman who says a patrolman is stalking her seventeen-year-old daughter."

"Don't presume to lecture me on why we began this venture," he says, whipping the handkerchief about to emphasize his point. "I've told you, we have to be scrupulous about what and who we investigate."

"No hope for the proletariats, then?"

"We're doing what we can," Bergman says, dabbing his forehead again before tucking the handkerchief into his pocket.

"This person you've got in the department feeding leads—I don't see how you can put so much trust in them . . ."

"Same way I trust you," he says. "We've had to evolve, adapt to circumstances."

"Circumstances?"

"What difference does it make how money moves if it takes dirty cops off the street?"

"Two exploited sex workers?" I say, rubbing my freshly shaven chin. "You're telling me your lead put you on to that?"

"That was a special request."

"I never signed up for smut work. I want to see these cops burned as bad as you do, maybe even more than you. But not like this . . ."

Bergman reaches into his drawer, pulls out an envelope, and drops it on the desk. He slides it over to me. "Go ahead. Open it." I pick the envelope up. The money must weigh a few ounces. I open it. Looks like a couple thousand. "From the client," he says, looking plaintive but satisfied. "Dropped by early this morning. She preferred to pay the remaining balance in cash. Even added a gratuity."

I flip through the crisp hundred-dollar bills and put the money back in the envelope. "What type of person keeps this kind of cash on hand?"

"If you want this firm to stand, this is how we do it." He takes a pen from his desk drawer. "Jobs like the one last night are why you're still employed."

He shuffles through stacks of paper on his desk, then pulls out a sheet and holds up the electric bill for the building. The total is over $1,000. "Meanwhile, we're losing money just breathing the air. You've seen them, Finnegan. The people this firm represents can barely cobble together enough to pay my retainer, let alone years of representation." Bergman rips a corner from the bottom of the bill and scribbles on it.

"I thought things were getting better?"

He sighs as if to summon assuredness. "It's a temporary dilemma," he says, arms outstretched, a mockery of a king confident his castle will stand. "Bergman and Associates will emerge victorious."

He hands me the note he scribbled. "Your next job."

Two names are written on the paper. I hesitate. "You sure this is correct?"

"Do you know them?"

"I recognize one name."

"I should be getting photos later today. You'll surveil them. If something catches your eye, take a few pictures."

"That's vague."

"It's what's been requested. Easy work, considering it's your last job for a while," he says snidely.

Bergman has plenty to be pissy about, but is my extended stay in France what's got him salty? "Both are detectives, right?"

"That's right," he says. "Narcotics, I believe. You think you'll have trouble?"

I shove the note into my pocket. "No."

"Once my contact sends word, I'll update you with where they'll be tonight. They've been spending most of their time in Venice Beach. Some surfers overdosed on heroin. The LAPD's worried some bad junk is spreading through the scene."

"Bad junk? Scene?" I say, rising from my chair. "You say *jive* next, and I quit."

"Please," he says, irritated. "I've never been one for colloquialisms."

"Shocking," I say. It seems like Bergman was born middle-aged. "Downstairs, a person was sweeping out front. Is that going to be a regular thing now?"

"For the time being," he says. "It's a pilot program with the city. Give a homeless person a job or something along those lines. They work a few hours, and I give them service vouchers for meals, clothing, toiletries . . . It's a tax write-off."

"It's just that Rusty isn't too keen on it. Says it could be a security concern."

"He isn't keen on anything. Our floors are locked down, and the tenants in insurance aren't bothered by it." Bergman glides and clicks the mouse.

"Sure, but this building isn't Fort Knox—"

"Is that all?" he asks, bluntly.

Worse things come to mind, but I settle on, "You've changed, David. Not sure why or when, but you're different."

My words strike a nerve. Bergman looks up from the screen. His stare is steeped in bitterness. Makes me wonder if he ever liked me.

"Live long enough and people may say the same about you." He returns to clicking his mouse. I button my suit coat, taking another look at his pale scalp, brazenly displayed despite his attempt at a comb-over. "Close the door on your way out." His words are hot, sharp.

I return to the lobby with the money snug in my pocket. "How was it?" Kimber asks. I notice her zipping a heart-shaped pendant back and forth along its platinum chain. She does this from time to time when she's thinking about her on-again, off-again girlfriend, Myra.

"About how I expected," I say, leaning on the desk.

Kimber receives another text. She picks up her phone, shakes her head dismissively, and then lays the phone back on the desk. "Can I ask you something?"

"I've got five minutes," I say, checking my watch. "What's up?"

"I think Myra's seeing someone else . . ."

"Cheating?"

"Yes," she says. "But I need concrete evidence."

"The answer's no."

"But I haven't even asked you anything."

"Still no," I say, moving toward the exit. "You think she's cheating, cut her loose."

"You're literally no help," she says. "Like, what's the point of me knowing a private eye? I need dirt, Finnegan!"

I want to tell her their relationship has run its course, but who am I to judge? So I say nothing and rush out the door.

CHAPTER THREE

"You're on time," Special Agent Brixton Hill says, climbing into the beige leather saddle. Given that he's a burly man, I feel sorry for the horse, who already looks worn out. "Easy, girl." He leans forward, rubbing his palm along the animal's neck.

Flies swarm around the horse's eyes, collecting in the corners. I keep my distance. "All these flies would drive me nuts," I say, stepping into what feels like mud or something fouler.

"You're missing out," he says, leading the horse away from the park's equestrian center. "A lot of people are intimidated, but they're gentle creatures. You respect them, they'll respect you."

"That's not it. I'm allergic, or have you forgotten?"

"Hives, right?" he asks.

"Swelling, too," I say. "Never got the horseback badge in Boy Scouts."

"A godforsaken ailment, that's for damn sure." Hill slides his aviator sunglasses down the bridge of his nose to get a good look at me. It isn't the first time he's looked at me like I couldn't be odder. Before Hill joined the FBI, he was my father's partner in the LAPD; they worked out of the Southwest Division. He'd come by on weekends to drink and play cards. Rock music was usually blaring from my room, but I could still hear my father and Hill laughing and joking that I'd never get laid listening to garbage, dressing in flannel shirts and torn jeans like Kurt Cobain . . . *the white boy who blew his brains out.*

"I can keep up on foot," I say.

Hill smirks. "I'll keep her at a trot," he says. "Wouldn't want you to have to run in your fancy shoes."

"You know, we can always meet in the café." I point toward the observatory on the hill. The large, white-domed building is an LA landmark, and the café serves decent food and coffee, though at tourist prices.

"What fun would that be?" Hill asks, tapping the horse's side with his boot's heel. The horse picks up speed. I'm forced to abandon my stroll and walk with purpose.

"So, any news?" I ask, looking up at Hill, who has a firm command over the horse. A straight back, hands tight on the reins.

"The wife's losing her gym business," he says, armpit sweat seeping through his shirt. He's the only black man I've known who tucks his Oxfords into Wrangler jeans and wears cowboy boots, typically oiled snakeskin, on most occasions. "IRS notified us last week. Missed mortgage payments for the last six months. It's looking like foreclosure."

"You think Cynthia losing the gym will draw Boston out?"

"The reason that she's losing it might be what compels Walsh to make an appearance . . ." The sun dips behind the clouds, darkening the trail. Hill removes his aviators and wipes the shine from his forehead and nose. "We think Cynthia's sick, and from what we've seen, it looks bad."

"Terminal?"

With a pull of the reins, Hill slows the horse, reaches into his pocket, removes his phone, and scrolls. "Take a look," he says, handing it over. "Surveillance team snapped these photos last week."

The last time I saw Cynthia, she was strong, toned, a walking billboard for Fitopia, the luxury gym she and Boston built in Sherman Oaks. If I didn't know any better, I'd swear the gaunt, feeble-looking woman in the picture is another person. It's a tragic revelation. Cynthia struck me as an honest, kindhearted woman clueless her wife was a homicidal sociopath.

"Still, it'd be risky for them to reach out to each other," I say, handing Hill his phone.

"She's sick. That does something to a person," he says. "They aren't always thinking logically, more with their hearts than their heads."

When my mother was ill, dying from cancer, all she wanted to do was talk with old friends and people she hadn't spoken to in decades. She longed to see those she had loved and lost to distance and time. "Does she have a family? Anybody coming around to look after her?"

"Not from what we can tell. Amanda Walsh was it."

"She was an Olympian, you know," I say, still unnerved by the image of an emaciated Cynthia. "Track and field."

Hill slips his sunglasses back on as the sun breaches the clouds, a blinding resurgence. "Tough break."

Two riders, young women in pastel leggings, boots, and windbreakers, approach. Not the usual attire for horseback riding. A blonde wearing a baseball cap with what could be a school mascot holds her phone high and angled, fixing her fingers in place to take a selfie. The women cock their heads and pucker their lips, expressions like dead fish. Then the blonde winks, and the other girl sticks out her tongue. The display continues for more shots. As soon as they're done, the blonde appraises the photos, sliding her finger across the phone's screen.

"Now I remember why I rarely ride here," Hill says. "Too much clutter on the trail."

I can tell Hill is annoyed, but he musters the courtesy to nod in greeting as the women pass. I try to give them enough space to maneuver around us without getting too close to Hill's horse. As they gain some distance from us, still within earshot, I hear: "You ever see one of them ride before?" It's followed by the kind of chuckle that begs for a tongue-lashing, a barrage of curse words sung as poetry they'll never forget.

I look to Hill, his face holding all the contempt of a black man who's ridden his entire life, a five-time rodeo champion from the age of sixteen, known from Dallas to DC, and one of the only African American officers in the mounted horse unit in LAPD history. I remember listening to Hill at our dinner table, recounting his glory days in black rodeos before becoming a cop. He'd tell stories of men roping and riding steers for sold-out crowds. I'd never seen a black man on a horse until Hill had us out to his ranch in Chino, where I watched him gallop on his prized Thoroughbred across a dirt field.

Hill looks back at the two girls. "Silly-ass tourists," he says. Even though I can't see his eyes, I can imagine the rage in them.

"I probably should get going," I say, feeling like the encounter with the riders has deadened the conversation, left Hill exhausted.

"I'll keep you updated on the Cynthia situation. Word is the gym will be officially foreclosed on by the end of the week. If Walsh is going to show, the next few days could be our window."

"Understood."

"How's the old man doing?" Hill asks, sliding his glasses back down his nose so that I can see his eyes.

"You know, same old Shaun Finnegan," I say. "It'd be great if you could check on him while I'm away."

"France, right?"

"Six months."

Hill's eyes widen discerningly. "Uh-huh." Hill doesn't keep up with my father, not as he should, given how close they were. When they fell out years ago, everything changed. Who knows the last time they've spoken? "Maybe I'll call him," he says. I know that call will never happen, but it doesn't stop me from trying to mend their friendship. After all, Hill's always been good to me.

"Be safe, kid," he says. "I'll be seeing you."

"Take it easy, Uncle Hill." He smiles. Being called "uncle" has always brought glee to his otherwise stoic face. I do it out of respect but also sympathy.

He nods at me, the way he acknowledged the bigots on horseback. I turn away, walking back along the trail to the parking lot near the stables.

It'll be sundown soon, rush hour. Traffic headed to Venice might be bad. I pull my phone from my pocket.

A text from Bergman.

Before I can read the message, I enter a security code required by my phone's encryption feature. Bergman's message is written with the matter-of-fact tone that's become his signature delivery: The Smokeciety. 20th and Ocean Front Walk. 7 p.m. Another text follows—a photo of the two marks, Detectives Munoz and Riley, standing next to a Crown Vic.

I'm not sure what Smokeciety is, but I'll need to change out of my suit if it's on the boardwalk. I keep a duffel bag of clothes in the Falcon's trunk for situations like this, a habit from my patrol days, when having an extra uniform was necessary. I never knew what type of bodily fluids would end up on me during a shift, and dressing to blend in helps me retain a semblance of anonymity. Though my job presents many risks, the greatest is being identified by the corrupt officers I bust. I head into the public restroom to change, hoping it smells better than the horse stables.

———

I've never liked Venice Beach or the boardwalk. There's something seductive yet distasteful about it that makes my skin crawl. It's dangerous, like most places where desperation resides. The police presence is decent most nights, but despite the endless flow of tourists and street performers strumming guitars for cash or breakdancing on cardboard, the boardwalk has had its share of muggings, carjackings, homicides, human trafficking rings, and sexual assaults. It's the type of place where people can slowly rot, disappearing into an underbelly of sex and drugs.

A boy wearing a multicolored poncho skateboards in front of me, then looks over his shoulder. "Spare a dollar?" he asks.

"Sorry, man."

He brushes me off and continues down the walkway, landing kick-flips while avoiding passersby. I've been sitting on a bench in front of the Smokeciety for nearly an hour and have yet to see my marks. People enter the neon-green building and come out ten, twenty, sometimes thirty minutes later carrying white paper bags sealed with an official-looking sticker. A sign in front advertises free medical evaluations by a certified cannabis doctor but doesn't say who or what medical body has issued the certification. I've come across all types of doctors in my work—doctors of metaphysics, Scientology, practitioners of chakra realignment. Most are frauds and quacks.

Venice is filled with these shops, what cops call "legal dope houses." The Smokeciety's windows are tinted. Judging by the exterior and the professional-looking security guard, it's one of the more successful weed spots. And success means a stream of customers purchasing legal marijuana to treat insomnia, eating disorders, chronic pain, and just about any ailment that might affect someone's life. All a person needs is a prescription, and they can indulge in potent to mellow strains of cannabis, infused oils, edibles, teas, and muscle creams. And to think, police officers used to kick down doors and arrest people for a few grams of weed.

The security guard is a tall, well-built man with a reddish complexion wearing an all-black tactical uniform and combat boots. He stares at me as if he knows I don't belong. I try to avoid eye contact, pretending to check my phone.

"Hey, my man," the security guard says, "you need something?"

"I'm good," I say, never looking up from my phone.

"You don't look good."

"I'm fine, man." My leg won't stop shivering from the chilly beach air, and I realize it makes me look more suspicious. It's colder than I anticipated. The only beach clothes I had in the Falcon were a pair of cargo shorts, a sweatshirt, and black Converse All Star sneakers. I'm beginning to think Bergman's LAPD contact furnished him with bad intel.

"You've been sitting there for a minute," the guard says, slowly stepping toward me. "Maybe you go find another bench."

"Last I checked, the city owned these benches."

The guard laughs. A chipped-tooth smile flashes across his face. "Nah, the city don't own shit right here, buddy. Best you step off."

"I said I'm good."

"You're looking like you planning to do something ignorant up in here. I'm here to let you know that you best not try it." He points to a collapsible baton on his belt and what might be a taser. "I've bodied suckas for less than what your little ass is thinking about."

"I don't know what you're talking about," I say. "I'm waiting for a friend."

"Yeah, right, a friend." He pauses and takes a few steps back. I realize he must remain within a particular distance to the building's door, like a family pet trapped by an invisible fence. If the pet ventures too far from home or out of range, its collar gives it a shock. The security guard can try to roust me all he wants, but he won't abandon his post.

I ignore the guard, listening to the low surf spilling onto the sand and pulling back into the ocean.

I check my watch again. Almost nine o'clock. I scan the boardwalk and notice that the security guard's attention is no longer on me. He's watching as a man and woman approach from the east end of the walkway. Both are casually dressed: the man in jeans and a bomber jacket, the woman in joggers and a baggy sweatshirt. I imagine there aren't many things that would make the thick-necked heckler with swollen biceps nervous, but these two people have him standing upright, looking goosey. I open the camera app on my phone, turn off the flash setting, and pretend I'm texting. The pair moves quickly, hands at their sides, facing the security guard. As they get closer, I'm better able to check them out.

Seeing someone from your past isn't easy if things weren't left on the best of terms. I hoped Bergman's intel was wrong, that the name written on the note was an error, and the photo wouldn't be of *my* Sally Munoz, the woman I called a partner for two years. Munoz was like a sister. I couldn't fathom not working alongside her when she went on maternity leave. It was months before I caught the Brandon Soledad case, and looking back, I've wondered if things would have been different if Munoz were working with me. By the time she returned, I was gone from the department, with the LAPD working hard to scrub me from its annals.

The security guard mutters a few words to Munoz's partner, Martin Riley, a dark-haired white man who carries himself more like a bruiser with a badge than a detective. Then he opens the gate. I snap a few pictures with my phone as they enter the smoke shop. The guard shuts the gate and stands out front, arms folded across his chest. For the next fifteen minutes, I watch him turn away patrons. I discern a few words he speaks to a mousy young woman in a UCLA sweatshirt. "Shop's closed," he says, his voice easy but stern, a departure from how he spoke to me. "Come back later." The woman draws back, throws her sweatshirt's hood over her head, and hurries off.

Whatever's happening inside feels important. I take a few more pictures of the building's entrance and of the watchdog standing firm. He reminds me of a painting I saw once on display at the Norton Simon Museum: a dismal depiction of Cerberus, the three-headed beast tasked with guarding Pluto's Gate. Though the entrance to the Smokeciety isn't a portal to hell, like the Greeks believed Pluto's Gate was, it might be as ill-fated.

When Munoz and Riley appear, they're eager to exit. I act like I'm tying my shoe, angle the phone upward from the ground, and take a few more pictures. Riley swings the gate open and steps onto the walkway with Munoz; they quickly make their way down the boardwalk.

I let them get about twelve feet ahead before following. I dodge a roller skater and a group of teenagers smoking cigarettes and playing loud music from a phone. The detectives pass rows of artisan booths. A woman selling handmade jewelry yells at Munoz, "You need this in your life, baby girl!" She holds up a beaded bracelet. Munoz keeps walking.

I'm nearly knocked over by a group of runners that moves from behind me, passing on my right side. I count five or six men and women wearing shirts, hats, and shoes with reflective silver and neon-green trim.

Munoz and Riley stop in front of a chili-dog stand. I look for another bench, finding one about ten feet from them, where an older man sits, slouching in a beige coat and holding a small dog in his lap. When I sit next to the man, his shih tzu begins to bark, baring its teeth, and I regret my decision.

"Don't worry, he doesn't bite," the man says, stroking between the dog's ears as it growls. "Calm down, Norman."

Having been attacked twice by dogs in my law enforcement career, I never take anyone's word when it comes to a canine's demeanor. "You're good," I say. "I'll find another bench."

"You don't have to do that. We've been sitting too long anyway." His feet look snug in orthopedic shoes. He wiggles them the way I might if I've got a cramp in my heel and lowers the dog to the ground. He cautiously stands, arches his back in a stretch, and grumbles the way old folks do when their joints start creaking.

"You OK, mister?" I ask, prepared to catch the man if he loses his balance.

"Just old," he says, laughing. "A condition we'll all be in if we're lucky."

"Sure," I say, keeping an eye on Munoz and Riley.

"The name is Chen," he says. He's a small Asian man, perhaps in his seventies. His beige coat looks out of fashion but classic, like the trench coat Bogart made famous in *Casablanca*. Chen seems out of place among the people who populate the boardwalk. His eyes are kind, warm; after a few moments of him smiling at me, I forget all about his overprotective dog.

"Douglas," I say, a name I use when I'm working. I like to think it sounds forgettable.

"Nice to meet you, Douglas," Chen says. "It's getting close to Norman's bedtime. We should probably be going." He looks down at the white, stringy-haired dog licking its paws.

"Have a good evening," I say, shifting my eyes from Chen back to the marks. He and Norman begin walking away, the dog's tail wagging as they pass the hot dog stand. I watch as Riley takes two chili dogs and a drink from the server. He sips from a straw and offers some to Munoz, who gladly accepts. She takes a long, confident sip. Though I never shared food with Munoz or anyone I worked with, watching her slurp the drink feels strange. Riley looks like he's twenty years her senior, but it's how he observes her that makes me cringe. It reminds me of how Garvey and Yoshida watched the surfer girls at the motel before joining them in the room.

The running club approaches in tight formation, and I notice an additional runner. The person isn't wearing clothes similar to those of the others—no high-visibility trim or expensive shoes; instead, they're dressed in a hooded black sweatshirt, dark sweatpants, and a baseball cap pulled down over their face. Chen dawdles in the runners' path, having not made it more than five feet from the stand. Before I can warn him, the hooded runner knocks him over, sending Chen to the ground.

"Shit," I say, getting up from the bench but hesitant to intervene for fear of blowing my cover.

Chen rolls to a stop and cries out for help, his body sprawled across the path, one leg tangled in the dog's leash. The runners collide, tripping over each other, while the hooded runner avoids a stumble. Munoz heads over to Chen, kneels, and asks, "Are you hurt, sir? Show me where . . ."

Riley continues to eat his chili dog, watching. Chen seems disoriented and powerless to get up. "Norman," he strains to shout. "Where's Norman?" Munoz looks to the dog, who's barking incessantly as a crowd forms around the commotion.

"Riley," she says, looking to her partner as he wipes a chili stain from his jacket. "Can you settle the dog down?" Riley looks bothered by it all, as if Chen falling is a colossal inconvenience. He sets his food down on a table, unwraps the gold foil around his other chili dog, and starts walking over to Norman.

Pop.

Pop . . . pop . . . pop.

Pop.

Gunshots ring out, scattering people in all directions. I dive behind the bench, taking hold of my Smith & Wesson .38 Special, holstered around my waist. I can only see legs and feet working to carry people to safety, along with trampled bodies. During the seconds when my view isn't obstructed, I catch glimpses of Munoz lying on top of Chen. Neither one is moving. I look to Riley, who's on the ground where he stood only moments ago. Blood has pooled around him. When I look at his face, I can only make out what used to be his mouth and part of his nose. The rest is gone, blown apart, reduced to skull and brain. What remains of his dark hair is clumped on top of his head like a rolled-up toupee.

I wait to be sure there aren't more shots. Then I get up, keeping my gun low, knowing that if a police officer spots me, I could easily be mistaken for the gunman and killed. I run over to Munoz, crouch next to her, and call her name.

"Munoz . . . Munoz."

She moves, then lets out an aching moan. "I think I'm hit," she says. I gently pull her away from Chen. I see he's breathing, and she's been shot in the arm. The bullet has singed her sweatshirt, exposing skin, a shallow cavity of puffy pink flesh. She's bleeding profusely. I tie my belt around her wound. "Chen . . . can you hear me?" He opens his eyes, his face flushed, wet, maybe from tears or sweat caused by Munoz lying on top of him. "Are you OK?"

"What happened?" he asks, looking to Munoz. Her weapon's in her hand, and she's trying to get her bearings. At the sight of Munoz's gun, Chen becomes hysterical and starts to crawl away, back toward the park bench. "No . . . please. Don't shoot!"

"It's OK, Chen. She's a police officer." Munoz is shaken and hasn't looked at me in a way that says she recognizes me. Blood is smeared down her cheek. It isn't until she sees Riley's lifeless body that she's overcome by a vicious tremor, like death rattling her bones.

"No! Riley—no!" Munoz crawls over to her dead partner and attempts to lift his head, tucking her knees under his body like a wedged pillow. Her screams are loud, deafening, and after a while it's all I can hear until more shots ring through the air. I look in the direction of the gunfire. They sound like they're coming from the parking lot. I turn to Munoz; she's covered in Riley's blood, trying to hold what's left of his face together. She looks up at me, agony and defeat in her eyes. "Finn?"

"Call it in," I say.

Munoz pulls her phone from her pocket, works to steady her hand, and dials. "Ten Ninety-Nine. Sh-sh-shots fired. Officer down. P-po-possible ambush. All available units at my location . . ."

I look at Riley's lifeless body. Behind me, Chen grips Norman so tightly that the dog looks distressed. I take off toward the gunshots, passing frantic people running in the opposite direction. Some people have taken cover behind vendor booths and food stands. Others appear dazed, running toward the beach, away from the boardwalk's lights, seeking refuge on the sand.

As I turn toward the parking lot, I hear sirens but see no police or emergency vehicles. I move down a row of taillights, crouching low. People hide in cars, windows clouded from heavy breathing, and a few huddle next to engine blocks. I hear murmurs of the Lord's Prayer, Hail Marys—fearful pleas for help. Bargains are struck with God and other unseen forces: "Let me survive this, and I'll change. Let me live, and I'll be better . . ."

Two people lie dead near the lot's entrance. Gunpowder lingers. My adrenaline is pumping; time feels off. The last series of shots could have been ten minutes ago or three. It's hard to be sure. I hear footsteps and take cover behind an SUV. I raise my pistol and look around the vehicle's grille to see the hooded runner standing with his gun pointed at me. I quickly whip my head back and draw my limbs into a ball behind the engine block.

The sirens are closing in. It won't be long. If the shooter intends to escape, the window is closing fast. But I've given away my position. I'm stuck. I won't get clear of the SUV before the suspect can shoot me. Even if I can take cover behind another vehicle, the suspect could open fire indiscriminately, killing passengers hiding in their cars. I have to stall, keep the suspect here until officers arrive.

I remember my training: Appeal to the shooter. Get them talking to buy time. "You need to know something," I shout for the suspect to hear. "I don't want to see you die." I tighten my grip on the revolver. "I don't know why you've done what you've done, but I trust you have a reason. Why don't you tell me what it is?" Silence. "What does it matter now?" I ask. "You've made your point. A cop is dead. Tell me, is this some kind of initiation? Somebody paying you? Or you just got it out for cops?"

More silence, then: "Don't follow me," he says before firing a fusillade into the SUV. I stay behind the engine block. Rounds pierce the door panels and shatter windows, sending glass crashing on top of my head. I'm breathing fast, sweating, my arms shaking. When the shooting ceases, I'm ready to return fire. I move to the rear of the SUV and look through what's left of a broken window, but I don't see the shooter.

I step out from behind the SUV, stay low, and run to another row. I take cover behind a Ram pickup truck and wait. LAPD SWAT should be arriving soon, but it's a large area to cover. What if they go to the wrong parking lot? Or what if they're here but attempt to set a perimeter around the entire boardwalk, which tactically makes sense but would be hell to coordinate?

An engine spits exhaust. It curls and disperses into the air. The revving grows louder, booming and growling, setting off car alarms two or three rows away. As I move in the direction of the rumbling, a motorcycle cuts down a row. I take off after it. As it nears the lot's exit, I try to intercept it, but I'm not fast enough. It's a dark bike, large trail tires, neon-green shocks—something I'd expect to see in a motocross race—and there's no license plate.

The motorcycle screeches out of the lot, nearly fishtailing before disappearing down the street. I holster my gun, mindful of the situation I've put myself in. It doesn't matter that I'm ex-police or a private detective. I'm a black man running around with a gun at a crime scene where the victims are LAPD officers and two bystanders. I may be the only person these witnesses can identify, not to mention I could end up in the crosshairs of a police department that despises me . . . I need to get out of here.

I race toward the Falcon, parked four rows away, near a cotton candy shop north of where Riley and Munoz were shot. My God, Munoz . . . I think of the officers I've known who've died in the line of duty and the partners who couldn't save them. It might be a cop's greatest fear: a partner dying. Most cops don't recover—dogged with survivor's guilt and PTSD, they never return to active duty. Those who do ride a desk and rarely spend time in the field. My old training officer,

Joey Garcia, talked about them as if they were zombies, the way they lurked around the division like the walking dead. Something was gone from their eyes, hollowed. Garcia called them "sad sacks."

I get into the Falcon, start the engine, and drive out of the parking lot, headed in the same direction as the motorcycle. Part of me hopes I'll find the shooter, maybe trying to ditch the motorcycle, make his way on foot. But another part of me is terrified of what I'll do if I cross him.

I head up Lincoln Boulevard toward Westchester, passing speeding police vehicles. I hear a helicopter flying low and see the searchlight's beam. I reach for my phone, digging into a pocket of my cargo shorts. It isn't there. I check the other pocket—nothing.

"Dammit!" I punch the wheel. *Where could I have lost it?* On the boardwalk or in the parking lot? The data on the phone is sensitive: text exchanges with Bergman, surveillance photos of officers, case notes—everything.

I must be cursed. That's the only explanation. It's karma, the type of cosmic rebalancing Sarada warns me about. Lightning has struck this investigation. I need to get home. I merge onto the 10 driving west toward the 110, tune the police scanner, and listen. It's pandemonium. The LAPD's requesting that the Santa Monica PD and California Highway Patrol send officers to canvass Venice and the surrounding areas.

I listen to the scanner the entire drive, afraid my description will be broadcast over the radio. I'm relieved when it isn't. Choking back tears, a female officer makes the end-of-watch call for Detective Martin Riley. The announcement doesn't veer from the script. It's straightforward. The particulars are read with a switch operator's cadence. The officer states simply that Riley was shot and died on the scene. "Detective Riley was a good man," she says. "He made people's lives better. He'll be missed." She composes herself, speaks louder, and closes. "Detective Martin Riley, you are end of watch." A moment of silence follows, and then the frequency clears. I turn off the scanner, still trying to grasp what transpired tonight.

What in the hell have I gotten mixed up in?

———

The Volkswagen Beetle parked in front of the townhouse looks familiar. It's filthy, with dirt caked on doors and windows. I watch as the driver reverses and angles the car multiple times to vacate the spot, even though there's plenty of room to pull out cleanly.

As I park in our driveway, the Beetle's taillights disappear into the darkness. I check my pockets again for my phone, then scrutinize the floorboards and the area behind the driver's seat.

Nothing.

I get out of the car and stagger along the walkway to the front door holding my keys, thankful I didn't lose them in the chaos. As I prepare to unlock the door, I hear the dead bolt click, and the door swings open.

"Have you lost your mind?" Sarada asks in a huff. Her hand's on the doorknob. She's blocking me from entering. "Why aren't you answering your phone?"

"Lost it," I say. "What's going on?"

"That's convenient."

Sarada doesn't yell, hardly ever raises her voice. Tonight, she's doing both. "Did something happen?" I ask.

"Did you really think you could keep this from me?"

"Keep what from you?" My brain is chafing. We might as well be playing charades. "Why won't you tell me what's going on?"

"She told me everything, Trevor. Everything!"

"She? Who the hell is *she*?"

"Tori, dammit," she says, trying to slam the door in my face. I brace my hand against it, apply my shoulder's weight to prevent her from closing it further.

"Tori?" I knew I recognized the car. The rear spoiler was missing, but it felt like her in my gut—Tori Krause.

"Don't play dumb, Trevor."

"I'm not playing dumb," I say. "I'm just confused. I haven't heard from Tori in two years. Why'd she come here?"

"I invited her," Sarada says, tears streaming down her face. "To talk . . ."

"What?"

"She came by Spinners." Sarada swallows hard, jaw clenched. It almost looks involuntary, like her mouth won't let her speak the words. "She said she tried to call you, but your number was disconnected. Lucky for her, she remembered me. Some nonsense about me having an *exotic* name. She searched me online, found my picture from an *LA Times* article about Spinners, and came in as we were closing."

"And you invited her into our home?" I ask, still bracing against the door.

"She had quite the story, Trevor. Very captivating. Started telling it in front of my staff and customers." She looks me in the eyes in a way she never has before . . . furious but heartbroken, too. "I've never been so embarrassed. I told her we needed a quiet place to talk. Thought our home was as good a place as any."

"Just tell me what she said." I think of the worst, knowing it will change everything. Maybe it already has?

"She named her Simone. Simone Finnegan," she says. "Your daughter." She overpowers my arm and slams the door so hard it shakes the frame.

The porch light goes off, and I stand in the moonlight. "Please, Sarada," I say, loud enough that she can hear me through the door. "Let's talk about this."

"Leave, Trevor," she says, weeping on the other side of the door. "Go, now."

"I can explain. Give me a chance." My forehead is pressed against the door. I'm afraid it'll mean we're over if I walk away.

"I said leave!"

Staring intensely, a neighbor watches from her window, the curtain pulled back. Nights here are subdued, especially by ten o'clock, with not so much as a TV at high volume. I wave to the nosy woman, hoping she'll get the message that things are all right. But I know people like us don't get to have public spats, not in places like Sierra Madre.

She closes the curtain. I begin walking back to my car. Sarada and I have always been able to talk things out. She's never cut me off before, but I suppose we've never faced something like this. I want to bang on the door, beg her to talk to me, but it would only make matters worse. Besides, the neighbor or someone else is sure to call the police.

I get into the Falcon. I've come up short plenty of times in my life, but tonight I'm reminded of my greatest failure—the last time I let Sarada down, a night that haunts me still.

If what Tori told Sarada is true, she didn't abort our baby, as she had threatened to do, which means I'm a father.

A father?

And my daughter is out there . . . somewhere.

CHAPTER FOUR

I haven't seen my father in more than a week. Work has a way of keeping me busy, and my free time is usually spent with Sarada, or at least it was. Pop will never admit it, but he's drowning in loneliness, which makes my coming to his condo at 11:30 p.m. opportunistic and selfish. But on a night like this, I don't want to be alone.

I press the button for his unit and wait. It's an ancient intercom. The panel's metal buttons remind me of the keypads on pay phones from my youth. I'm old enough to remember the Pacific Bell phone booths erected on corners around the city.

Static blares from the intercom. "Who is it?" Pop asks. He sounds drunk.

"Trevor."

"Trevor?" he says, startled. "What you doing here at this hour?"

"I need someplace to stay."

A buzzer sounds. I open the door and enter the lobby. I pass a row of mailboxes. Newspapers and grocery store ads are scattered on the floor. The elevator hasn't worked for months; a cardboard sign reading OUT OF ORDER is taped to the doors.

As I climb the stairs to my father's second-floor unit, I notice paint peeling from the walls and the fetid odor of pet urine. I knock on Pop's door.

"That you?" he asks.

"Yes. It's me, Pop."

He unlocks the door, opens it slowly. "Come on in." It's not unlike Pop to keep a junky place, but I can barely see the floor. Envelopes and junk mail are strewn everywhere, along with forms and documents. Pop shuts the door behind me.

"Sorry if I'm interrupting something. I didn't know where else to go."

"People always say that, like hotels don't exist." He locks the door. "I slept in my truck bed once. Nearly froze my balls off."

"Well, I don't want to impose . . ."

"I'm kidding," he says. "You aren't imposing on anything. I'm just doing some spring cleaning."

"It's November, Pop."

He kicks a stack of newspapers into the corner. "Gon' have a seat," he says, hurrying me toward the couch.

"The elevator's still not fixed?" I ask as I sit, unable to ignore the frayed fabric and lumpy cushion.

"I thought I told you. The HOA is broke, defunct. Not a dime for repairs." Pop sits next to me. "The president cleared out the account, ran off with everybody's dues. Police are looking for him, but I'm sure he's long gone by now. Had a young thing with him, too. Pretty little Spanish broad. They probably living it up in Mexico by now, sipping piña coladas."

Pop speaks like he's still holding court with officers outside a 1970s bullpen. No matter how often I discourage him from using words like *broad*, he says I'm too sensitive and calls me "the PC police." I've learned to pick my battles.

"You have a burger or something earlier?" Pop asks, pointing to a stain on my shorts. "Looks like ketchup. I wish you would have picked me up something."

There's a red smear near a cargo pocket. Blood, likely from when I tended to Munoz's wound. Or it could be splatter from when the bullets hit Riley. "Eating on the run. Been a crazy day."

"Bergman keeping you busy?" Pop doesn't know what I do for Bergman, only that I'm a PI for his firm. Most established firms have in-house investigative services, but some contract out, which Pop presumes is the situation.

"Money is good. No sense in complaining."

"You're starting to sound how I used to. Just grinding out a living, aren't you?"

"Guess so."

"You want to tell me what happened between you and Good Genes?"

"C'mon, Pop," I say, visibly annoyed. "You know I don't like when you call her that."

"There you go getting all sensitive again," he says, stretching his arms above his head, putting them behind his neck, and leaning back. "I've been calling her that since she was fifteen; I figured you'd both be used to it by now."

"There's more to her than looks, Pop." I ponder the right words to describe her. "She's everything—"

"Well, she's got your nose open. Not that I blame you." He gets up from the couch and walks toward the kitchen. "So what was the fight about?"

I've never thought much about Pop as a father. Caretaker? Sure. Provider? Absolutely. But being a grandfather fits him even less than being a father or husband.

"Not sure how to explain it," I say. "I'm still trying to make sense of it."

Pop comes back with two longneck beers. He sits, slides one over to me. "Best to come out with it. She caught you cheating, didn't she?"

"What?" I nearly knock the beer to the floor. "Of course not."

"OK."

"That's not me."

"OK."

"I told you before, I'm not made like you."

"Oh, don't be a Pollyanna," Pop says, twisting the beer's cap and taking a swig. "You're grown now. Enough to know men got needs, and if those needs aren't being satisfied, then a man is going to find someone who will."

"What a load of . . ."

"Watch it," he warns.

"Don't sit there trying to justify what you did to Mom."

"Your mother and I had our issues," he says. "We were never compatible in that way . . ."

"So you slept with whatever badge bunny came along . . ."

"Our married life was none of your damn business," he says with a wag of his finger. "It still ain't. And remember, you came out of my batch." He grabs his crotch and squeezes. "Whatever's in me is in you."

"For God's sake, I hope not," I say, realizing coming to Pop's place was another misstep in a night full of mistakes.

"Then out with it, golden boy. Why's your ass on my couch right now looking like you ain't got a friend in the world?"

I work the cap off the beer, take a long sip, then place the bottle on the coffee table. Water marks—white rings overlapping—tell the story of my father's countless nights drinking beers, shuffling thoughts. I'd felt sorry for him, believing he was suffering in solitude. But he always does something to remind me he deserves isolation. His loneliness can't hold a candle to the years of pain he caused my mother and me.

"Well?" he asks, staring at me the way he did when I mouthed off as a teen. Back then, he'd call me something ugly—punk, sissy, faggot—and I'd run to my room and slam the door. He probably still thinks those things, or worse, but he has enough decency not to say them.

"I have a daughter."

"You have a what?" Pop freezes, slack-jawed.

"That's why Sarada's pissed. She learned about her today. We both did."

Pop stands, bringing his hands to his hips, as if stumped by a complicated math problem. "So you're certain you've got a kid out there?"

"Not certain, but there's a good chance . . . a very good chance."

"The mother?"

"A woman from two years ago. Sarada remembers her from the Soledad case. She's the one who brought me to the hospital when I took that beanbag to the ribs."

"The white girl?" Pop asks, his voice elevated. "With all the fluff?" He makes hand gestures in front of his face, recalling Tori's thick, skillfully applied makeup.

"I'm not sure what to do," I say.

"Dammit, boy. Talk all you want about me, but I always wore a rubber. I thought I taught you better than that."

"Really? That's the conversation you want to have right now?"

"I'm just saying . . ." He returns to the couch and sits on the sinking cushion. "You know what her showing up means, don't you? She's come for the money, the child support."

"That doesn't make sense. Tori told me she wasn't going to keep the baby and cut me off completely."

"Guess she changed her mind," he says. "You know, these new-age types are fine raising babies on their own, say they don't need men anymore. We're just sperm donors until that purse is empty."

I watch Pop for a moment, his face dry, with more age spots than when I saw him last. His eyes are pink and milky from advanced glaucoma. He's rarely correct about much and never about women and relationships. But there's one thing I fear might be true: what's in him may be in me. I know I'd never cheat on Sarada or berate my children, but he might have felt the same way once. Then his best intentions dried up, flaked off like the dead skin along his cheeks. And what shone through instead was his intrinsic nature, that of a detached, abusive man.

If Simone is mine, I refuse to be like Pop. I can't be.

"You're not even a little excited, are you?" I ask.

"Excited?" Pop grunts. "Shit—what do I need to be excited about?"

"You might have a grandchild."

"Look here," he says, leaning in, his beer breath on my skin. "Blood doesn't make family. My father was no better than dried dogshit, and if someone had told me they were going to put a bullet in him, I would have asked to watch."

Pop's fair complexion tells an American story. My grandfather was a white farmhand and one of the only Irish people who settled in Goldsboro, North Carolina. He married my grandmother, a local black seamstress, and, as my father tells it, promised to move her to Chicago. That never happened, and Goldsboro became a kind of perdition, which was fitting, since Pop swears the devil possessed my grandfather with a brutality that knew no bounds.

"If it's true, that ain't no grandbaby of mine," Pop says, gulping more beer.

"I can still fix things," I say, not sure if I'm trying to convince Pop or myself.

"Shit," Pop says, drawing out the vowel. "That snow bunny's going to take everything you've got. Every red cent." He sighs and gets up, his back stooped.

"Why would I expect anything different from you?" I say, exercising the chip on my shoulder. "No one should have a bigot for a grandfather."

"What's that?" Pop says, frowning hard.

It's the first time I've called my father anything besides "Pop" and maybe "Daddy" when I was a boy. He looks not mad but assured, like I've proven myself to be what he's always seen me as—a disappointment.

He chuckles. "And here I was feeling sorry for your ass. You can stay here for a week. If she doesn't take you back by then, find some other place to lick your wounds."

Pop tilts his head, making a spectacle of beer drinking. He heads toward his bedroom at the end of the hall. "Don't stink up my couch, either. You smell like you've run a mile. You know where the towels are." Before shutting his door, he shouts, "Bar soap is under the bathroom sink!"

I touch the perpetual crater in the cushion from Pop sitting for hours in the same spot. He wants me out, and I value my back too much to sleep on the couch for long. I only hope that a week will be enough time, but who knows how long it'll take for Sarada to hear me out.

———

Pop's place smells of canned tuna, scorched popcorn, and beer. *Is that what he had for breakfast?*

My back is sore, and so's my neck. I sit up and rub a tender spot from my tailbone to my hip, feeling like I slept on a boulder. Since my stabbing two years ago, my back hasn't been right, and I worry the couch will trigger spasms. I slowly stand and bend at the waist, incapable of reaching my toes. My hamstrings burn like something's going to burst. I roll my shoulders forward, then back, then forward again.

I turn on the TV and flip to the local news. The headline "Shooting at Venice Boardwalk" scrolls across the chyron. A well-manicured anchor lays a sheet of paper before him, looks into the camera with calculated sincerity, and says, "Police are investigating last night's shooting in Venice Beach. Three people are dead and several others injured after, police say, a gunman opened fire at the popular hangout. Authorities have no suspects at this time but believe the shooting might have been gang-related. If you have any information related to the shooting, you're urged to call the LAPD's tip line."

Gang-related. What police call a shooting when there aren't any suspects or leads. It means they've spoken to witnesses, and nobody offered anything definitive, no detailed accounting or solid clues. A shooting that isn't solved within the first forty-eight hours can deflate whatever gusto a detective brings to the investigation, and the chances of finding the culprits decrease exponentially. Along with shell casings, my phone may have been collected as evidence. Right now, detectives could be trying to tie it to the shooter or victims. My only consolation is that the phone has adequate encryption. Bergman doesn't know shit about tech, but I'm relieved he listened to me when I told him our modes of communication needed to be highly secure. The phone's two-step authenticator means it could take police weeks or months to access its contents, and they'll need a warrant and an expert to do so. Returning to the boardwalk has become too perilous, and finding the phone would be a long shot.

Maybe Bergman's trying to reach me? He hasn't heard from me in hours and could be thinking the worst. I need to get to the office. Let him see I'm alive.

I brush my teeth, wash another roach and two water bugs down the tub's drain, then shower and put on last night's clothes. "I'm leaving!" I shout at Pop's bedroom door. "Be back later tonight!" He doesn't respond.

I press my ear against the door and hear the cold snap of a beer's tab, then the hurried guzzle. The TV is blaring the news. "That poor son of a bitch," Pop says, and then there's a thud that shakes the wall.

I move away from the door and back into the kitchen, where I take a set of spare keys from a brass tray on the counter and pocket them. Pop might be too drunk to buzz me in when I return in the evening.

I drop twenty dollars on the dining table in case he gets hungry for something besides tuna, and I leave.

———

"Shit, you're here!" Kimber declares, the expletive marking a crass and unexpected departure from her tame office vocabulary. "David's been trying to reach you all morning." She pops up from her chair, hurries around the front desk, and throws her arms around me. "We thought you were . . ."

"Alive and kicking," I say with clumsy coolness. She brings my head to her shoulder, and I inhale her floral fragrance. We've never touched or been this close before . . . I guess I'm really growing on her.

"David didn't know what to do. He was afraid to call your father."

"Afraid?"

She ends her embrace and straightens her ruffled blouse. "He didn't want to be the one to tell him something horrible might have happened to you."

And if I were lying dead in Venice Beach, I'm sure Bergman would find a way to disavow me. It wouldn't be difficult. I'm off the books. A hired contractor paid in cash. Disposable.

"Bergman in his office?" I ask.

Kimber nods, and I head down the hallway. I knock hard on Bergman's door, then enter before being given the green light. Bergman's on the phone when I come in. "I have to call you back," he says before hanging up. "Trevor, you're all right. I thought you were—"

"Dead?"

"I was going to say *hurt*." He gets to his feet. "What happened last night? Can I get you water, tea?"

"Water."

Bergman pulls a bottle from his mini fridge, hands it to me, then sits back down. "Is it as bad as the news is saying?"

"One gunman." I twist the cap off the bottle. "He shot one of the detectives I was surveilling. Killed him right in front of me."

"Did you see the shooter's face?"

I drink half the bottle before answering. "Not really. It was dark."

"And the other detective?"

"Munoz," I say. "Shot in the arm. I think she'll be OK."

"I don't know what to say . . ."

"I need to use your computer." I walk behind Bergman's desk and prod him out of the seat. He moves aside, and I set the water bottle on his desk. I sit in his leather executive chair and click an icon on his desktop as he hovers over my shoulder. "I lost my phone last night and need to locate it."

"Lost it? You mean at the murder scene?"

"Possibly."

"This is a nightmare," he says. "Should I even ask why you're dressed like that?"

The mobile phone's security app opens. I select the phone number from the device menu and click the "Search" button. "Rather not get into it." I wait for the phone to appear on the map. A small red dot pulses over LAPD's Central Division. "I knew it."

"LAPD headquarters?" Bergman reaches a new threshold of alarm, exceeding his daily neuroticism about the firm going under. "This can't be happening . . . How the hell do we get it back?" He covers his face with his hands. "If what's on that phone gets out, we're over."

"Let me think for a minute," I say, gaining enough confidence for both of us. "It's probably sitting in an evidence locker, where it'll stay until they get a warrant to unlock it, and even then, it's damn near impossible to crack."

Bergman paces. "Near impossible, not impossible," he says. "We don't know. They could be cracking it as we speak."

"Doubt it," I say. "That phone is tagged, bagged, and sitting while the department gets the proper clearances." Bergman's pacing is going to work the carpet bare.

"Maybe I can go there," he says. "Tell them I lost it. They'd believe me, right?"

"More than they'd believe me? Is that what you're saying?"

"Given your history . . ."

"And what would you say when they ask you how your phone ended up a few feet from the victims?"

"I . . . I don't know."

"There is one way we can get it back."

"OK?"

"Your source in the department," I say. "Have him get it for us."

"Oh, I can't do that . . ."

"Right . . . right. It's too risky." I mock him in a voice that irritates even me. "But I'm the only one taking the real risks out there." I get up from the chair and head toward the door. "This cloak-and-dagger shit isn't going to fly much longer, Bergman. Maybe I should walk? Let you sort it out."

"You're not making this easy," he says, running his palm across his brow. "All I can tell you is that the contact is someone of high rank, and he's been with the department for a very long time."

"OK," I say, unimpressed. "There some reason he can't bust these cops I've been chasing down?"

"Many of these officers are protected. They have connections deep within the department. Opening an investigation with their names at the center raises red flags. That means the investigation is shut down instantly and my contact put out to pasture."

"Then have them exercise the consent decree? Go to the feds; I'm sure they'll listen."

"You don't understand," he says. "It's all show. Once DOJ is off LAPD's back, it's a return to business as usual. You need to understand that it's a fragile alliance we have here."

"I don't care about that. It's time your contact starts showing some goodwill." I finish the rest of the water and drop the empty bottle in the blue recycling bin next to the door. "Shared risk," I say. "Your contact is going to get the phone and bring it to me."

Bergman starts shaking his head as he returns to his chair. "What if he gets caught?"

"That's why it's a risk," I say.

"Evidence tampering is a felony."

"I know what the hell it is!" I sound like my father, coming off the hinges. "Dammit, Bergman, just do what I'm asking for once. Have the contact swap the phone out with a dummy."

"A dummy?" he asks, like I'm speaking a foreign language. "This is something you're acquainted with?"

"If you're asking if I've ever switched a piece of evidence, no. But I know of cops who have . . ."

"And they were caught?"

"Some. Never the first time, though."

Bergman brings his hand to his chest, mulling over what I've said. "I don't know . . ."

"You have a better plan?" I ask.

He reads my expression, which says I'm unwavering and unwilling to stomach more of his excuses. "Fine. I'll call him," he says.

"Go ahead. I'll wait."

"I'd prefer you to wait outside."

"Come again?"

"Outside, please?"

I wait outside the door until Bergman calls me in. When I enter, he's finally taken off his suit coat, and his shirt is blotched with sweat. "So?" I ask. "What's the plan?"

"Echo Park. Thirty minutes."

"Where in the park?"

"He said to find a seat, and the phone will come to you."

"Bergman, I told you to cut that cloak-and-dagger shit . . ."

"I'm just relaying what I was told."

"Fine," I say, leaving him looking disgruntled behind his desk, surrounded by bills and a tower of case files. He's staying afloat with a few troubles less than what I've got, and we're both trying not to drown.

CHAPTER FIVE

I drive north to Beverly, make a right onto Silver Lake, merge onto Sunset, and park a block away from Echo Park Lake, a refuge in the heart of the city. It's a five-minute walk through the park to the man-made body of water. The lake is the busiest area of the park's thirty-three acres, boasting the kinds of wildlife many Angelenos rarely see outside zoos and aquariums—fish, geese, frogs, ducks, and finches. I walk past people relaxing on the green, eating lunch on blankets, reading books, and flipping through magazines. I smell tart wine and follow the aroma to a couple cozied up, drinking blush from sippers. They could be inebriated, which would explain their groping and hard kissing, or just plain audacious, lewdly shoving their tongues down each other's throats.

The lake looks deceptively vast in the distance, but I've seen ones on golf courses that are larger and better maintained. Having branded the lake an "impaired body of water" requiring cleanup and revitalization, the city has been restoring it for the last decade. In an *LA Times* article, the LAPD police chief called the surrounding park a "hotbed of crime." Dope dealing, assaults, rapes, and shootings are common occurrences once the sun goes down. I like to think of it as LA's socioeconomic epicenter, one of the only places in the city where you'll see the wealthy, the broke, the artists, the junkies, the models, and the bangers all converge. High-fashion photo shoots happen feet away from drug sales.

I sit down on a park bench and watch the paddleboats—gigantic molded swans—take laps around the lake, drawing wake lines and ripples. A water feature explodes like a broken main, spraying high into the air. Mist blows in my direction, cool against my skin. I seize the moment, clearing my mind as my therapist, Dr. Angell, encourages.

I go over the objectives in my head: *Get the phone. Call Sarada; see if she'll talk with me. Then find Tori and my daughter.* I know I should reach out to Munoz somehow, make sure she's OK. But I'd rather not have to lie about why I was at the boardwalk and potentially jeopardize my and Bergman's operation.

"Hello?" A young woman in her early twenties, maybe older, walks toward me. A fine breeze lifts strands of auburn hair; her hand coddles a camera strapped across her body. "Got a minute?"

"I'm busy."

She's dressed in black: distressed jeans, Vans, a denim jacket over a low-cut top. She smiles, and I notice a silver ring in the crease of her lower lip. "I like your look," she says. I'm not sure what look she's referring to. I didn't sleep well last night, and dark circles sit under my eyes. I haven't shaved, so a shallow beard has set in, and my usually bald head is covered in short black hairs. Plus, my father's off-brand bar soap dried my skin, which feels like it's burning under the brutal sun.

"Come again?" I ask, not sure if the girl's hitting on me or just pandering for change.

"I'm not a weirdo or anything," she says. "I want to know if you'd let me take your picture. One shot. I can even send you a print if you give me your address."

It's a first-time request from a stranger. "There are much better-looking people in this park," I say.

"It's not about that. I'm doing a series on expressions."

"OK?"

"You've got a nice face, but . . ." She seems to search for the right words. "There's a sadness," she says, soft and true, like she knows the emotion intimately. "Please don't take that the wrong way . . . I'm just trying to build my portfolio."

"So how's this work?" I ask. "I let you take my picture and I get the phone back?"

"Phone?" she says, presenting her 35-mm Pentax. "I'm more of an analog girl . . ."

I look her up and down again. She doesn't look suspicious, or how Bergman described his contact. She's younger than a seasoned high-ranking officer would be, and nothing about her says "cop." Even when undercover, police officers move and look a certain way—stiff and square-shouldered with wide struts and beady, paranoid eyes.

"Hey!" a man shouts, closing in on my left. "You Finnegan?" he asks, holding a brown paper bag like a sack lunch.

I spring up from the bench and step in front of the woman, instinctively shielding her from the man. "Who's asking?"

"I got what you need," he says, holding up the paper bag. "Want it or not?"

"Stop," I say, motioning for the man to halt. "There's good."

He freezes about three feet away and offers me the bag. "It's your phone, man. Take it."

I step closer, snatch the bag from his filthy hand, and look inside. The phone is sealed in a separate Ziploc bag. "Who gave this to you?"

"Same guy who paid me fifty bucks," he says, swinging his tattooed arms like flimsy noodles. "Are we good?"

"What'd he look like?"

"Man, I don't know . . . a white dude. Old."

"He say anything?"

"Look," the man says. "I'm just supposed to give you the phone."

"Answer the question."

"Nah," he says. "Didn't say shit really."

I stare him down, reading his body language. He's jumpy, eager for a fix. "All right, fine. Get out of here!"

The man turns on his heels, scratches a cluster of lesions on his arm, and scampers back the way he came. I look to the photographer, who appears more fascinated than shaken. "What the hell was that about?" she asks, energized by the scene.

I evaluate the phone, looking for signs it was tampered with. It's dirty but otherwise in the same condition as when I lost it. I press the "On" button. The phone vibrates, and when the display screen glows, it shows multiple missed calls and a voice mail.

"Must be an important phone," she says, watching me. "Now you have no excuse but to call me."

"I have to go."

"What? You're just going to leave like that?" She brings her hands to her hips and tilts her head to one side. "I'm not your type?"

"It's not that . . ."

"Let me guess—married?"

"Not exactly." I'm still uncertain how the conversation turned to romance. "I'm involved," I say, feeling defensive but unsure why. I begin walking quickly in the direction I parked.

"Sounds like drama." She sounds mildly aggrieved. "Fuck drama."

My sentiments, exactly.

Once in the car, I scroll through the missed calls. Besides Bergman and my father, Sarada is the only person who has my number. She called twice this morning and left a voice mail. I play the message: "I guess you really did lose your phone. Anyway, we need to talk. I'm sure you and Bergman are sorting the whole phone thing out. Call me when you can. Bye."

She sounds weary, brokenhearted, and I think she's been crying. Dr. Angell says every relationship gets tested. I was confident that Sarada and I had already gone through the worst, our gauntlet of fire, but I was wrong.

I call Sarada. She answers. "Hello? Trevor?"

"You still want to talk?"

Chapter Six

"I know you weren't trying to keep things from me," Sarada says, dressed in her robe and slippers. It's her day off. She hands me a cup of coffee and sits next to me in the sunroom. She sips her tea, holding the cup with both hands.

"I didn't think she wanted the baby. She ghosted me, but that isn't an excuse. I was afraid."

"Afraid of what?"

"That you'd leave me."

"Because the baby might be yours?" Sarada frowns.

"Well, yes," I say. "I've always thought if I had a child, it would be with you and only you."

"Technically we weren't together when she got pregnant, Trevor."

"I know . . . but why do you think she showed up now? I was sure Tori hated me."

"I don't think Tori hates you." Sarada sets her tea down on the bistro table between us.

"Tell me," I say. "Did you see Simone? Did she seem OK?" I gaze down into my cup, watching the coffee ripple like silk, anything to avoid having to look Sarada in the eyes.

She lets out a penetrating sigh. I know she may have forgiven me, but she'll remember last night for years to come. "Oh, Trevor." Sarada quivers, overwhelmed with emotion. "She's beautiful." Tears well in her eyes, and I realize Tori showing up with my child has triggered more than anger.

"I need to find them," I say. "Did Tori say where they're living?"

"She didn't tell me much besides Simone being yours," Sarada says, dabbing her eyes. "Maybe she would have told me more, but I kindly asked her to leave." She gets up from her chair. "But she left you something." She goes into the study. When she returns, she hands me an envelope. "I was too angry to give it to you last night."

I open the envelope and remove a handwritten letter. I read it silently, then slip the letter back into the envelope. "What's it say?" Sarada asks. "Are they in trouble?"

"No, but I know where they're staying." I get up from the chair. "I should see them today."

"OK."

"Should I come back here after?" I ask. "I get it if you need time alone."

"Where'd you stay last night?"

"My father's place," I say. "It wasn't my first option. I had a terrible night working a case. Didn't feel like finding a hotel." Telling Sarada I was involved in the Venice Beach shooting will only cause her to worry, and today, the last thing I want is her thoughts to become even heavier.

"And how was it?"

"My back isn't great. He's a pain in the ass, as usual." I shake my head. "He's fine, I guess."

Sarada cuts me a look. I can never shine her on. "You can take the couch in the study tonight," she says. "I'd hate to see you in traction."

"OK," I say, knowing I'm still in the doghouse but happy to be back home. There's a hard knocking at the door, three heavy pounds. "Are you expecting anyone?"

"No," she says, her grip tightening on the teacup. "Are you?"

"You don't think it could be—"

There's another knock, followed by two more. Sarada doesn't speak. Hurt and resentment haven't left her eyes since I arrived. My neck's growing hot. I'm beginning to sweat. Sarada clears her throat. "Are you going to get it?" she asks.

"OK," I say, wanting it to be Tori and Simone but knowing that them showing up would be salt in Sarada's wounds.

Downstairs, the knocking continues. "Coming!" I yell before I look through the door's peephole. "Shit," I say, seeing Sally Munoz standing on the porch. I breathe a moment, gather my thoughts, and then open the door slowly.

"Finnegan," she says. Her face is scrunched, jaw tight. She's dressed in boots, jeans, and a studded leather jacket. One arm's cradled in a sling.

"Crickets?" Her nickname when we were partners. "How are you?"

"How's it look? Too many stitches to count," she says. "Went by your father's place. I don't remember him being so chatty."

"He drinks."

"I got that impression," she says. "Wasn't sure he'd given me the right address." She surveys my sweatpants and the long-sleeve shirt I usually reserve for working out. "Arts District wasn't doing it for you anymore?"

"Needed a change."

"Not sure it suits you," she says, staring at the garden gnome anchored in our flower bed. "We need to talk about last night."

It was only a matter of time before Munoz came knocking. Didn't think it would be this soon. "Now isn't the best time. Tomorrow, breakfast. Machaca burritos at that hole-in-the-wall?"

"I'm not asking, Finn." She bares the gold shield clipped to her belt. "You were there last night. I need to know what you saw." Munoz wants me to believe she's here in a law enforcement capacity, but I know the LAPD hasn't cleared her for duty, not after what she went through last night. And there's no way her sergeant assigned her the homicide investigation of her partner. "Or we can always do this at the division . . ."

"It's like that?"

"I need answers."

I know how pain can strip a person of their warmth and endearment, turn them cold, make them betray their character. But something tells me Munoz didn't become this way overnight. Two years working as a narc. Undercover investigations. Handling informants. Having to contend with drug dealers and killers brings about an inevitable hardening, like calcified stone.

"I did what I could," I say. "There isn't much more to tell."

"You witnessed a crime. Didn't you think you should give a statement?"

"I didn't think I'd be much help."

"What the hell, Finn?" she asks. "You left me." Munoz can't know why I didn't stick around. Any involvement with the police could mean the end of my and Bergman's crusade. It's a risk I can't take, not even for her.

"I know a place we can go," I say. "But I need to change."

"Go," she says, adjusting her arm sling. "I'll wait here."

I close the door and go upstairs to the bedroom. Sarada's sitting on the bed's edge near the window. "Who's that at the door?" she asks. "What's going on?"

I grab a pair of dark jeans from the dresser and snatch a black button-down from a hanger in the closet, tossing them on the bed.

"She's staring at me," Sarada says, looking out the window. "Who is she?"

"Sally Munoz," I say, pulling up my jeans. "My old partner."

"The one with the weird nickname? Dragonfly or something?"

"Crickets." I unhook a belt hanging from the closet door and feed it through the loops around my waist. "I'm helping her with a case."

"A case?" she asks. "Doesn't she have a partner for that?"

"She did." I work my arms through the shirtsleeves. "I shouldn't stay here tonight. Better if I crash at Pop's."

Sarada says nothing as I reach for the top shelf of the closet, drag down my duffel bag, and begin filling it with clothes—boxers, undershirts, socks, collared shirts, a sweater, and two pairs of wrinkle-free pants. I toss in my travel Dopp kit, which contains deodorant, a toothbrush and toothpaste, soap, and moisturizer.

"Well, are you at least going to tell me what kind of case?"

"It's more of a favor," I say, picking up my holstered snubnose off the dresser and putting it in the duffel bag. I don my brown suede jacket, last year's birthday gift from Sarada, and throw the duffel bag over my shoulder. "I've been thinking . . . maybe it's better I don't go with you to France."

"You've been thinking this since when?" she asks.

"I don't know," I say. Before talking with my father last night, the thought hadn't entered my mind. But now I wonder if we're made of the same stock. Am I destined to hurt Sarada, bring chaos and pain into her life? I don't want to believe that, but Crickets at the door feels like a bad omen.

"You don't know whether or not you want to see me for six months?" she asks. "Trevor, we leave in a few days."

"I know . . . I know," I say.

"Is this about Tori?" she asks. "You don't even know if Simone is yours."

"It's just a feeling . . ."

"I can't believe this."

"I just want us to be in a good place. Having me there could be a distraction for you," I say. "I know how long you've waited for this opportunity."

"If you don't want to go, Trevor, just say it."

I take a deep breath, push it out quickly. "Of course I want to go."

"Then what's all this about?"

"I don't know . . . I'm . . . I'm tired. We should talk later."

Sarada shrugs, bites her lower lip. "Fine."

I leave the room, feeling like a failure, and head downstairs. When I reach the front door, I look back to see Sarada standing on the top step.

"Trevor . . ."

"Yes?" Our eyes lock, and I wait for her to speak. No words come. "I love you," I say, breaking the silence. "Never doubt that." She looks as if she's pondering a response, but says nothing. I walk out the front door, locking it behind me.

Outside, Munoz stands on the lawn, looking up at a large oak tree. "Nice neighborhood," she says. "Lots of foliage. That's how you can pick out the good neighborhoods in LA . . . by the number of trees."

"And grocery stores," I say sharply, already tired of her musings. "So where do you want to go?"

"Leaving town?" she asks, looking at the duffel bag.

"I'm staying with my father."

"Trouble in paradise?"

"I'd rather not get into it with you."

"Never thought I'd see you settled," she says. "She's pretty, by the way, but they always are . . ."

"Dammit, Crickets," I say, reaching the peak of tolerance. "What the hell do you want from me?"

Munoz pumps her fist, her voice a rasping growl. "People don't call me that anymore. Got it?"

"Easy, easy," I say, my hands up, yielding. "I got it. Munoz it is. Now, please, where do you want to go?"

"Any decent happy hours around here?" she asks, tempering her attitude.

"I know one."

"That narrows it down. We can take my car."

"You can follow me," I say, heading toward the Falcon.

"What?" she asks. "Is it the arm?"

"No," I say, treading lightly. "I have somewhere to go afterward."

"We're not going far, are we?"

"Couple blocks east," I say.

"Just hop in. We'll leave when you're ready."

"If I have to, I'll walk back home."

"Since when did you get so anal?"

"I'm serious, Munoz."

"Sure, whatever."

"You got the first round," I say, secretly feeling nostalgic for riding in the Crown Vic.

I put my duffel bag in the Falcon's trunk, then get into the late-model sedan, navy with tinted windows. Munoz works her way into the driver's seat and settles behind the wheel. It's the same model we used to work out of. We sat in the bucket seats for hours, and they never felt comfortable, not after eighteen-hour stakeouts or the time we spent two grueling days tailing homicide suspects into Bakersfield and Oakland. The seat was always firm, like my grandmother's living room sofa, which people rarely sat on.

Munoz starts the car. I look back at the townhouse and see Sarada staring out the window, an unmeasurable amount of hurt in her face.

We drive down Sierra Madre Boulevard to the Swashbuckler Lounge, a pirate-themed bar. According to Sierra Madre's free paper, the *Foothill Gazette*, it's known for cheap beer and stiff cocktails and is the "best place to drink" in the northern San Gabriel Valley, though the pickings are slim.

We park in front. If it weren't for the green awning reading SWASHBUCKLER LOUNGE, we would have driven past the spot. Munoz gets out of the car, slamming the door behind her. I take a moment, touching the dash, feeling the cheap plastic and stitching . . . then hop out.

"They serve food in here?" she asks. "Haven't eaten in hours."

"Don't know," I say. "Never set foot in here."

"Then why are we here if you can't vouch for it?"

"This isn't a social call, Munoz. You're the one who banged on my door. This place has alcohol and that's good enough for me."

She follows me into the bar. "An unusual dive"—that's what the article dubbed the Swashbuckler. The description fits. It's dimly lit, not unexpected, and behind the bar, liquor bottles clutter mirrored shelves. Fancy bourbons, gins, and rums sit at the top, collecting dust. It doesn't seem like the type of place where patrons order pours from one-hundred-dollar bottles of booze. The bar's a home for hard drinkers, people like my father who want to forget the past. But drunkenness doesn't conquer anything. It only defers sorrow for a few hours, a day if you're lucky.

Munoz looks around. The bar is nearly empty. Two older white men are ordering drinks. A group of men shoots pool in the back.

"Jesus, Finn. Where did you bring me?" Munoz's head tips toward the tacky paintings that line the walls: pirates drinking from foaming mugs, fondling maidens, and brandishing cutlasses. "What's with all the pirate shit? And that smell . . ." She turns her nose up, trying to handle the odor of skunky beer mixed with a tinge of pine deodorizer.

"Let's just order," I say.

We approach the counter. Two older men drinking beer stare at Munoz. I know she can feel it, their eyes studying her in a way that couldn't be confused with flattery. When they notice me watching them, they look away, laughing among themselves.

The bartender, a man wearing a knit cap and a lumberjackish green flannel shirt, grips the counter's edge. "Can I get you something?" he asks. The pinkish skin on his neck looks irritated, like he has psoriasis or a severe sunburn. "We only serve beer and liquor," he says curtly. "No wine." He looks to Munoz, then eyes me like a spotlight. "Or malts."

In a place like this, it's best to order bottled. "Two golden lagers," I say.

The bartender doesn't acknowledge my order but reaches below the counter and comes up with two cold beers. He removes the caps with an opener and slides them forward. "Ten bucks," he says.

Munoz slips me a ten-dollar bill and two singles, and I hand him the money. She rolls her eyes. I'm not sure if it's intended for the bartender or me. He doesn't thank me, and we leave to find a booth. Finding a place to sit with Munoz is on my short list of annoyances. She always needs to see the front door. Like most cops, she closely monitors who comes and goes, and she wants to be near the establishment's restroom. Munoz never mentioned it while we worked together, but after riding in a car with her for three weeks, I suspected she suffered from IBS. A good number of cops are afflicted with the condition. It was so prevalent that the department shrink hosted a mandatory seminar in which he named some of the major triggers—stress, lack of sleep, and poor eating habits. He taught us breathing exercises, highlighted the importance of exercise, and gave us handouts: "10 Foods to Avoid" and "Living with Irritable Bowel Syndrome."

Given Munoz's experience last night—the severe emotional toll—it could be a bad night for her. "This spot looks fine," I say, standing by an empty booth. Behind it hangs a large painting of a topless woman cozied up to a toothless brute.

Munoz surveys the booth and slides across the ragged vinyl seat. I sit across from her as she places a cardboard coaster under her beer.

"It was hard when you left the department," she says, taking a swig. "No one in RHD wanted to ride with me."

"I didn't know—"

"How could you?"

"Right," I say, tasting the bland lager. "I never imagined the Soledad case would hurt your career."

"Me either," she says. "Guilty by association, I guess."

"I'm sorry."

Munoz ignores my apology and drinks more beer. "But narcotics is always in need of fresh blood," she says, mouth wet with ale. "Riley took me under his wing, made me feel at home. He was a good partner."

The men huddled around the pool table are shouting, cursing, talking money. We both glance over as an overweight man in paint-stained overalls racks the balls. "They're probably drunk," I say, dismissing their rowdiness.

"I need to know what you saw last night," she says insistently.

"OK." I visualize the shooter in my mind, but nothing's clear. It's like looking through a smudged lens. "I went after the gunman, but I couldn't catch up." Condensation beads over the beer bottle's label and collects on the table. "I lost him in the parking lot."

"Him?" she asks.

I take a long sip, then say, "Pretty sure the shooter was male."

"And that's it?" Her elbow on the table, she leans forward. "He evaded you?"

"Yes."

"What were you doing on the boardwalk?"

"Thought I'd walk the beach," I say, having anticipated her line of questioning. "Clear my head."

"I thought you hated sand."

"I kept on the path . . ."

Munoz takes another sip of beer. "I haven't been able to sleep," she says, rubbing her shoulder. "I just keep seeing Riley's face."

"You talk to the department shrink yet?"

"I'm dragging my feet, but I'll make an appointment."

"It helps, you know."

"What does?"

"Talking to someone," I say. "A professional."

"Didn't take you for the therapy type."

"I had a change in perspective," I say.

Munoz looks at the men playing pool behind her. I count four of them, along with more than a dozen empty shot glasses on a barstool. "The chaplain said I should take some days at the Sanctuary," she says.

"You going to go?" I ask.

"Joshua Tree?" She takes another sip of beer. "And do what? Stargaze?" Munoz pushes a few untamed strands of her hair out of her face. It's the first time I've seen Munoz with her hair down. She notices me looking. "What is it?"

"Nothing . . ."

"Just say it, Finn."

"I've never seen you out of a ponytail."

"Kinda hard to manage it with my arm in a sling," she says, tapping her nearly empty beer on the table.

All those hours together, and never once did Munoz let her hair down. It was part of her persona—by the book, sometimes terribly rigid, but she always appeared to be squared away. Stakeouts were spent talking sports—Clippers, Dodgers, Galaxy. I feigned interest so we didn't have to talk about her failing marriage. Pregnant with her first child at twenty-two. Husband in the army. (Or was it the marines?) Both career-driven workaholics with no time for each other. Marital strife and divorce are common for cops. When Munoz went on about her loveless relationship, it felt like a family drama that should have been canceled after the first season, and I had watched the reruns too many times.

"So what else do you want to know?" I ask.

"That's everything?"

"I wish I could give you more. But as I said, I didn't see much."

"A mystery gunman on a motorcycle. Might as well be the one-armed man." Munoz takes the coaster from under her beer glass and bends the corners. Good dexterity. It must be her shooting hand.

"You've got to have some idea who's behind it," I say.

"One name . . . Cassandra Boyle."

"The socialite?"

"That's right," Munoz says, like thinking about Cassandra puts a bad taste in her mouth.

"Didn't she come close to getting pinched by vice for running an escort service?"

"Well, close only counts in horseshoes," she says. "She's got a new venture. Marijuana dispensaries."

"So goes the whole city."

"Yeah, well, the bureaucrats fucked up, and no one's playing by the rules."

"You mean Cassandra?"

"She's been funneling dope through the dispensaries—pills, heroin, and coke, mostly. She's opened a slew of places around the city, but the Venice location is her most lucrative."

"Who's her supplier?"

"We don't know. Riley and I were only three weeks into the investigation."

My mind is trying to make sense of the information, to connect the few dots I have. Cassandra Boyle is a known undesirable who's hidden behind money and influence for years. But if Munoz and Riley were trying to make a case, why did Bergman's contact have me surveil them? What happened inside the dispensary? What isn't Munoz telling me?

"What happens now?" I ask. "With the case, I mean . . ."

Munoz doesn't answer. She's still watching the pool game. "What is it, Munoz?" I ask, looking in the direction of the men.

And that's when I hear it: "All I want is for him to build that god-damn wall."

She slams her beer glass down. I turn to see the players watching us.

"You got a problem, señorita?" the pudgy player asks in a singsong taunt, something more fitting on a grade-school playground than inside a bar.

"You should keep all that bullshit to yourself," Munoz says.

"Free country, last I checked. Ever hear of freedom of speech?"

"Go back to your game, asshole, and keep it down."

"How about you go back to your goddamn country," he says, pool stick resting on his shoulder like a Neanderthal's club. True to every bigot I've encountered in life, once the dam of civility breaks, the slurs come flooding. "And take the rest of the border jumpers with you."

Munoz stands up, knocks her beer to the floor. The glass shatters, spilling the little beer she had left. It's loud enough to be heard by the bartender, who enters from what looks like a storage room behind the bar. Munoz steps toward the slobbering man, who I'm betting is as nasty sober as he is drunk. He sizes her up. Munoz is petite, but I can tell she's been lifting. She's put on muscle in her arms and shoulders, maybe more than twenty pounds since last I saw her. "You want to say that shit again?" she asks.

"You heard me, chica," he says, turning to his friends, who look thrilled by the prospect of violence. He holds the pool stick like a batter squaring up at the plate. Munoz doesn't budge. Cops never do.

"Go ahead," she says. "Let's see what you've got."

I get up from the table and approach, hoping to defuse the situation. "Screw them," I say. "Let's just go."

"After he apologizes," she says, her hand on her belt.

"Apologize? You serious?" The man's hearty laugh turns to a phlegmy cough. He flaps his husky jowls. "I'm not apologizing for shit."

There's the distinct sound of pulled Velcro, and then the collapsible baton appears in Munoz's hand. I never saw her pull it. I might be fatigued, or the alcohol's impeding my focus. The baton extends with a snap of her wrist. She makes a cutting motion, like swinging a driver into a golf ball, striking the man's leg. It buckles at an unnatural angle.

"Ah, shit!" he cries. He drops to the floor, gasping for air and gnashing his teeth. "You bitch!"

Before I can pull Munoz out of the fray, she stomps her boot's heel into the man's face. Blood, dark and rich, gushes from his nose. His drunk buddies rally around him, trying to shake off their stupors, raising their fists, cursing and spewing slurs: *Filthy wetback . . . Greasy Spic.*

They stumble toward Munoz. She swings the baton with menace, sending the black steel through the air. "You want some, too?" she screams. "Come get some, las conchas de su madre!"

I watch the men's hands for weapons, bottles, anything they could harm us with. "Munoz, we need to go," I say.

"Hey!" the bartender shouts from behind the bar, holding a cordless phone. "Get the hell out of here. I'm calling the cops!"

Munoz swings again, wide and wild. The men trip over each other, trying to dodge the strike. "I am the fucking police," she says, her rage reaching a crescendo. The bleeding man lies on his side, as helplessly still as a beached whale. Blood collects under his nose, runs into his mouth, drips onto the floor. He looks up at Munoz. The smugness is gone. He's small, broken.

"That was fun, cabrón. We should do it again sometime." Munoz collapses the baton, winks at the fat man, and runs toward the exit, never looking back.

———

I follow Munoz through the door to the Crown Vic. "We better get out of here, in case he does call it in," she says, opening the car door. I lag, trying to get my thoughts straight. "What are you doing? Get in . . ."

"What the hell for?"

"How are you going to get home?"

"My legs work."

"Don't be so dramatic," she says. "Officers might be here any minute."

"I'll take my chances," I say, walking in the direction of the townhouse.

"Finn, hold up," she says, but I keep walking. "Wait, dammit."

"Good luck with everything, Munoz."

"Finn, will you listen a moment?" she asks, hard up for my attention. "I need your help."

I stop and face her. "What can I possibly help you with? You have more bar brawls on your itinerary tonight?"

"You think I should have let that slide? It's bad enough I have to hear that shit around the division," she says. "But now I can't even have a drink in peace."

"I live around here. I have to see these people."

"That's unfortunate . . . I hope the whole town isn't like those dicks."

"Bye, Munoz."

"No, Finn, wait!" she shouts. "I'm sorry. I get it. I'm just on edge . . ."

"Clearly."

"That's why I need you to keep my lid on tight. Just come take a ride with me."

The bar's door swings open, and the bartender stares us down, the phone to his ear. I'm sure he's giving the operator our descriptions. I turn away from him. "Look at this shit you got me into."

"We could be miles away if you get into the car . . ."

"And go where?"

"Malibu."

"What the hell's in Malibu?"

"Cassandra Boyle."

"Are you out of your mind?"

"I just want to talk to her."

"Why don't you leave it to the homicide detectives?"

"Puga and Wilton? They're second-rate, out of their league," she says. "Riley was my partner. It's my responsibility to find out what happened to him."

"News flash, Munoz. I'm not a cop anymore."

"You're not sworn," she says. "But you'll always be blue like me . . . like Riley."

"It's a bad idea . . ."

"Stay in the car if it makes you feel better." I hear sirens in the distance. A benefit of living in a small town with a minimal amount of crime is that emergency services are immediate, especially when the fire station is three blocks away. "All I'm asking for is company. I'll drop you back home when we're done. I promise."

Munoz gets in the car. The sirens are on the move, a block or two away. Sounds like an ambulance, a police car, maybe a fire engine. "Come on, Finn," she says, her head out the window as exhaust pours from the tailpipe.

"Shit, Munoz," I say, opening the passenger-side door and getting into the Crown Vic. Before I can put my seat belt on, Munoz reverses quickly, makes an illegal U-turn, and heads south toward the freeway.

———

We ride in silence until Munoz accelerates onto the 210 on-ramp, driving west toward the 134. "How long are you going to give me the silent treatment?" she asks. "You're worse than my kids."

I ignore her, looking at my watch. It's six minutes past five o'clock. I'm driving to Malibu when I could be on the way to see my daughter in Orange County. Another ruined night. I pull Tori's letter from my pocket and read it again.

> Dear Finn,
> I'm writing this for our daughter, Simone. She was born on June 9, 2015, at a hospital in Irvine. My parents refused to come; friends were too busy. I know that I should have told you, but I was still so angry with you. I was blinded by it. I couldn't see how her

knowing you would make her life better. We've been living in Vancouver, Canada, where a friend got me a job in the wardrobe department on a TV show. Simone likes to visit the set and knows most of the crew members' names. She's so smart, Finn. Reminds me of you. I think it's time you meet her, if you're willing.

We're staying in Orange County while I get some things in order. The High Tide Hotel in Newport Beach. Room 222. Please, see us.

—Tori & Simone/604-552-5555

"What you got there?" Munoz asks, glancing over at the letter.

"Nothing," I say, shoving it back into my pocket.

"If you're worried about earlier, I'll take care of whatever heat might come your way," she says, switching lanes without signaling. "You didn't do anything to that piece of garbage, anyways." Not doing anything in the radius of a crime has never made much difference. Plenty of black men are locked up right now for the offense of "not doing anything."

"Whatever, Munoz." I look out the window at a passing motorist. The Crown Vic's dark tint makes everything appear surreal, a netherworld.

"Your father said you were working as a PI for a law firm. That true?"

"Yes," I say. "Just something to keep me busy."

"You know," Munoz says, "we didn't use to lie to each other." I feel her eyes on me.

"And who's the liar in this car?" I ask.

Munoz sits up in the seat and repositions her hand on the steering wheel. Driving with one arm must be tiring, and she's too proud to let on that swinging her baton like she'd lost all sense probably made it worse. "Maybe we both are," she says. "I know you weren't at the boardwalk by chance."

Does she know? But how?

"It's like I told you," I say. "I needed to clear my head."

"Did he hire you to watch me?" she asks.

"Hire me?"

"Rodrigo," she says with spite. "That chickenshit."

"Your husband?"

"Separated."

"Since when?"

"Last year," she says.

"Sorry to hear that, Munoz," I say. "But I was just there for the ocean."

She reads my face, combing it for evidence, collecting every bit of truth. "Rodrigo took the kids, and he wants a divorce, full custody," she says. "They're living together with his mother in Fresno." I tally up the heartbreak in Munoz's life: a dead partner, separation, absent kids. "He blamed the job. Said I stopped making time for the family. He didn't understand, never could."

"Understand what?"

"Who I am," she says. I wonder how my life might have turned out had I remained a detective with the LAPD. Maybe it would have been me spilling my troubles to Munoz? "It's a terrible feeling knowing you can't give your children anything more than what you've already given them." And like that, the old Sally Munoz returns. "I've never been able to breastfeed. I mean, I've wanted to. I tried, but nothing. 'If you relax, like the doctor said, the milk will come,' Rodrigo would say. Always if I would just relax . . . like it was that fucking easy. That's what I get for marrying that kind of man."

"What kind of man?"

"Rodrigo's first love, maybe even his truest love, has always been the army," she says. "The man can assemble his rifle in five minutes flat, but he treated my postpartum like trigonometry. Never bothered trying to understand it." Munoz accelerates to pass a slow-moving car. "But that's life, isn't it?"

"Not always," I say. "People can change."

We travel under the sign for the Golden State Freeway, the 5, toward Los Angeles. "I guess we all have problems." Munoz pushes past the emotion. "I'm sorry I didn't reach out after what went down in the alley. By the time word of it got to me, I didn't know what to say. I should have been there."

"You had a baby, Munoz."

"Maybe things wouldn't have gone south, and you wouldn't have been"—she looks at me compassionately, a look once reserved for assault victims—"stabbed."

"Don't worry about it. Family comes first."

"You were my family," she says, the emotion returning. "We're the same, aren't we? Both of us have suffered because of this job." She grimaces as if the thoughts are poison. "It's given, but it's also taken its fair share."

My father always said becoming a police officer is one of the most self-destructive choices a person can make. He likened it to drowning in a lake. The deeper one sinks, the darker things get. It can be unbearable, and soon the last and only light is the shimmering sun on the water's surface. When that's gone, it's over.

"It's in the past," I say, knowing I can't provide her any comfort. I can't see past my own pain.

We merge onto the 110 south, passing through downtown. There's a game tonight. In a few hours, the Staples Center will be lit purple. Brilliant white beams will crisscross the night sky. I lower the window some, pining for fresh air, but it's tainted by diesel exhaust from a semi commanding the center lane. We take the curving on-ramp to the Santa Monica Freeway. We're ahead of rush hour, and vehicles are just beginning to clutter the lanes. If the 405 is this clear, it won't be long until we reach the winding coastline of Malibu. Maybe I can still make it to Orange County before ten p.m.

"I knew when this job owned me," she says. "The last week of my maternity, I couldn't sleep. Most moms suffer insomnia over worry, knowing they won't see their babies. Me . . . I was excited, couldn't wait to get back to the division." Munoz brakes behind slow-moving traffic. There's a squeal and cooked brake dust. "I told Rodrigo that, and he said—"

I notice blood on Munoz's ear. "You got something."

"What?"

"Your ear."

She looks in the visor's mirror, turning her head for a better view. "El Gordo's blood," she says. "Grab me a tissue from the glove box."

I reach into the glove box, pull a tissue from a travel-size packet. "Here," I say, handing it to her.

She dampens the tissue with her tongue and wipes the blood from her earlobe. "I get it?"

"Yeah," I say. "You're good."

"Thanks, partner."

CHAPTER SEVEN

The Crown Vic is at half a tank as we travel Highway 1 into Malibu. The traffic was hectic on the 405, and it took us two hours to reach the coastline. Munoz turns on the high beams, and light stretches a little farther into the darkness. The GPS says Cassandra Boyle's residence is another ten miles.

Munoz is quiet, watching the road. She isn't familiar with the curves, and the area is crawling with wildlife. Animals likely skitter across the two-lane highway at all hours, apparent by the roadkill.

Homes are lit in the distance. Golden lights gleam along the expansive crest, nestled in affluent enclaves where owners relish views of the Pacific from verandas. "Must be nice," Munoz says, "living out here."

"Oh, I don't know . . . I hear the salty air is bad for your car's paint."

"That's what you're worried about?" she asks. "Hell, I'd be able to buy as many cars as I'd want if I could afford to live in this place."

The GPS alerts Munoz to make a right onto Malibu Canyon Road. We drive through a lit tunnel. My eyes adjust to the bright concrete tube after staring into near blackness. Munoz dims the high beams so she doesn't blind the driver in the oncoming lane. We reach the end of the tunnel and cross the threshold back into the pitch-black night. A road sign warns of sharp curves ahead. Munoz steadies the Crown Vic between double-yellow, never topping thirty-five miles per hour. The road cuts through the foothills and carries us over a bridge. A truck passes, headlights filling the car's cabin. I glimpse Munoz's hand tight on the wheel.

"You nervous?" I ask.

"What?" There's a sting in Munoz's voice, like my question has offended her. "No, why? Do I look nervous?"

"Just checking on you," I say. "So what's the plan when we get to Cassandra's?"

"I'm going in," she says, her eyes tracking the twisty road. "Stay in the car if you want."

"Yeah, I got that . . . I mean, how certain are you that Cassandra killed Riley?"

"Pretty fucking certain, Finn. Motive and opportunity and all that . . ."

"Even if that's true, she isn't going to confess because you lean on her."

"You think I don't know that?" Munoz takes her hand off the wheel and quickly rolls her wrist, then grips the wheel again. "Contrary to what you may have thought when we worked together, I'm a good detective—"

"I never doubted your abilities, Munoz," I say, though it's not completely true. When we were first partnered together, I had reservations about Munoz's street IQ. Neither of us had spent much of our careers investigating homicides, but we grew together, learned to trust each other. At least, that's what I thought . . .

"You didn't have to say it, Finn . . ."

"Was it something I did?"

"It's what you didn't do," she says. "You never once suggested the sergeant assign me point on a case. I literally walked in your shadow, even though I'd been a detective six months longer than you. Your shield was gold, same as mine, but somehow I got treated like your sidekick."

"I didn't realize," I say. "Is that why you don't want to be called Crickets anymore?"

"I've never wanted to be called Crickets, dammit!" I always thought the nicknames doled out in the academy were amusing, but Munoz rightfully disagrees. "You know why they called me Crickets?" she asks. The entire department knows why. Munoz's academy drill instructor felt it took her too long to sound off, to answer questions. She couldn't get her words together under pressure. "All I hear is crickets," he'd say. "Goddamn crickets!"

On the stand, Munoz dreaded cross-examination. If the defendant's counsel were any good, they would make her out to be a bumbling fool, seeding enough doubt in a juror's mind to successfully argue that the LAPD had planted evidence or forced a confession. Munoz's stutter and her failure to answer directly became every prosecutor's horror, an Achilles' heel that could destroy a solid case.

"Riley finally got the few assholes in narcotics to call me by my real name and show me some respect."

"I didn't realize it bothered you," I say. "I should have said something." The truth is my voice wasn't much louder than Munoz's. I wouldn't have been able to end the taunting, not like Riley had. I learned during my time on patrol that I didn't have the agency to change anyone's mind on the streets or in the department. Riley and I were nothing alike—the only thing we both had in common was that we left Munoz on her own. "If I could go back and change it, I would," I say. "I'd change that and a lot more."

"We all wish that, don't we?"

"I don't want this night to be added to my list of regrets, Munoz. I just want to know the play. Humor me, please?"

"Fine," she says with a wearied sigh. "I'm going to ask Cassandra a question."

"OK."

"I want to know why . . ." Munoz's voice cracks. "Why she didn't kill me, too."

Grief? Survivor's guilt? She's rolling the dice. No strategy, all chance. The likelihood of Cassandra taking the bait and bragging about her crime or divulging information is astronomically slim. Still, any line of questioning will produce a result. It's cause and effect. Suspects may remain silent, but their faces can tell a story, revealing something true, giving detectives something to work with, anything that could be used to tip the scale. But if Cassandra is as sharp as I hear, Munoz has driven us fifty miles to have a door slammed in her face. Or, worse, not opened at all.

We take a left onto a long paved road leading to a large white house on a hill. It's modern, evocative of a shoebox. We pull into a driveway lined with mushroom-shaped lights. A floodlight over the garage turns on, along with additional lights on the side of the home.

"So much for the element of surprise," I say, realizing sensors have detected the Crown Vic and the abundance of light probably means the home's surveillance system is recording us.

There are cars in the driveway: a German coupe and a luxury SUV. Munoz parks, and we sit for a moment, watching the house. "You think anyone's home?" I ask.

"Doesn't matter," she says, pulling a picklock from her pocket.

"You can't do that," I say. "What the hell are you thinking?"

"There might be evidence in there. Something that I can use to implicate Cassandra in Riley's death or at least tie her to the drug ring."

"That's what warrants are for. Anything you find in there won't be admissible. You'd be effectively killing the case."

She unfastens her seat belt. "Maybe it isn't about the right way anymore."

"It's the only thing it should be about," I say, ignoring my checkered law enforcement career. "What if you trip an alarm? In this neighborhood, cops will be here on the spot—what then?"

"I know Cassandra," she says. "There's no alarm. She doesn't want cops showing up to her house, ever."

Munoz opens the door, gets out. "Think about this," I say.

"Sit tight, Finn," she says as she shuts the door behind her. Everything in me is saying I shouldn't follow her, that she's heading down a disastrous path, and that the outcome will be dire.

And that's why I hop out of the Crown Vic and join her at Cassandra's door. I'd want Munoz to do the same for me if I were thinking illogically and about to commit a crime.

"Couldn't stay away, I see," she says before ringing the doorbell.

Coming to a suspected drug dealer's home without a warrant, backup, or reasonable suspicion isn't wise, but breaking in is downright idiotic. I know Munoz is better than this, smarter than this, but Riley's death has thrown her off her game. Tonight I'm here as a failsafe. Munoz had enough foresight to know that if left on her own, she could do something worse than violating Penal Code 459: Breaking and Entering.

"Someone's home," I say, struggling to hear what could be heavy feet against hardwood. We stand clear of the door, Munoz on the left, me on the right, just as we would if we were executing a warrant or responding to a high-risk call.

"Announce yourselves," a man demands in a baritone voice.

"LAPD," Munoz says. "Is Cassandra Boyle home?"

I glare at Munoz, mouthing the words: "I'm. Not. A. Cop." Impersonating a sworn officer, even in the company of one, is a felony.

"I got this," she says. "Just watch my back."

"I was never here. Understood?"

Munoz nods, and the door opens slowly to reveal a towering, muscular white man with wavy gray hair down to his shoulders. He's dressed in what could be pajamas or a martial arts gi.

Munoz flashes her badge. The gold shield is wrapped with a black ribbon symbolizing that an officer has fallen in the line of duty.

"LAPD," the man says. "Malibu isn't your jurisdiction."

"I'd like to speak to Cassandra Boyle," Munoz says.

"Do you have a warrant?"

"I've come to talk." Munoz puts her badge away. "Not planning to arrest her . . . yet." If this is Munoz's strategy to sit down with Cassandra, she was better off trying to question her over the phone.

"This is private property," the man says, expressionless. "You're trespassing. Please leave."

"And who are you supposed to be? Lurch?"

"He's whomever I tell him to be." The man steps aside, and Cassandra Boyle comes into view. "Tonight, he's my yoga instructor." She's dressed in a sheer chemise, something between a nightgown and a robe. I'm drawn to her eyes—big emeralds that sparkle in the porch light's incandescence and pop with an exuberance seldom demonstrated for police. "Detective Munoz, to what do I owe the pleasure?" Her smile reminds me of Tori's. Ultrabright. Perfect teeth. It was one of the first things I noticed the night Tori and I met. I've always thought her mega-white ivories were the work of a craftsman, the sort of cosmetic dentist sought after by celebrities. The same goes for Miss Green Eyes.

"We need to talk," Munoz says.

"Consider it a one-time courtesy, Detective." Cassandra is about five foot ten and thin. Standing barefoot in the doorway, she looks to be in her mid- to late forties under forgiving light. "Oh dear . . ." She looks at Munoz's arm in the sling. "Is this from the attack?" Before Munoz can answer, she resumes: "I'm so sorry to hear about Detective Riley. I didn't realize the department would replace him so quickly."

"Riley wasn't replaced," Munoz says, perturbed. "This isn't my partner."

"Oh," Cassandra says. "Who might you be?"

I don't answer. Cassandra looks at me oddly. Munoz says, "He's a special consultant working the case with me."

"A consultant?" Cassandra tongues her pouty lips, unquestionably plumped with filler. "Well, this is interesting. Please, come in."

Munoz enters first, and I follow. Standing in the foyer, I notice blank white walls and a flowering plant that looks alive but could be synthetic. Cassandra doesn't strike me as the nurturing type. Maybe it's Lurch who has the green thumb? Everything feels fake, like the inside of a model home. Nothing's out of place.

"Lock the door, Nigel. You can go back to the yoga studio."

Nigel gives a disapproving grumble, locks the door, and begins to walk down a hallway toward the rear of the house. When he's no longer in sight, Cassandra leads us down the same hallway. It's a departure from the sparse foyer. The walls are adorned with framed photos: Cassandra posing with former and current politicians of various stripes, spiritual gurus, tech entrepreneurs, and sheriffs and police chiefs.

"I must say, I usually don't open the door for unsolicited visitors, but something tells me this is important, Detective."

"It is," Munoz says.

"How can I help?"

"I've got questions."

"Anything for the LAPD." Cassandra leads us into a bright kitchen with black countertops, maybe marble or quartz. "My grandfather was a staunch supporter of the department. Even hosted the policemen's ball at his film studio in the '80s."

"I'm aware," Munoz says.

"He always said things were different back then."

"Different how?" Munoz asks.

"Well, for starters," Cassandra says, "there weren't many female detectives, especially with the last name Munoz. But it's good to know things are changing."

"Sure," she says. "Changing every day."

Adjacent to the kitchen is a family room. A large gray couch hosts three girls watching TV. I glance at a brunette in rhinestone sweatpants and a fitness bra. The other two are dressed similarly. At first, I'm not sure, but the distinct pink hair color confirms it. I recognize her and the shorter blonde as the sex workers from the Surfside Motel. I immediately turn away so they don't see my face. There's not much chance they'd recognize me, but I don't want to test the waters.

"These are my daughters," Cassandra says, pointing to the girls. They're cleaned up, not nearly as disheveled as the night I saw them. I'm grateful they don't acknowledge us, too entranced by a reality show starring buxom women with plastic faces.

"Daughters?" I ask, breaking my vow of silence. Munoz cuts her eyes at me.

"He speaks," Cassandra says. "They're adopted, but our bond is no different than if I had birthed them. I have two others as well."

"A full house," I say. "I've got one myself. Not quite 'going out' age yet."

"Well, enjoy it. Once they turn eighteen, it's like the trials of Job."

"What are your other two doing tonight?" I ask.

"Working," she says. "I always tell them there are no free meals in this house."

"Working at this hour? Doing what, exactly?"

"Cocktail waitresses," she says. "Some Hollywood nightclub where they charge people five hundred dollars for bottles of cheap champagne."

"You don't know where your daughters work?"

"The name escapes me right now." She's defensive. "A new club opens every month. Who can really keep up?"

"And all they sell is champagne?" Munoz asks.

"Yes," Cassandra says. "If it means they can pay their car insurance, it's fine with me. Like I always tell them, don't waste the pretty."

Munoz sucks her teeth. "How progressive of you . . ."

"I didn't catch your name," Cassandra says, looking at me and conspicuously irritated.

I pretend I don't hear her question. "The champagne any good?"

"I don't know," she says, her tone less friendly. "They wear glitter thongs, shove sparklers into the bottles, and carry them to VIPs. I don't think the champagne needs to be good."

"You must be proud," Munoz says with a sideways glance.

"I am," she says, looking over at the girls, now occupied with their phones. "My daughters have accomplished quite a bit, despite adversity. We should speak in the study." Cassandra's terse, nearly abandoning her pompous charade as a concerned citizen. "It's much more private."

Munoz grins. "Lead the way."

We follow Cassandra into a large room with built-in bookshelves and a baby grand piano. Vast glass panels offer a breathtaking view of the Pacific. Munoz takes a moment to look out at the ocean. I peruse Cassandra's books. There are numerous titles related to high fashion, the golden age of cinema, politics, architecture, Californian and European histories, vintage automobiles, and trains, along with a collection of travel guides from the 1950s to the '70s.

Cassandra sits in a cream-colored leather chair, wide and plush. The seat swallows her slender body, and she sinks into the cushion. "It's something, isn't it?" she asks. "I've always been terrified of the ocean."

Munoz clears her throat. "Why's that?"

"There's so much we don't know. Species that have lived for thousands of years. Fish that exist in pure darkness." Cassandra brings her hands together, tickled with excitement. "They say scientists know more about space than they do the oceans."

"And that frightens you?"

"The unknown . . . yes."

"That's something we have in common, then," Munoz says, moving closer to Cassandra. "It's my nature as a detective to want to know things."

Cassandra crosses her legs in the chair. The gauzy fabric hikes up her tanned thigh. "Like what?"

"Information."

"All right." Cassandra looks up at a looming Munoz. "Ask away . . ."

"How exactly can you afford this place?"

"Excuse me?"

"I'm curious. Stocks? Bonds? Real estate investments?"

"Well, if you must know, the home was a gift from my grandfather. Of course, there have been some upgrades since I took possession of it."

"That's right!" Munoz declares. "What did they call him . . . Mr. Hollywood, or was it Sir Casting Couch? The Admiral of Auditions, perhaps?"

"Mr. Tinseltown," Cassandra says, a fraction of courtesy left.

Munoz grins again. She's enjoying provoking Cassandra. Maybe too much. "He must have been *very* fond of you," she says.

"He was generous to all his granddaughters."

"But a house like this? You had to have been his favorite, right?"

"What is it I can help you with, Detective?"

"Well . . . I'm pretty sure I know why you did it," Munoz says, fighting to keep her emotions at bay. "I just need to know why Riley and not me?"

Cassandra sighs. "And what is it you seem to think I did?"

"You had someone put a bullet in my partner's skull."

"Sounds like you're accusing me of a crime," Cassandra says without a trace of concern. "Does your sergeant know you're here?"

"Riley was a good man." Munoz's tone is growing more hostile. "I'm going to prove you had him killed."

"Detective, I can't tell you how to spend your time or the city's tax dollars." Cassandra rises from the chair. "I'd think long and hard about accusing people without a shred of evidence. I understand it's rather hard for a woman to become a detective, which means it's even easier for her to be fired."

"I know what you did, and you're going to burn for it."

"You should leave," Cassandra says, moving in the direction of the front door.

I tap Munoz's shoulder. "Let's go."

Cassandra ushers us to the front door and opens it. Once we're outside, she doesn't close it right away. "It's curious, though," she says, half of her face visible. "Why would someone kill one cop and let the other live? Maybe whoever killed Detective Riley thought, 'What good is a dead cop without a partner left to mourn?'"

Munoz reaches forward to snatch Cassandra, but the door shuts. The porch light goes off, leaving my old partner seething in darkness.

We walk to the car and get in. "That bitch did it," she says, pulling the seat belt across her body before starting the engine. "She all but admitted it." Munoz's looking for validation, but she won't get it from me. This entire venture was sloppy, half-assed. "Why so quiet now? You were so chatty in there."

"What do you want me to say? She gave up nothing and worked your nerves pretty good."

"I'm not so sure about that," she says, shifting the gear from park to reverse and slowly backing out of the driveway. "You seemed to think her daughters were of interest. You care to clue me in?"

"It's a hunch," I say. "Maybe her daughters aren't what they seem . . ."

"You think she's trafficking them?"

"Could be worth looking into. Check for rap sheets and warrants. Both in and out of state."

"If that's the case, she's looking at 'pimping and pandering' along with the narcotics charges and Riley's homicide. She could go away for life." Munoz shifts into drive and makes a wide turn. She applies the squeaking brakes, so we're not flying downhill. "You pulled a major one out of your ass back there," she says.

"What?"

"That business about having a daughter . . . What the hell was that?" Should I tell her it was a ruse, a way to get Cassandra comfortable, establish a rapport? Munoz looks at me with keen perception, and I clam up. "Wait," she says. "You were for real?"

"Just found out," I say, sparing her the details.

"You're a father?" Munoz asks. "I mean, that's crazy." She looks over at me, momentarily distracted from the road. "No offense."

"None taken."

"You don't seem too happy about it."

"It's not that," I say. "It was a surprise, that's all."

"Makes sense now."

"What's that?"

"The duffel bag," she says a bit cheekily. "Please, tell me you have pictures on your phone. Let's see the little Finnegan."

"Nothing to show yet." *Had I not gotten hung up with you, maybe I could've met her tonight.* But saying that would only exacerbate an already volatile situation. And I can't blame Munoz, not entirely. I should have demanded that she drive me back to the Falcon after the bar fight. But part of me, something I'm afraid still holds favor, missed the thrill of riding in the Crown Vic, chasing down leads.

"Get some pictures, man. It's your damn kid."

"Yeah, all right. I'll work on it."

———

Munoz drops me off in Sierra Madre close to midnight. I get in the Falcon and look up at our bedroom window, hoping to see the blue flicker from the TV or the warm glow from Sarada's reading lamp, but everything's dark. Our relationship's been derailed before, but not like this. I can't lose her. Not after all we've been through.

I back out of the driveway and head south, then drive for about fifteen minutes. When I arrive at Pop's, my eyes twitch from fatigue, and my stomach growls with hunger. I park on the street, under a tree that functions as a toilet for what I figure are nightingales. An entire side of the tree trunk is bleached white by bird droppings, and I know the Falcon will need a wash come morning.

I enter Pop's condo carrying my duffel bag. The place smells awful, killing my appetite. Doesn't matter, I know Pop's fridge is void of food anyway. Streetlights shine through the kitchen window. Empty beer bottles are collected next to an overflowing trash can. If I weren't so tired, I'd carry the garbage to the dumpster, but I'll have to endure the stench of fetid tuna until morning.

I toss my duffel bag onto the floor, head over to the couch, sit, and remove my shoes. I don't bother washing the day's stink off or brushing my teeth. I rest my head back, close my eyes, and think about happier times with Sarada.

When my thoughts drift to Simone and Tori, I'm overcome with remorse. I can hear Dr. Angell in my head, coaching me through the gloom: *Think of how you've contributed to the lives of those around you. Remember the good you've done.*

The idea of good deeds might as well be gutter water swirling down a drain.

I'm so tired of feeling broken . . .

———

A dry palm slaps my cheek. My face tingles with pain. I open my eyes. Moonlight spills through the window curtain, washing the shadow from Pop's grizzled chin. A gun comes into focus. He cocks the hammer.

"Pop?" I try to determine how close the gun is to my face. "What are you doing?"

"How'd you get in my house?" He steadily aims the barrel between my eyes. "You came to rob me, didn't you?"

"Rob you?" I ask, still trying to get my bearings. "I was asleep. What are you saying? Put the gun down."

"You can't take from me!"

"Put the gun down. It's me, Trevor!"

"Someone put you up to this?"

"I'm your son."

"Son?" he says, looking down the pistol's sight. "My son's in Nevada."

"Nevada? I'm right here, Pop." I'm careful not to make any sudden movements. Pop's hammered. "I need you to put the gun down, now."

"I'm not putting down shit," he says. His feeble arm is showing fatigue. He strains to keep the long barrel revolver balanced at my head. "Matter of fact . . ." He stares toward the empty kitchen. "Glenna!" he cries into nothingness. "Glenna, call the police."

"Mom's gone, Pop."

"Glenna!"

"It was cancer." I try to bring him back to reality. "Remember?"

"What are you talking about? My Glenna's fine . . ."

"Please, Pop, I need you to listen to me," I say. "You have to put the gun down."

"Glenna!" It's a strident plea, one I'd never expect to hear from my father. "Glenna, answer me, dammit." Pop shudders, as if struck by an unsettling thought, and I wonder if he's breaking from the delusion. "Please just answer me, Glenna!"

"You don't want to shoot me." Sweat coats my skin. Fear sets in. "I'm your son!"

"Trevor?" Pop's eyelids flicker. He looks at me with faint familiarity, as if trying to place the face of someone he hasn't seen for years.

"I'm not trying to get shot, Pop," I say. "Not by anyone's hand, especially not my own father's . . . so put the gun down."

Pop slowly lowers the pistol. "Trevor?" he asks, free from the list-lessness. Light is restored in his eyes. "What's going on?" he asks, breath sour.

"Just take it easy, nice and easy." I guide the gun from my face, pull it from his grasp, and set it on the couch.

"Shit, son, I'm sorry."

I hug him tightly, holding on to his weathered body. I feel his protruding shoulder blades and the space between them. I held him this way when my mother died—so tightly. He stood at her graveside, watching over her casket resting at the bottom of a six-foot-deep hole. Mom's death was a stark reminder that life could be vicious. Standing beside the grave, he might have wanted to be alone, but I didn't care. He was marooned, washed ashore. Uncharted territory. I went to him, wrapped my arms around his waist, and squeezed. "It's going to be OK," I said, not knowing how else to console him. He looked down at me, eyes encumbered with grief. "What the hell do you know?" he muttered. "She was my life."

"I'm all right," he says, slipping out of my arms. He brings his palms to his eyes, rubs them hard. "I need to sleep."

"Hold on a sec," I say. My father stumbles backward. I quickly grab him by the arm and steady his body. "This is getting out of control, Pop."

"Let go of me! I told you I'm fine." He jerks his arm away. "You know better than creeping in here late at night." Pop turns and shuffles back toward his room, leaving me to feel how I often do when it comes to him—useless. I'm that same boy at my mother's graveside, clinging to him, waiting for him to admit that he needs me.

I get a better look at the gun, a long-barreled revolver. I engage the safety and tuck the gun under the couch cushion. I'll need to find some-place safer to hide the weapon, but keeping it close to me and far from Pop is the priority now. There's no telling what he has stashed in his room. He could be packing higher-caliber pistols, rifles, a shotgun . . . I'll need to assess the situation when I can—look in his closet, see where he keeps his gun safe. Maybe I can go in when he takes a shower and shaves? But that doesn't seem to be a daily occurrence.

Wide awake, I lie back on the couch and stare at the ceiling. The thought of Pop's mini arsenal is keeping me from rest. No use in trying to sleep. My adrenaline is already revved up. I wonder what Munoz is doing. Probably somewhere looking into the bottom of a bottle. I can't help but feel sorry for her, even though her campaign against Cassandra feels misguided. My gut's telling me there's more to Riley's murder than Cassandra ordering a hit . . . and for what? To protect her illegal drug pipeline? She's smarter than that. If Munoz weren't sinking in grief, she'd be able to see that Cassandra's well insulated. I wonder if the weed shops are licensed in her name. It's worth looking into . . . but right now, I should try to sleep.

———

I wake after ten o'clock to soreness and a pounding headache. I put my feet on the floor, tuck my head between my legs, and take three deep breaths, the way Sarada does after her yoga sessions every morning . . . something about finding her power animal and aligning chakras. I text Tori, letting her know I'm coming to the hotel. After a few minutes, she responds:

OK. See you soon!

In the kitchen, I open the fridge to find three eggs left in a carton. I scramble them in butter. I thought Pop might emerge when he smells the cooking, but when I go to his door, he's snoring.

I shower, shave, and put on slacks, a sweater, and polished dress boots. I don't leave Pop any money, since he spent the last cash I left him on booze. I throw my duffel bag over my shoulder and leave. Staying a few nights in a hotel might be nice, especially if the room has a Jacuzzi tub. An hour-long soak could ease the tension in my neck caused by sleeping on Pop's raggedy-ass couch.

Outside, I put my duffel bag in the Falcon's trunk, get into the car, and enter the High Tide Hotel's address into my phone's GPS. Forty-eight minutes to Newport Beach—less time than I thought. I drive Mountain Street toward the 2 and accelerate up the on-ramp heading south. I cross two lanes, gassing the Falcon until it reaches eighty miles per hour. I slow when I see a chippy on the shoulder, aiming a speed-measuring device at passing cars. The 2 isn't congested. It's less traveled compared to other LA freeways, and it invites drivers who speed along its bends like it's the autobahn.

I merge onto the 5 south, darting in and out of lanes until I clear a cluster of slow-moving vehicles. Sarada hates my driving; it makes her nauseous. She's ridden in the Falcon only twice, and both times she looked as if she were going to vomit. During her last stint as a passenger, she said, "You still drive like a cop." It wasn't a compliment, though the remark brought a smile to my face. When I pressed her for an explanation, she toiled for the words. "I don't know exactly," she said. "It's like you're so confident, believing you're in control. But anything can happen. What if a driver cuts you off? Slams on their brakes? You wouldn't have time to react."

"I've spent my life anticipating what people might do, starting with reading my father's moods," I said. "And isn't confidence a good thing?"

"Not blind confidence," she said, head drooping toward her lap.

I approach a wall of traffic. My phone rings. The caller ID reads "Bergman's Office." I slow down, reaching for the phone in a holder that's suctioned to the dash. I press the green button to answer. "Finnegan."

"You've recovered your phone," Bergman says. There's a crackle when he speaks, a bad connection. "I take it the handoff was uneventful?"

"The handoff, sure!" I shout into the phone's speaker, uncertain if Bergman can hear me well. Even if he can't, it's satisfying to holler at him.

"You sound miffed," he says. "Everything all right?"

"I know Cassandra Boyle hired me to take photos of Garvey and Yoshida."

Bergman is quiet, but I know he's still on the line. I can hear his machinelike breathing. "It's complicated," he says. "We can discuss all this at the office."

"She's pimping those girls." My words are hot with indignation. "Please tell me you didn't know that?"

"God no," he says. "She told me they were her daughters. That they had gotten mixed up with the wrong kinds of people . . ."

The line starts to clear up, enough that I don't have to shout. "C'mon, Bergman . . ." I check my side-view mirror before switching into a faster lane. "You didn't consider the woman had ulterior motives?"

"I don't make it a habit to cross-examine potential clients. I was thinking about keeping our firm afloat."

"Our firm?"

"Of course," he says. "I couldn't do this work without you."

"We don't do business with criminals," I say.

"I have no knowledge of Ms. Boyle's crimes." His breathing grows heavier. "Do you?"

I know more than I should about Cassandra's business. If the California Bar Association found out we exposed two crooked cops so that Cassandra could recover her working girls, Bergman would be disbarred, and I'd lose my PI license. "It isn't negotiable," I say, holding strong. "Just stay away from Cassandra Boyle, or we're done."

"Drawing the line in the sand, are we? All right, Mr. Finnegan. You have my word."

"Good."

"How'd you find out she was the client, anyway?"

"Don't worry about that." I can sense our measure of friendship slowly evaporating.

"This partnership doesn't work unless we can trust each other."

I'm 14.2 miles from the hotel, according to my phone's GPS. It's the only thing I trust right now.

"All right," I say. "Then tell me. Is Mitch Beckett your contact?" I remember the description the junkie gave in the park. Captain Beckett was my LAPD supervisor. Last I heard, he had salvaged his career, finding his way to the Internal Affairs Division. Beckett effectively threw me under the bus when the Soledad investigation went to hell. My hate for him is unbridled, and Bergman knows this.

"What?" he stammers. "No! What makes you think that?" I don't respond, listening as he grows more flustered. "Trevor," Bergman says. He's never called me by my first name, and something about hearing him say it makes him sound desperate. "Cassandra was a mistake. It won't happen again . . . Hello . . . Are you still there?"

I let him hang on the line a bit longer. "Yes," I say. "I'm here."

"Will you be coming in today?"

"No," I say. "But I need a favor."

"A favor? All right."

"Pull the licenses for Cassandra Boyle's marijuana dispensaries."

"And why would I do that?" he asks.

"What's that you like to say? The less you know, the better."

"Guess I earned that," he says. "And what am I looking for?"

"I want to know what's on paper," I say. "Names, dates . . . call me with the info when you get it." I leave Bergman ruminating to the dial tone and roll the window down. A vortex of air fills the cabin. I hear a loud thrashing. The headliner's cream fabric, ripped and loose, whips violently in the gale. Paired with the engine's soothing hum, it's a signature cacophony that comes only from driving the Falcon.

The car hits smooth pavement, leaving behind a roadway riddled with potholes, hard shoulders strewn with garbage and remnants of blown-out tires. I don't have to look at the freeway signs to know I've left LA. I can see the Orange County tax dollars at work. Yellow and violet flowers flourish in the median. Blacktop with perfect white lines has been recently laid. The Falcon travels steadily between them, and

I can't help but feel envious of the county with an airport named after John Wayne.

Even though the OC is home to some of the most beautiful beaches in Southern California and touts less crime than LA, it's all overshadowed by a shameful legacy. Orange County is the birthplace of, and headquarters for, nearly a dozen white supremacist groups, from Nazi prison gangs to groups portraying themselves as benignant social clubs focused on improving their communities and "preserving white culture." They've all been emboldened by this election cycle and the anti-immigration talk of faux patriots spewing hate on TV and the radio. Dog whistles beckoning them out of the gutters, gassing them up to believe they wield power and hold dominance in a world growing more multicultural by the second. I think of Simone, wondering about the world she'll inherit. Will it still be dominated by racism and prejudice along with rising temperatures and sea levels and endless wars? All the bullshit of callous humans. Not enough love, copious amounts of hate and destruction.

But I have to believe on some level that, despite all the horrors of living on this planet, her life will be better . . .

I look at the GPS. In thirteen minutes, I'll see my daughter. What do I say to her? How do I introduce myself? What should she call me? *Dad? Daddy? Pop? No, certainly not Pop.*

I nearly miss my exit and cut in front of another motorist, who lays on the horn. I can hear the sustained barrage long after I'm off the freeway. I drive a busy street populated by shops: T-shirts and souvenirs, bike rentals, and surf gear. In the distance, the crystalline ocean twinkles beneath the sun. Another block and I'll be at the High Tide Hotel. I haven't felt this nervous since my first day in the academy, standing on the black line. I didn't know what to expect, and I feel the same way now, driving into the hotel's parking lot. What if seeing me causes Tori to recall our last conversation, when I told her I didn't love her, that our relationship was one of convenience?

Not my finest moment . . .

I park the Falcon close to the hotel's entrance. The car elicits a few stares from a man pulling luggage from the back of his luxury SUV. Most of the cars in the parking lot come with expensive price tags— rows of vehicles valued at more than a million dollars.

I get out and walk toward the hotel's entrance. The grounds are immaculate, boasting birds-of-paradise and baby palm trees amid a range of tropical greenery. Outdoor speakers play music I'd expect to hear during a yoga class. When I enter the lobby, the polished marble floors and Grecian columns further suggest that the High Tide offers five-star accommodations. If the lobby's any indication, Tori isn't hurting for money.

"Hello?" the woman behind the reception desk asks. "May I help you?" I'm not surprised by her accent—it fits the digs. It sounds European, could be French. Or it could be all the hours spent listening to Sarada playing language tutorials that has my hearing off.

"I'm here to see Tori Krause."

"And you are?"

"Trevor Finnegan."

"Oh, yes, Mr. Finnegan," she says, glancing at a sticky note on her computer's screen. "Ms. Krause is expecting you." The woman hands me a small envelope holding a key card. "She said for you to go up when you're ready. You can take the elevator to the second floor. Room 222." She points down the hall, where a few people are congregating.

"By chance, is there a gift shop here?"

"Yes, of course," she says. "It's out near the pool area." She points to double doors that lead outside.

"Thank you."

I walk the second-floor hallway to Room 222 holding a fuzzy dolphin. Its eyes are like shiny black stones, and its white underbelly is extra soft. Even though Tori left a key for me, I'm hesitant to walk in. I knock gently and wait. When I don't hear anything, I knock harder. "Come in," Tori says. I slide the key card into the electronic slot. When a small light blinks green, I turn the handle and push. "We're just enjoying the view." Tori's standing on the balcony and holding Simone. She's bouncing the baby on her hip, pointing to the seagulls gliding through the sky, which grows more ashen with a coming storm.

Tori greets me with her perfect teeth. "You made it," she says. "What's that you've got?" I show the dolphin to Tori. Simone lights up and reaches for the toy.

"She likes it," Tori says, mirroring Simone's joyous face. "You're getting dad points already."

"Caught my eye in the gift shop," I say, enamored by Simone. She has Tori's smile, wide with endearing dimples that only add to her sweetness. Her complexion is fairer than mine: red and brown in her cheeks, copper hair. "She's beautiful, isn't she?" Tori asks.

"Yes," I say, looking into Simone's brown eyes.

"Go ahead. Hold her."

Tori hands me Simone. Her plump body's warm against my chest. I try my best not to wrinkle her royal-blue-and-cream dress, but I don't know what to do except hold and rock her.

I carry Simone around the room, her tiny hands barely able to hold the dolphin. When she reaches out for Tori, I place her back in her mother's arms. "Is it how you thought it would be?" Tori asks.

"No," I say, thinking of the disparities my father tried to cast, filling my head with doubt. I know Simone is my daughter, and Tori doesn't look like she has money woes. Her sky-blue dress, with its spaghetti straps and florid print, is what I'd expect her to be wearing. She always seemed to have the perfect outfit for every occasion. Today she looks carefree, far from worry. Confident as she stands feet away from her ex-lover. She hasn't changed much. She's still blonde, though with shorter hair, and her makeup is expertly applied.

I remember why I swiped right those many years ago.

"You want a beer . . . a cocktail? I can have room service bring you something."

"I'm fine," I say, taking a seat in a wicker chair. "How is she?" I ask, looking at Simone, wondering what could be happening in her body, hoping the heart beating in her chest is strong. "I mean, she's healthy, right?"

"Oh, Finn, this little one is perfect."

"Good," I say, relieved. Terrible thoughts can plague a parent's mind, stoking all kinds of fears. It's more than worrying about Simone's physical health. I've dwelled on what might blight her spirit. After all, she's got Finnegan blood running through her veins.

"Penny for your thoughts," Tori says.

I'm staring at nothing again. "Just wondering . . . why'd you name her Simone?"

"After Nina," she says.

"I had no idea you were a fan."

"Not at first, but 'Feeling Good' was playing in the pub the last time we saw each other."

"I don't remember that."

"I'd never heard her version," Tori says. "I played it all while I was pregnant. Anytime I thought of you." I think back to our breakup in the downtown pub, only able to remember the rain after months of drought and the people marching in the streets demanding justice for Brandon Soledad. "Is it weird?" Tori asks. "Seeing us?"

"Weird?" I repeat back. "No. I'm glad you found me. But I have to ask, why now?"

"I had to come." Tori sits on the bed. "My dad passed away last month from a heart attack. I needed to see my mother."

"I'm sorry."

"My parents and I hadn't spoken since Simone's birth. My mother would email me now and again, just making sure things were all right, but never called."

The dolphin drops to the floor. I pick it up and hold it while Tori cradles Simone. "I always thought you were close with them?"

"Me too."

"Can I ask what happened between you?"

Tori swallows hard. "Let's just say my parents weren't as open as I was raised to believe. How'd my mom put it? *Simone won't belong anywhere.* She wanted me to give her up for adoption."

"I don't know what to say." Trying to contain my ire is like smothering a brush fire with a cocktail napkin.

Tori sweeps her hand over Simone's loose curls. "There may be some hope for my mother," she says. "Now that she's seen her granddaughter, she can't stop talking about her. Unfortunately, my father never had the chance. I don't think it would have mattered, though."

"I'm sure he went to his grave regretting his decision."

"Maybe." Tori snickers. "Or he just regrets dying before voting for the Second Coming." Her words are bitter, and rightfully so.

"Did you tell them about me?" I ask.

"I did," she says, pulling one of her dress straps down. Simone works her way to Tori's breast to nurse. "They searched you online. Read about Brandon's murder. They said I should keep as far away from you as possible."

Two years ago, I'd say Tori's parents were right. But I'm not the same man. I've changed. "About the letter," I say. "Did you mean it?"

"Every word," she says. "I want you to be a part of her life, Trevor."

"I'd like that. I've already missed so much . . ."

"Which is why we're going to stay."

"Here in LA?"

"A friend got me a gig in the wardrobe department of a TV show shooting in Burbank. I start next week."

"Wow—OK." I jump up from my chair. "Where are you going to live?"

"I found a few places in Burbank, Glendale and North Hollywood, but the deposits are killer. With moving expenses, it's going to be tight."

"I can help," I say. "Whatever you need."

Tori smiles. "I'll give the property managers a call," she says. "Maybe we can see them together?"

My phone rings; it's Bergman. "Sorry, have to take this," I say. Tori nods and returns to the balcony. I answer. "Go ahead."

"You were right," he says. "Nothing appears to be licensed in Cassandra's name."

"Then who owns the business?"

"Trisha and Dawn Boyle," he says. "According to public records, it's two of her adopted daughters. Sure you can't tell me what this is all about?"

"It would put the firm in legal peril."

"I'm the lawyer," he says. "Let me make that determination."

"It's better this way, Bergman. I'll be in touch," I say before ending the call. Either Cassandra's using her daughters as fronts, or the entire family's a criminal enterprise. What if Munoz is right and a hit was ordered on Riley? Maybe Cassandra wasn't the one who called it. It could have been anyone in that household. But that supposition feels weak. Those girls didn't strike me as having the wherewithal to know their mother's "true business," let alone be so deep into it that they'd order a cop killed.

Munoz should have known about Cassandra's daughters. A preliminary investigation would have turned over records showing who owned the dispensaries. Hell, Bergman found it easily, so why did Munoz act like she didn't know her daughters existed?

Tori steps back in. "Everything OK?"

"Sorry, work stuff," I say, a little embarrassed the call disrupted my visit with Simone.

"I understand," she says. "So are you up for some apartment hunting with us?"

"I wish I could . . . It's just my schedule, and I might be going out of town for a while."

"Sounds familiar."

"I guess some things don't change," I say. "Whatever place you choose, I'll cover the deposit and anything else you need."

"That's generous," she says, looking surprised. "You want to tell me what you're doing these days?"

"I'm a private investigator."

"Makes sense," she says. "Not sure if I should ask this . . . I don't want to pry."

"Go ahead."

"You and Sarada? Married?"

"No," I say.

Tori's silent, then says, "I was seeing this guy in Vancouver, but it didn't work out. Simone's my priority. Some men don't get that."

I hadn't considered the prospect of other men coming into Simone's life. I'm unsure why, but it makes me queasy.

"Please tell Sarada I'm sorry for showing up as I did. I didn't know what else to do."

"You followed your only lead, same as I would have done." Simone finishes nursing, and Tori pulls her dress strap back up. "I better get going," I say, looking at my watch. "Can I ask a favor before I go?"

"Of course."

"It'd be nice to have a picture with Simone?"

"Just one? This little girl's a ham."

"Wonder where she got that from?"

Tori laughs. "Trust me, she has plenty of your idiosyncrasies."

"Like what?"

"For starters, she's headstrong."

"Oh really?"

"Don't bother denying it," Tori teases.

"Oh, I'm not," I say, somewhat proud and grateful that Simone likely won't grow up to be a pushover.

I hold out my arms. Simone reaches for me, and I nestle her against my chest. I give Tori my phone, grinning wide. Tori takes a few pictures—one with me kissing Simone's cheek, another with Simone drooling onto my shoulder. I gently rock my daughter, looking at her with admiration before giving her back to Tori.

"I see you still have the Beetle," I say, nearing the door. "I saw you drive off . . ."

"Oh," she says, taking on a cheerless mood, "you did?" Perhaps the night wasn't humiliating for only Sarada?

"How's the car holding up?" I ask, hinting at the broken spoiler.

"Aside from some jerk rear-ending me on the 5, it's fine," she says. "Insurance will cover the damage. Thankfully, neither of us was hurt."

"The Beetle might not be the ideal car long-term. Maybe we can discuss getting something larger, more accommodating?"

"We can talk about it, but"—Tori pauses—"you don't have to do that."

"What do you mean?"

"You know . . . save us. We're doing OK."

"I didn't mean it like that. You've done amazing, Tori. I just want to help however I can."

"OK." Tori rubs Simone's back as she starts to fall asleep on her shoulder. "She *is* precious cargo."

"Yes, she is," I say.

"And we made her . . ." Tori's brimming with pride. "Not a bad collaboration."

"Thank you for this."

"You're welcome," she says. "Oh, and Finn?"

"Yes."

"About what I said last time"—she speaks with a tremble—"I was wrong. You're a good man. Talk soon, OK?"

I nod, and Tori shuts the door. I walk down the hallway to the elevator and descend to the lobby, where I return the key card to the woman at the front desk. "Enjoy your day, Mr. Finnegan," she says.

Outside, I breathe a sigh of relief and get into the Falcon. I must have done something right in my life to deserve the few good things that have come my way.

I check my phone. There's a text from Munoz:

Can you come to Riley's memorial?

Bethesda Mortuary in Torrance @1300.

I don't respond. As much as I'd like to support Munoz, the more I help her, the greater the risk she'll find out why I was in Venice the night she was shot and Riley was killed. I know she's withholding details about her and Riley's investigation into Cassandra's drug business, but why? And if Cassandra is pimping her daughters against their will, they need help. She could have forged the girls' signatures on the dispensary paperwork, too. There's no telling.

I start the Falcon, type Cassandra's street into my phone's GPS, and peel out of the parking lot, leaving hotel guests gawking.

CHAPTER EIGHT

Driving Highway 1 into Malibu is different in daylight. Rolling green hills look rich in the distance despite the unrelenting drought. And to the right of the twisting blacktop, sandstone borders the lane. The Pacific Ocean demands attention to the left. Surfers are lured by its cerulean waters like neophytes enchanted by a charismatic guru. Today is unseasonably warm. The official weather of Malibu, and most beach communities in Southern California, is mild temperatures paired with overcast or sunny skies.

When I arrive at Cassandra Boyle's home, Nigel, her "yoga teacher," stands outside looking up at the rain gutter. I get out of the Falcon and start walking up the driveway.

Still waters run deep. That's what Pop says. I take it to mean you never know what crazy lurks below the surface. I approach Nigel slowly. Everything about him makes the muscles in my shoulders tighten. He moves methodically, incessantly aware of his surroundings, and looks poised to react to whatever situation presents itself.

"Pulling double duty," I say. "Yoga teacher and groundskeeper?" I stop about six feet away, watching as he uses a long pole to clear the gutter. He's wearing attire similar to what he wore last night—loose-fitting beige pants and a pullover shirt. They look to be made from some earthy material. Raw hemp or cotton. His shoes are thin-soled tan slippers that remind me of the training shoes I wore in karate dojos as a kid. "I sure hope she's paying you well," I say, followed by an uncomfortable laugh.

"Why have you returned?" he asks.

"Is the lady of the manor in? I need to see her."

"Ms. Boyle isn't interested in hearing anything that you have to say." He flicks a bird's nest out of the gutter. It falls to the ground.

"It's about her daughters," I say.

Nigel groans. I move closer to see the source of his distress: two shattered bird eggs among twigs and leaves. He bends over, scoops the eggs' remnants into his hands—pieces of shell and tiny feathered masses coated in xanthous liquid. "She abandoned them," he says.

"Who?"

"The mother." He kicks the pole away in frustration. "They didn't hatch, so she abandoned them."

"What are you going to do?" I'm somewhat curious and want to emulate his concern, hoping it'll win me his favor.

"Make use of them." Nigel begins walking toward a gate that leads to the rear of the house.

"You need any help?" I ask.

Nigel stops and looks at me. "Are you armed?"

"Yes."

"Leave it in the car," he says. "There can be no weapons near Ms. Boyle during her yoga session."

I return to the car and place my revolver in the trunk. Maybe it's not a wise choice, but it's a good-faith gesture, and if my plan is going to work, it means playing by Cassandra Boyle's rules.

Nigel walks toward a security gate that automatically opens once he approaches. It's some sophisticated tech and might be calibrated to a key card in his pocket or it's remote operated. Maybe a concealed camera scanned his retinas? We enter the backyard. The gate shuts behind us and seals heavily, like a bullpen's door.

The homes in Malibu are lavish. Backyards with infinity pools, eight-person hot tubs, and professional-grade outdoor kitchens. Far better equipped than the kitchen I grew up with, watching as my mother dropped pancake batter onto a hot griddle. But what Cassandra has created is far beyond palatial. It's a flourishing oasis. There's the greenhouse, a dome-shaped bubble for plants and produce, and an elaborate pond, home to colorful fish and turtles that sunbathe on smooth rocks. Screeching parrots and other tropical birds jump from one wooden rung to the next in multilevel cages. And there's Cassandra in the center of it all, her body bent in the flamingo pose, clad in a white bikini top and spandex shorts.

"Do you practice?" she asks, switching to another pose that looks comparatively more difficult but showcases the flexibility of her torso.

"It's not my thing."

"It's really about holistic health," she says. "Relaxation. Better sleep. Calmer thoughts. And best of all, an increased libido."

Nigel mutters in Cassandra's ear. She looks at the feathered mess in his hands and then points to the greenhouse. He carries the birds' remains toward the dome. She releases her pose and picks up a towel from her yoga mat. "There's just been so much death lately," she says in the blasé way rich people sometimes talk.

"I don't think birds live long," I say.

She looks at me peculiarly. "Does that make it better?" she asks.

"Maybe."

"You've got a morbid streak."

"If you say so . . ."

"And what do others say about you?" she asks, dabbing sweat from her arms with her towel. Her copper skin looks tight, stretched over discernible muscles. Her arms are long and lean, the way Sarada's are, likely formed from hours of yoga.

"Plenty, I'm sure."

I hear what sounds like a wood chipper and look to Nigel. He's turned on a metal contraption, a little larger than a portable refrigerator, with a hole in the top and a spout extending from its side. It's something I've never seen before, and I suddenly determine its purpose. He drops the bits of bird and shell into the hole, and the device spits out thick, chunky soil through its curved metal spout.

"Nigel makes the best mulch," Cassandra says. "Things that shouldn't grow this close to the ocean manage to thrive." Nigel turns off the machine, collects the mulch, and works the soil into a heap. "From death comes life." Cassandra claps her hands, marking her observation the way a magician would a magic trick. "Harmony."

"Well, at least they didn't die for nothing," I say. "Too bad we can't say the same for Martin Riley."

Cassandra sighs and wraps the towel around her neck. "Is that why you've come? I'm disappointed. I thought we already went over this."

"You're right," I say. "Probably just need a refresher."

"I had nothing to do with Riley's death," she says. "And I still don't know your name?"

"Trevor Finnegan. I'm the man you hired."

"Hired? You must be mistaken."

"I took the photos of Officers Garvey and Yoshida." Anytime a client hires us, Bergman is explicitly clear that they'll never meet me. It's the one rule he seems to follow religiously, and usually I abide by it, but there's no point in pretense with Cassandra.

"I'm confused. You work for Bergman?"

"Bergman doesn't know I'm here, and I'd like to keep it that way."

"All right," she says. "Then why are you here? And why were you here last night with that detective?"

"I thought I was helping a friend."

"That vulgar woman is your friend?"

"Detective Munoz is my old partner," I say.

"She's an astounding fool if she thinks I had her partner killed." Cassandra laughs. "Be careful with that one." She walks over to the heap of soil, where Nigel is funneling buckets of waste into the machine. "But I will admit, the thought of harming Detective Riley did cross my mind."

"Well, thoughts don't constitute crimes," I say. "But why the consideration?"

"Riley and Munoz are no different than Garvey and Yoshida," she says, choosing her words carefully. "Certain behavior is to be expected among some of our members in law enforcement."

"Certain behavior?"

"They're human beings," she says. "No different than the rest of us—governed by wants and desires."

Flies hover over the soil. It reeks of decay. "Those photos I took . . ." I turn my back to Nigel and his pungent mound. "What do you intend to do with them?"

Cassandra smirks deviously, as if the thought of the photos brings her unparalleled pleasure. "I'm not sure," she says. "I considered asking Garvey and Yoshida to work for me. Part-time, of course, in addition to their sworn duties."

"Blackmail?"

"A job offer," she says sharply.

"Why not give them to the police? End their careers."

"Interesting." She brings her hands together, interlacing her fingers. "Why would I do that?" She looks to Nigel, who's stopped dumping waste into the machine and seems to be listening to our conversation. "Those pictures are worth far more if their existence is only known to the parties involved."

"Understandable," I say. "But they're still on the streets and could be harming other girls."

"So it's an ethical thing?" She sucks her teeth.

"Call it what you want," I say. "I was hoping it was to keep your daughters safe."

"But I'm confused . . . You want me to report them to the same police department you work to expose?"

"Do you care about them, your girls?"

Cassandra pauses. I may have pressed the envelope too hard. "My girls have been through a lot," she says. "They mean everything to me. I saved them from a life no girl should know."

"Saved them?" I ask. "So they could work for you?"

"No girl *works* for me," she says. "They have been, and always will be, free to make their own choices. Sometimes I don't agree with those choices, and I choose to intervene, as any good parent might. But what I won't stand for is some man thinking he can do whatever he wants with them."

Nigel empties the rest of the bucket into the machine. "Anything else, Ms. Boyle?"

"The leftovers in the garage. Bring them out."

"Are you sure?" Nigel asks. "Perhaps once our guest leaves?"

"No," Cassandra says, sterner than I've heard her speak to him. "Bring it, now." Nigel leaves with the empty bucket, taking ungainly strides toward the door leading into the garage.

She watches him dismissively, then turns to me. "What were you before?" she asks. "I mean, before you began working for Bergman."

"A police detective."

"Why aren't you that anymore?"

"I was injured and became temporarily disabled. Wasn't useful to the department, so I was fired."

"Fired for an injury?" she says. "Sounds like grounds for a lawsuit." She removes the hair tie from around her ponytail and lets the dark strands fall down her back.

"One of the largest in the city's history," I say.

"Wait," she says, shaking her pointer finger in my direction. "It's you, isn't it? You're the guy . . . the detective from that case. The dead recruit." Her eyes twinkle. "You wear infamy well," she says. "But why reveal yourself to me?"

"Because I helped your girls, and I need to know they're OK."

"Well, I'm telling you they're fine . . ."

"I'd like to hear it from them."

"Your persistence is admirable, but you're mistaken," she says. "I'd never hurt my girls."

"Why'd you make them owners of your dispensaries?"

"Why not?" she asks. "If anything happens to me, I want them to be taken care of."

"An inheritance . . ."

"Yes, Mr. Finnegan. It's something parents do."

"Of course . . . some," I say.

"So you're satisfied?"

"Almost," I say, as Nigel returns with the bucket and walks over to the machine. "Why is Munoz so sure you killed Detective Riley?"

"I think she'd be better at answering that question," Cassandra says.

"I tried to get the truth, but she lied to me."

"Pesky things, aren't they?"

"What's that?"

"Lies," she says. It's like I can smell her complacency; it's how I'd expect a big-game hunter to smell after killing a defenseless elephant. "You're a detective, Mr. Finnegan. What do your instincts tell you?"

"She and Riley worked for you, didn't they?"

Cassandra brings her finger to her lips. "Nice try, but you won't get a peep out of me."

I wonder how many crooked cops Cassandra has employed. I'm sure it's far more than Bergman and I can expose, which only depresses me further.

There's a horrendous crackling, as if sticks or rocks are lodged in the machine, followed by the uncanny drone of a broken motor and the odor of scorched metal. "Not again," Nigel says, banging the machine's side with his palm. "I'll get my tools." He stands up, sulking, and walks back toward the garage, his shirt damp with sweat.

"Then our business is done," Cassandra says. "Unless there's something else?"

"I don't get it," I say. "Why?"

"What's that?"

"You're not hurting for money. Why not stop while you're ahead?"

"I'm just a businesswoman, Mr. Finnegan. Would you question a man's success?"

"Depends how he made his money." I stare into her big green eyes, pondering why some people are criminals. Especially people like Cassandra, whose privilege is only heightened by her intellect and allure.

"Did they ever find that woman responsible for killing the recruit?" she asks. "What was her name?"

"Amanda Walsh," I say.

"That's right—Walsh."

"Still at large."

"Pity," Cassandra says. "That must get under your skin. Anyway, stick around if you'd like. I'm going to shower. The kitchen is fully stocked. You can help yourself." She walks toward the house, doesn't look back, doesn't have to.

More flies have swarmed the machine, crawling all over it. I take a step closer and look down into the shaft. I pull back when I realize what I'm seeing. Bloody bits of flesh have gummed up the blades. Butchered fingers, bone, gristle, and tissue still encased in skin—a feeding frenzy for the flies. I step away, walking to the gate at a moderate pace. The gate doesn't open. I push against it, then jiggle the handle. It doesn't budge.

I study a keypad. It looks like a code is needed to exit, unless, of course, you're Nigel or Cassandra. I jerk the handle again, hard, then mash a few buttons on the keypad. There's a long staccato of beeps suggesting an error. Panic sets in, pinpricks erupting down my back. I reach into my pocket, take out my phone. I should call for help. Maybe Munoz? She can notify the local authorities and have the place teeming with sheriff's deputies.

No reception.

What the hell?

Malibu isn't a city in the wilderness. I shouldn't have one signal bar. Is Cassandra restricting cellular reach? I look toward the mansion's roof and notice a group of pricey-looking antennae. Whatever operations she's running out of this house, they're complex and far-reaching.

A long shadow falls across my feet. I turn around. "Leaving so soon?" Nigel asks, standing over my right shoulder. He's holding a red tin toolbox, the handle gripped firmly in his palm. "I thought I'd prepare lunch . . ."

"Thanks, but I can't stay."

"I see," he says. "Ms. Boyle so enjoyed your visit. You'll have to return soon." Nigel nudges me aside and assumes my position, standing square in front of the gate. There's a sustained beep, friendlier than before. Access is granted, and the gate swings open. "You're on your way." He steps aside so that I can leave. "Drive safely, Mr. Finnegan."

"I'll do that." I walk through the gate, holding my breath until I reach the Falcon. I feel Nigel watching. It isn't until I'm safely inside the car that I breathe easy, stealing a final glimpse of his menacing mug as the gate closes.

———

I should've been at Bethesda Mortuary ten minutes ago, but traffic determines arrival times in the city, and people drive terribly when there's even a slight drizzle.

I exit onto Western Avenue and drive south to Torrance Boulevard. A large white sign reads Bethesda Mortuary in black letters. I pull into a relatively empty parking lot—not what I'd expect for a fallen officer. I park the Falcon. Before getting out, I consume a protein bar from my emergency stash, which I keep in the glove box along with a bottle of water. I step out of the car when I'm finished and open the trunk. Digging around in a bag of clothes, I remove a charcoal-colored suede sportscoat with elbow patches. It's slightly wrinkled, but I doubt others will notice. I walk toward the exit, passing two white men in dark suits smoking cigarettes. One of them reeks of liquor. Both stand like cops.

Inside, I'm struck by the bloodred carpeting and intricate stained-glass windows depicting Jesus as a shepherd, crucified, ascending into heaven. I'm reminded of my mother's memorial and how I never wanted to see stained glass again. At the front of the mortuary are an organ, a brass podium, and an easel displaying a poster-size photo of Detective Riley in his dress blues, looking younger than the night he died.

I notice Munoz speaking to a white-collared priest. They stand next to a blue-and-gold floral wreath arrangement presented on a wooden tripod. Munoz nods when she sees me but doesn't come over. I'm relieved more than offended. Though I need to speak to her and get to the bottom of what she and Riley were involved in, this isn't the setting.

More people enter the mortuary and begin filling up the first three rows. Some are in uniform, others in suits. Gold and silver shields are fastened to their belts, firearms in burnished holsters. No one seems to notice me sitting at the end of a bench, farthest from the front and close to the door. Munoz finishes with the priest and sits in the front row. A few people join her. One woman puts her arm around Munoz's shoulder and pulls her close.

I hate memorials.

The priest, a husky black man with a prominent forehead, adjusts his wire-framed glasses and looks out at the small crowd. "I didn't know Detective Martin Riley, but you all, his colleagues and fellow officers, tell me he was the type of man many aspired to be like. See, we all know that police officers face dangers every day. They're tasked with being the peacekeepers, embodying the laws of the land, and it isn't easy. But each time Detective Riley put on that shield, he understood that and knew the risks, yet he soldiered on because that's what he was called to do—it is a calling!"

Munoz sobs. A gray-haired man sitting behind her reaches forward, places his hand on her shoulder, and lets it rest there for a moment. "And when you've been called to do something," the priest adds, "there's nothing that can deter you from your path. Detective Riley walked the path that God set out for him, and in doing so, he fulfilled his purpose."

As much as I'd like to believe that Riley deserves this kind of eulogy, I'm thinking otherwise. I don't know why Munoz wanted me to come. There are enough people here who can offer her a shoulder to cry on.

I stand up, leave the row, and head toward the exit. I can feel people staring at me. When our eyes meet, some show faint recognition, struggling to place my face. For those who are certain they know me, there's only contempt.

I push the mortuary doors open, clear the lobby with broad steps, and leave the building to breathe the smog-filled air. I start removing my sportscoat as I approach the Falcon, which seems farther away than I remember.

I'll have to meet up with Munoz later. There's never a good time to ask an ex-partner if they've violated their sworn oath. I only hope she hasn't veered so far from her vow to uphold the law that I can't help her.

"Leaving so soon?" Agent Hill approaches from his truck, parked a few spots down. He's wearing a black suit, matching cowboy boots, and a wide-brimmed gray hat with a red feather tucked in the band. He looks like he's going to perform an exorcism or rob a stagecoach.

"Uncle Hill?" I ask. "What are you doing here?"

"Paying my respects. Riley and I worked out of Southwest."

"Didn't know that . . ." I toss the sportscoat into the trunk.

"You ill or something?" Hill adjusts his hat and squints. "You're not looking too good."

"Tired, that's all."

"Well, I'm glad I ran into you."

"What's up?"

"The bank will officially acquire Fitopia tomorrow."

"And what about Boston? Anything come over the wire?"

"Nothing," he says.

"You still have eyes on Cynthia?" I ask.

"For now," he says. "She's spending the day clearing the place out. But come tomorrow the surveillance detail ends."

"So that's it?"

"Sorry, kid. I wish we had something, but we don't."

The heaviness in my chest is gone. Anxiety is replaced with disappointment. "Yeah . . ." I say, trying to think of something positive, hopeful.

"It was worth a shot," Hill says. "Tell you what, come by the house later on. I'll grill up some steaks. Get your mind off that godforsaken Amanda 'Boston' Walsh."

Pop might have ended his friendship with Hill, but I still drop by his place from time to time to enjoy a beer and watch him groom horses. Even so, his offer couldn't have come at a worse time.

"I don't know, Uncle Hill," I say, looking at my watch. "I've got a lot going on." It's almost two p.m. I should be going home to talk things over with Sarada.

"I've got T-bones," Hill says, puffing out his chest as cops often do when *no* isn't an option. "I won't even get pissed when you drown it in steak sauce."

Hill must be aching for company. He's not backing down. "All right," I say, figuring I'll stop in Sierra Madre, then go to Hill's afterward. Depending on my conversation with Sarada, T-bones and beers could be a good way to cap off the night.

"All set, then," he says, relaxing his chest. "Come before sundown. I'll have the grill good and hot."

"You got it," I say, thinking the steak dinner might also be a good time to clue Hill in that I witnessed Riley's murder, and he and Munoz might have been involved in something illegal. I wanted to keep the little I know under my hat until the particulars weren't so blurred, but Hill's a career cop. I know he's met his share of sullied officers. He might be able to give me advice and help save Munoz if it isn't too late.

"I better fall in with the mourners," he says, looking back at the mortuary as more people enter.

"One more thing, Uncle Hill."

"Sure."

"Did you know Riley well?"

He pauses. "Not really," he says. "Sad thing is, these funerals are more like reunions for us retired LAPD. The only time we see old faces from the beat."

"That's sad," I say, remembering how Riley's face exploded in a hail of bullets.

"How'd you and Riley cross paths?" Hill asks.

"Never met him," I say. "Came for Sally Munoz. She was his partner."

"Well, I wouldn't wish what happened to him on anybody. It's a real shame."

"Yeah," I say. "Real shame."

"We'll pour some liquor out for him tonight," Hill says. "Mourn him properly." And with that, he heads toward the mortuary as thoughts of Cynthia bombard my mind.

———

After fueling the Falcon and stopping at a sandwich shop for a turkey club and coffee, I start north on the 110 bound for Sierra Madre, missing Sarada. But I don't get far, merging onto the 405 headed toward Sherman Oaks. The last time I was at Fitopia was two years ago, but it still feels fresh. I stood face-to-face with Boston and confronted her for helping my training officer, Joey Garcia, kill Brandon Soledad and Ruben Montgomery. She laughed off my accusations and said none of my evidence would stick, convinced she'd never be charged or set foot in a courtroom.

I drive down Ventura Boulevard, a clean, well-lit, heavily patrolled street. This is the Valley, where LAPD officers stay busy citing drivers for parking violations and not much else. Officers out of the Van Nuys Division used to call it a glamour beat, as they mostly had to contend with celebrities, paparazzi, eccentrics, runaways, and panhandlers. Crimes are rarely sensational enough to make the prime-time news. Then the case broke, and Boston was implicated. Protestors descended on Fitopia, the place where Brandon took his last breath. She became another LAPD failure, emblematic of egotism and barbarity, as she apparently thought she could kill Brandon Soledad and have a soft opening at her gym the next day.

The parking meters are all taken, along with the ten-minute loading zone. I drive a couple of blocks farther, then turn down a dead-end street. I park across from a used-car lot and get out. It's a few minutes' walk to Fitopia. The building's defaced; concrete walls are spray-painted with JUSTICE FOR BRANDON . . . BLACK LIVES MATTER . . . NO MORE KILLER COPS . . .

I wonder why Cynthia never bothered to paint over the tagging. Or maybe the defacing was so incessant that she gave up trying to blot it out?

Three men in matching long-sleeve shirts and work pants exit Fitopia. One man carries a box. The others bookend a weight bench and walk toward a moving truck parked on the street. They load the box and bench inside, then go back into the gym. Cynthia hobbles out moments later, arms wrapped around a smaller box. She inches her way up the loading ramp. Hill wasn't exaggerating. She's gaunt, her clothes sagging from her bony frame.

She goes inside and returns moments later with a medium-size box. Fearing she may stumble, I run to her aid and brace the bottom of the box with my palm. Cynthia manages to stay upright. "What the hell, man?" she says, looking at me cockeyed. "You!"

"Can we talk?" I ask.

She tries to adjust her grip on the box. "I've got nothing to say to you."

"I'll put it in the truck for you."

"I don't need your help."

"Look, you could get hurt, break something."

Cynthia drops the box. The contents rattle inside. Flushed, she's panting hard and sweating. "My God," she says as a severe cough sets in. She presses her hand to her chest, struggles to speak. "Just . . . leave."

"Are you OK?" I ask, knowing she's far from it. "I mean, should I get someone?"

"I'm dying." She seals her hand over her mouth, removing her hand when her cough subsides. "There's no one to get." I look at her palm to see blood droplets. "Just take the damn box and put it with the others."

I carry the box up the ramp and stack it in a corner with the rest. When I come back down, a mover is standing with Cynthia. "Everything cool, Cyn?" he asks, legs stout as tree trunks. "Didn't know you needed an extra man."

"I don't," she says. "I guess he was trying to help."

The man sizes me up. "Let the professionals handle it," he says, taking on a crass tone. "OK, fella?"

"Sure," I say. The man goes back inside, bopping as if he holds authority over me.

"Why are you here?" Cynthia asks.

"I'm not exactly sure . . ."

"Maybe you've come to gloat?"

"I take no pleasure in this."

Cynthia adjusts her knit cap, pulling it lower over her ears. I can tell most of her hair is gone, and her skin looks dull, the way my mother's did after years of chemo. "Winners and losers," she says. "That's how it's always been . . . the world." She coughs, then draws a long breath. "For the first time in my life, I know what it is to be a total loser."

"You're not—"

"Don't patronize me!" she says, shaking her fist. "And don't try to tell me how to feel. Men have been doing that my entire life. Manipulating. Trying to psychoanalyze me. First my father, then coaches and trainers. And none of them ever got it right because they didn't know me. No one did . . . not until Mandy." Cynthia puts her hands into her coat pockets. The sun has set, and the mild temperature feels somewhere in the sixties, but she's dressed for a blizzard. "Mandy murdered people. I know that, and no matter how much I wish it weren't true, I know the woman I loved—my wife—was a killer. And you know what I've come to realize?"

"No," I say.

"I'm just another one of her victims . . ."

"Boston kept a lot of secrets. She's the only one to blame."

"You think so?" she asks. The movers carry another load of boxes into the truck and watch me with distrust. "Because Mandy wasn't alone."

"I don't know what you mean."

"It's in the quiet moments," she says. "The moments I'm dying in now. I think back on the past. Things she said about suspects. And I wonder if she was trying to tell me then. Does that happen to you? Has your mind wandered back to that night?"

"Sometimes."

"You ever think that maybe you could have done something? Reported what Mandy and Garcia did to Ruben Montgomery? Raised hell, told anyone who would have listened and those who wouldn't?"

"I tried."

"Maybe you should have tried harder."

"You think I don't have regrets? It's all I've got."

"Good," she says.

"I want to know where she is," I say. "Tell me how I can find her."

Cynthia rolls her shoulders forward to a hunch, as if to make herself small. "I don't know," she says. "And as much as I hate her, I'm not sure I'd tell you if I did."

"Withholding information about her whereabouts is a crime. You could be charged as an accessory after the fact."

Cynthia's weak laugh threatens a coughing fit. "I'll be dead by then. Nothing matters anymore—not you, not Mandy, and not that poor recruit. But if you do happen to find her, tell her she's the worst thing that's ever happened to me." Cynthia begins her slow return to the building.

"I'm sorry you're ill," I say.

She stops to look at me, longer than what seems ordinary. "No, you're not," she says, walking away.

I head back to the Falcon and get in. My cell phone vibrates. It's a text message from Tori:

Found the perfect place!!!

Simone seems to love it. <Smiley face emoji>

The deposit is $1,500.

She attaches photos of the unit. It looks lovely: white walls, bright, spacious. I ask for her account information and immediately transfer her the money. She responds with Thank you!!! and an excited-face emoji followed by a thumbs-up and a picture of Simone looking precious in her stroller. I respond: You're welcome. Then I text Hill to let him know that I'm on the way and starving.

I make a U-turn and drive back to the freeway feeling sorrier for Cynthia than when I arrived.

It's close to five o'clock. There's not enough time to go to Sierra Madre before heading to Hill's place. Traffic is moderate when I merge onto the 10 driving east. My stomach rumbles as I think about Hill's steaks searing on the grill and the frosty longnecks waiting for me in Chino. I've been dreading the visit, not being in much of a sociable mood and unsure if I can manage to hoot and holler through Hill's one-man rodeo show—jumping over steeples, roping pegs in the ground, and shooting beer bottles with a Civil War–era revolver—but it might be the reprieve I need.

It's about forty-five minutes on the 91 east before I'll arrive in Chino. I smell the cow dung and know I'm close. Aside from its state prison, the city is known for its produce and dairy farms. Hill says the terrain reminds him of Texas, especially during the summer months, when the sweltering heat bakes the dung and the city is blanketed in a lingering stench.

I exit onto Prairie Road, which is lined with large plots of land. Some are barren; others cling to life. Fences have been chained and bolted, affixed with FOR SALE signs and auction notices.

I turn onto Hill's private road, driving toward the large white ranch house. Dust kicks up behind the Falcon, billowing in the air and collecting on the windshield. I park next to Hill's pickup truck, an old Chevy with two-tone paint and an American flag bumper sticker. I get out of the car, walk the stairs onto the porch, and ring the doorbell. A few minutes pass, but Hill doesn't come to the door. Thinking he may be in the backyard, I walk around to the rear of the house.

"Uncle Hill! Where are you, man?" The backyard is fenced with a three-foot barricade made of wood and chicken wire that Hill constructed himself. It isn't elegant or passably up to code, but it keeps the horses in. I climb onto the fence, throw my legs over, and drop onto the soft dirt. My LAPD detective days left me with not only occasional back spasms but also a sensitive receiver. When something isn't right, my stomach tightens like a sponge being squeezed hard, and it's happening right now.

I pass the barrel barbecue shedding rattan-colored rust. Propelled by sporadic gusts of wind, a dented beer can rolls along the patio table. Wood chips are soaking in a bucket. Hill usually soaks hickory or mesquite hours before firing up the grill. He says it gives the beef a delectable flavor that most steakhouses can't come close to achieving. I'd never say it, but having dined at some of the best steakhouses in LA, I've concluded that Hill thinks much too highly of his wood chips.

The hoof impressions in the dirt look fresh; he's been riding. "Hey, Uncle Hill. Come on. I'm starving!" I knock on the back door, then twist the handle. It's locked.

I climb back over the fence and walk toward the barn, a tin-roofed structure of rotting wood. My father used to warn Hill that the whole thing would collapse one day. "It's a damn hazard," he'd say. "Bulldoze it and use the wood for a bonfire." But Hill refused, convinced it was a historical structure and that the City of Chino would come knocking one day with a preservation grant to cover its restoration. Twenty years later, no one's shown up.

Inside the barn, his horse, Monte Cristo, eats from a pile of hay. The brown-maned steed is usually stabled when it isn't being ridden. "Uncle Hill, your horse is having a buffet over here!" I yell. "What's the deal?" Still no answer. I walk toward the stalls at the rear of the barn, expecting to see Hill shoveling the horse's dung into a wheelbarrow. Monte Cristo's stall door is open. The two others are locked as usual. Last year, Hill sold the occupants; he didn't have time to care for two saddlebreds.

My stomach drops. "No! No! No!" Hill's body swings from a rafter, the rope stretched around his neck. Everything's accelerated—my heartbeat, thoughts, movements. I kick over a stool next to him and grab his legs, trying to hold him up. "Uncle Hill," I say, "come on! Please!" He's limp. The rope resembles blood-soaked licorice twisted into a noose. I need to cut it. Letting go of Hill's legs, I sprint to his workbench across from the stables to search a toolbox for anything sharp enough to cut the rope. I find a rusted hacksaw.

I return to the stall, stand on the stool, and begin cutting the rope until the fibers fray and the rope gives out. Hill drops, and I stumble backward. His body lands on top of my legs, pinning me between his thick torso and the sawdust floor. "Help!" I yell. "Somebody, help!" Monte Cristo scampers out of the barn. I suck air, then gather the strength to roll Hill off me. I brace him on his side and try to untie the noose. I contemplate cutting it but come to my senses when I look into his bulging eyes. Blood vessels have burst, a dark redness having gathered in the tear ducts. I note his blue tongue; flecks of white mucus have collected on his gums and in the corners of his mouth. He's been dead for some time.

An engine revs; it's familiar. I rush out of the barn. In the distance, a black-clothed figure is mounted on a motorcycle at the start of the private road. I run in their direction. "Stop!" I shout. "Don't move!" What good are commands without the threat of force? My gun is locked in the trunk. The rider may be armed. I keep moving forward, staggering my pattern, taking wide steps to the right, then angling to the left.

I'm closing in. The rider's less than fifty yards away. I notice the neon-green shocks. The motorcycle's rear tire whips into a half circle, producing plumes of smoke and dust. There's a loud squeal and popping, the same sound I heard that night in Venice. Rubber burns across the blacktop. The engine whizzes as the motorcycle speeds down Prairie Road, heading south.

I ditch my foot pursuit and return to the Falcon. I get in, turn the key in the ignition. The car doesn't start. I try again . . . then again, but there's only a clicking sound. "Fuck!" I slam my palms against the steering wheel, then get out. I open the trunk and remove my revolver. I attach the holstered weapon to my belt. I pop the hood and confirm what I feared. The battery has been removed—no doubt by the prick on the motorcycle.

Back in the barn, I stare at Hill's body. I've seen plenty of DBs, but Hill's is different. Even if I never told him, he might have been my only friend and sometimes more of a father to me than Pop. It doesn't seem real. How can Hill be dead?

The entire scene is off. I'm sure the motorcyclist took my car battery to strand me here, but what's the play? Prevent me from following? Leave me to haggle with the police? Hill's been dead for an hour or more, judging by his skin coloring. The longer I wait to get the police out here, the more suspicious things start looking. When it comes to suspicious deaths, homicide detectives pay close attention to timelines. They're trained to identify gaps—say, from the moment I found Hill dead to when I called 911. A skilled detective will notice a span longer than fifteen minutes between actions.

I dig into Hill's Wranglers for anything to shed light on what transpired. His right pocket is empty, but I pull a set of keys from his left. Two of the keys look like they might open the doors to the house. There are three additional keys: one to his truck, another made of brass, and one that's longer and silver, stamped with an equestrian insignia, which means that it probably locks the stables. I attach the keys to my key ring so I won't lose them.

I run back to the rear of the house, climb over the fence, and unlock the back door that leads into the kitchen. I cross the threshold into the dated galley kitchen. The hardwood flooring, once cadmium, has turned coal black, ruined by rot. Capless seasonings sit on the Formica counter: Kentucky bourbon dry rub, celery salt, garlic powder. Shucked ears of corn are stacked in an aluminum bowl.

I head upstairs. The floor creaks loudly in the stairwell. I draw my weapon. The motorcyclist may have been a lookout. There could be people in Hill's home. When I reach the second-floor hallway, I head to his study. Like my father, Hill spent the most time in one room. If there are clues to what happened, the study is a good place to start. The door is slightly ajar. I raise my weapon and nudge it open with the tip of the gun's barrel. The room is empty but smacks of body odor, musty and acidic, and there's the vinegary stench of urine.

Hill's desktop screen is black, but the small orange light tells me the monitor is on. I touch the mouse, and the screen comes to life. An open document reads:

I'm sorry. Mateo deserved better. I deserve worse.

—Brixton Hill

Who the hell is Mateo? The office chair looks damp. I bend down to get a look under it, where I find a puddle of piss, the source of the awful smell. There must be more than a few liters. Presuming it's from Hill, why didn't he get up to relieve himself?

The piss inches toward the corner of the room, propelled by the sloping, uneven floor. I taste vomit and swallow it back down my throat.

Keep it together, Trevor. Focus on the scene.

I continue to assess things, looking for objects that stand out and might be out of place. His bookshelf looks undisturbed, and there's a file cabinet where he kept copies of cases. I check whether it's open. Both drawers are locked.

Even before I discovered the piss and the suspicious note, the room felt ominous. It'd rival a basement if not for the large casement window. The window allowed Hill to see his private road, part of Prairie Road, and most of his property. The way he surveyed his land with discernment made me think of his study as the upper deck of a watchtower.

I urged him to get a security system with motion-detector cameras, but he regarded it as a waste of money. "No one's coming up in here unless they want to leave in a body bag. All those cameras do is entice people. It'll have them thinking I've got something worth stealing."

I wasn't surprised by Hill's refusal. He was raised how my father was, country and keen to the dangers black folks faced daily in the South. Life meant staying under the radar. Keeping a gun loaded and handy, prepared for anything: vandals, lynch mobs, thieves coming to lay claim to the little they had.

My watch's minute hand ticks—it's 6:30 p.m. Realizing fifteen minutes have passed since I found Hill's body, I go downstairs and leave out the back door, locking it behind me. Monte Cristo still hasn't returned. He likely watched Hill die, and if animals suffer shock the same as humans do, then wanting to flee isn't a sign of a primitive mind but intelligence.

I unlock Hill's truck and lift the hood. The battery's terminals are caked in chalky white powder and blue crystals. Baking soda or cola usually does the trick, dissolving the sulfuric acid so it can be scrubbed off with a toothbrush, but I don't have the time or the means to clean the corrosion and hope that once the battery is transferred into the Falcon, it'll work fine. I pull it from the truck, hug it like a brick, and drop it into the Falcon's compartment. I connect the red and black cables. It's a snug fit. The Falcon's hood barely closes. I start the engine, letting it run as I dial 911 from inside the car.

"There's been a death," I say to the operator. "I found him . . . Yes, I'll remain at the scene."

———

Nightfall—always harder to work a crime scene once the sun goes down, and that's what this is, a crime scene. Hill didn't commit suicide. Someone sat him down, forced him to type the note, and then marched him out to the barn under threat, likely gunpoint. It's beyond a gut feeling, something honed from years of standing over dead bodies, working homicides till they ran dry as brittle bones. Between conjecture and conviction is knowing that the deceased had no say in the matter. Someone took them from the world with designs, motives, and opportunity.

I stand in the road with arms raised high. My state-issued private investigator's ID dangles around my neck, twirling in the light wind. A police SUV nears, flashing red and blue. An ambulance follows behind. The vehicles come to a stop, headlights bright in my eyes. Two officers get out of the SUV, step into the light. I remain still.

"You the one who found the victim?" one officer asks as they approach slowly. He's a man with a military fade, skintight on the sides, thicker on the top. The cut doesn't suit him. Maybe ten years ago, he had a soldier's physique, but now his neck is a fatty buttress for the water jug of a head on his shoulders.

"Yes."

"Identification?"

"Around my neck," I say. "And I've got a licensed firearm."

The officer studies the snubnose that I've placed on the ground in front of me and says, "You can put your hands down," without questioning why I had them up in the first place. "I'm Officer Vasquez. That's my partner, Officer Stewart."

"OK," I say, picking up my gun.

Stewart is a petite white woman with a familiar face, though I'm certain I've never seen her before. Without asking, she takes hold of the ID around my neck, studies it, then lets it slip from her fingers. "Trevor Finnegan, private investigator," she says, staring back at me. Behind her dark eyes, belligerence seems in conflict with her need to be professional.

"Are you working a job out here?" Vasquez asks, taking out his field notepad and pen.

"I came for dinner and found him hanging in the barn . . ."

"A dinner invitation?" He points his pen at me. "A special occasion?" I don't respond right away. "Or something routine?" He flicks the silver pen like a conductor bringing the orchestra to tempo. I don't know how to interpret the gesture, but it isn't a show of respect. "The dinner, sir?" he asks.

"Sorry," I say, remembering how people looked at me when I questioned them in uniform. Afraid. Apprehensive. Despondent. Studying my face for an inkling of how I might use my power with impunity. "We try for once a month. Sometimes it works out, sometimes it doesn't."

"And who is *he*?"

"Brixton Hill."

"He family?"

I pause. "Yes, a family friend. He's like an uncle."

"OK," Vasquez says. "Stewart is going to take a look in the barn."

Stewart pulls her flashlight from her Sam Browne and turns it on, directing the white beam in front of her. She moves the flashlight from side to side, shining the light into the barn's darker corners. I listen as her boots press against the dirt, crushing sand and pebbles. With each step, she ventures farther into the barn. Then there's silence, and I know she's found Hill. "Let's have the EMTs back here," she says, sounding relieved she didn't have to see Hill's skull blown apart. There's nothing uncommon about police officers taking their own lives, but suicide by hanging is rare. A bullet is a preferred method.

"Billy," Vasquez says, summoning the lead EMT with a wave. The EMT is a fit white man about my height and younger.

"He's dead," I say. "There isn't anything they can do for him."

"It's best to be sure." The EMTs rush past Vasquez and me, carrying equipment bags, and join Stewart in the barn. "We had a case a while back. This kid overdosed on something nasty. The mom was sure he was dead. Ten minutes of chest compressions and his mama praying to Jehovah and presto! Resurrection."

"Street miracles," I say. "That's what we called them."

"Oh, were you on the job?" he asks, his shoulders dropping, his posture less authoritative. "What department?"

"LAPD."

"You look young for retirement."

"Took an early pension."

"Let me guess," he says. "Detective?"

"Robbery-homicide."

"I knew it," he says. "So you've seen this sort of thing before?"

"Far too often," I say.

Stewart approaches, pointing her flashlight at my face. The EMTs return to the ambulance. "You cut him down?" she asks in the way officers sometimes do—an ineludible statement posing as a question.

"Yes, I cut Hill down."

"How long ago did you find him?"

I look at my watch. "About an hour ago." Stewart shoots Vasquez a look, the same one I used to give Munoz the instant I regarded a scene or someone as suspicious. "Any idea why he'd want to kill himself?" She takes her field notepad and a pen from her pocket and begins to write.

"I'm hoping you'll be able to tell me that," I say. Neither officer looks pleased with my suggestion. Nothing good will come out of riling them. Best to play nice, compliant. "No—I've got no idea."

"How has his behavior been?" Stewart asks. "Anything bothering him? Marriage? Work? Family issues?"

"He didn't mention anything."

"What's he do?"

"He's a special agent with the FBI."

Vasquez makes a strange noise, not far from a snort. "An FBI agent?" he asks. "Oh boy." Stewart steps away. I can hear her mumble into her radio, requesting to have a supervisor on the scene.

"He worked out of the West LA field office," I say.

Vasquez tilts his head forward so that I can see the precise edges of his hairline. He drills the pen into the pad and writes faster. Then, as if

I've told him tomorrow's weather, he casually says, "OK," and slips his pen and pad back into his chest pocket.

"OK?"

"Feds like to do their own autopsies. My partner is working on getting someone down here who can coordinate all of the particulars."

"What happens to him until then?"

"If they don't collect him in a few hours, we'll transport the body to the county morgue."

"Collect him?"

"Yeah, like I said . . ."

"Can you at least cover him up?" I ask. By now, rigor mortis is compounding in his muscles, causing them to grow rigid. The rope has caused necrosis around his neck, turning it violet and black. In an hour or so, his skin will feel like wax paper coated with oil, and his umber pigment will transmute to the color of whey.

Vasquez shrugs. "We've got a sheet in the trunk."

"I'll get it," Stewart says, having ended her radio call. She gives me a chiseled stare that could split me in two, then walks to the rear of the SUV, opens it, and begins riffling through gear.

The EMTs are perched on the ambulance's bumper smoking cigarettes. I didn't observe them closely before, but they're young and burly men who look like they drink off-brand beer and refer to themselves as "Grade-A all-American." When they finish their smokes, they flick the cigarette butts into the dirt, get back into the ambulance, and drive down the private road.

"I am sorry for your loss," Vasquez says.

I can't gauge if it's heartfelt, but I present my hand for him to shake. "I appreciate that."

Vasquez's calloused palm usurps my hand. "You miss it?" he asks. "Being a cop?"

"Some days," I say, thinking if I were to answer no, it'd become a longer conversation.

"You ever consider going back? We could use more good soldiers."

"No," I say. "I watch the news."

"Tell me about it . . . Every day it's another group claiming brutality or some bullshit. Doesn't matter if the arrest is clean," he says. "If it's caught on video, you know the shit's been edited."

"I was talking about the crime stats."

"Oh, yeah, right," he says. "I'm sure patrolling Chino is nothing like working streets in LA." His lips are pursed as he looks at me longingly, a dog dying for a bone.

"I'm sure you've got your hands full here."

"Oh, do we ever . . . meth and opioid addicts," he says, bucking with more urgency than he's previously displayed. "But all that's going to get sorted out once we get the big guy in the White House."

"You believe that?"

"I sure do," he says, brimming with unabashed pride. "He's going to give law enforcement our balls back." He makes his hands into fists and shakes them vigorously. "I'm telling you, it's going to be epic. A show of force that reminds people we're not some kind of joke."

"The people I hauled off to jail usually weren't laughing."

"Yeah, and that's how it needs to stay," he says. "Finally, an ally in Washington, and it's about goddamn time, brother!" He gives my shoulder a frat-boy slap. It's hard enough to register as pain. I ignore the urge to hit him back. He adds, "Blue lives matter, and they always will."

Stewart drapes a gray sheet over Hill's body. A tremor commandeers my hand, moving up my arm toward the shoulder that Vasquez slapped. When I have anxious fits like this, I twitch. Dr. Angell says it's a corollary of my anxiety and PTSD. I usually manage by breathing slowly and shoving the afflicted hand into my pocket until it passes. But I'm alone in a field with Vasquez and Stewart, and I should keep both hands visible.

"You OK?" Vasquez asks.

No, I'm not OK. How the hell can I be . . . OK?

The gray sheet settles atop Hill, tracing his contour. His beating heart is gone, along with memories, experiences—everything that made him *him*. He's now codified as a victim to be carted to the morgue, toe-tagged, cut open, and examined. Another puzzle to be solved.

"It's getting late."

"Hopefully it won't be much longer," Vasquez says. "Was he a big deal?"

"What do you mean?"

"You know? A honcho in the big bad FBI."

"He was a career agent. Closed plenty of cases. What's it matter?"

"Just curious," he says. "I don't get to interact with too many FBI agents."

"Well, you didn't interact with him," I say.

Vasquez smiles crookedly. "Sure . . . since he's dead and all."

I look at my watch. I'm not trying to be out here with Vasquez and Stewart any longer than I have to be. "It normally takes this long to get a supervisor on the scene?"

"Yep," Vasquez says. "You going to turn into a pumpkin or something?"

I don't respond, but my face surely translates to *Fuck off.*

When FBI agents finally show up, they'll look in Hill's house, sift through his office, and find the "suicide note" and dried piss. If they've got eyes, they'll rule his death suspicious. I've worked cases like this, weird ones that only stand to get weirder, and Hill's death has the makings of a long-hauler. The type of case that could take months to clear, if ever. But I have an advantage, the missing piece: the motorcyclist. I've got at least a day or two before the FBI will finish turning Hill's house upside down, only to rule what I already know—somebody killed him. Forty-eight hours should be enough time to find out who Mateo is, and maybe it'll lead me to the motorcyclist.

"So are we good here?" I ask. "I really need to be going."

"You don't want to wait for the FBI?" Vasquez looks surprised, his droopy chin fitting his dimwitted persona. "Otherwise, I'm going to need to get your information."

"Go ahead, whatever you need."

Vasquez removes a field-interview card from his pocket and starts asking the standard questions: full name, occupation, date of birth, height, race, eye color, and my reason for being in the area. "You might want my phone number," I say when it becomes obvious he may forget to ask how to reach me.

"Oh, right," he says. I tell him my number, speaking faster than normal so that he's forced to write quickly. Then he shoves the card into his pocket and says, "You're good to go."

"All right."

"Oh," he says. "You probably want to stick around. No domestic or international trips. Just until things get sorted."

"I'll be around . . ."

CHAPTER NINE

"Shit, Finn, I'm sorry," Munoz says before gulping down the last of her amber ale. "Your uncle sounds primo." She slides the empty stein, still chilled, to the edge of the table. She drank the beer so fast the glass didn't have time to thaw. She throws her good arm over the top of the booth, something I'd imagine she does at home on her sofa.

The Golden Gopher has a way of disarming cops. They unwind, let their guards down. And some, like Munoz, hold bar tabs that are never called in. Located a few blocks from Skid Row, it's a refuge. One of the last drinking holes still welcoming to cops. The other cop bars have been shuttered or co-opted by LA's hipsters, celebrities, and socialites, who are willing to pay fifteen dollars for Moscow Mules.

In all its dark, faded beauty, this vintage booze house is one of the last places where officers can be *nobodies*, disappearing into the red shadows cast long by dusty Edison bulbs that burn faintly in copper and crystal candelabras.

"He was *primo*," I say, holding the shot glass queued below my lips. The other shot, topped to the brim with dark liquor, is waiting on the table. "To Hill!" I take the shot down fast, breathing out the burning.

"And Riley," Munoz adds. "Both good cops."

Good cops? I can vouch for Hill, but I'm less enthused about Riley, and Munoz isn't far behind. I spent the entire drive to the bar working out the best way to interrogate my ex-partner while crying over Uncle

Hill. Then there's the matter of the biker. Even if Munoz is dirty, I need her help to find out who the motorcyclist is and what they have to do with Uncle Hill's death.

"Drink up, Finn," Munoz says. "Tonight, we're keeping them coming."

I drink the other shot, regretful I don't have a beer to chase it with. My eyes water, blurring slightly, and when they return to focus, I notice the news broadcast airing on the TV behind the bar. Mary Ling for Channel 7 reports: "Tonight, our special investigation has revealed that two LAPD officers have been suspended without pay pending a probe into misconduct. Officers Chris Garvey and Brian Yoshida of the Pacific Division have been placed on a fifty-five-day suspension. An LAPD spokesperson familiar with the investigation says the department is looking into allegations that both officers may have engaged in on-duty sex acts with two women suspected of prostitution." Photos of both officers smiling in uniform before an American flag backdrop appear side by side on the screen.

"These clowns," Munoz says, passing judgment as if her record's spotless. "Watch those girls be underage or something . . . Sickos."

Did Cassandra grow a conscience and turn them in? But that would mean bringing her daughters into the light. Not the move if she wants to protect them.

My cell phone rings. I look at the caller ID. Bergman. "I better take this," I say to Munoz.

"Go right ahead," she says, bubbly from the booze.

I slide my finger along the screen and put the phone to my ear. "Hello?"

"Are you watching the news?"

"I am," I say.

"I did it," he says. "I leaked the photos to Channel 7."

"You did what?" I ask, tongue heavy.

"Have you been drinking?"

"Might've had a few . . ."

"Don't worry. There's no chance of it blowing back on us," he says. "My contact doesn't even know."

I sigh. "You should have talked to me first."

"I needed to make it right."

"I still should have been looped in," I say, trying my best to be discreet. "What's next?"

"I was thinking, and you're right," Bergman says. "It's time to return to our mandate—working for the people of this city."

"What happened to hooking the big fish?"

"We can manage both."

"You believe that?"

"I do," he says, sounding overly confident. "Which is why I want to talk about making you a partner."

"You're serious?" I ask.

"I am," he says. "We can figure out how best to keep your investigations covert, but I want you to have insurance, a pension, vacation time . . . I want you to know you have a future at the firm."

"Kind of difficult if you're bankrupt."

"Well, yes," he says, "but don't worry. Things are looking up."

Munoz looks askance. Paranoid? What if she can hear Bergman on the other end? "Might be best we discuss this another time," I say.

"Of course . . . It warrants a proper conversation, face-to-face. Maybe before you leave for France?"

"All right," I say. "I'll try." I end the call and return to drinking.

"What was that about?" Munoz asks. "Somebody going bankrupt?"

"My dad," I lie. "He's never been good with money."

"How's your lady? Still drama at home?"

"Seems like the season for it."

"Don't worry," she says. "She'll come around."

"I guess there are worse things than having a secret love child."

"Hey! Please tell me you have a picture of that darling?"

"I do." I smile wide, certain every tooth is showing. "Here she is." I present Simone's picture on my phone.

"She's beautiful, Finn, a little angel," Munoz says, leaning in closer. "Isn't it just the best feeling?"

"What's that?"

"Unconditional love." Munoz's cheerful grin recedes. She brings her hand to her mouth and is silent for a moment. Then she says, "I remember no matter how bad my day was, seeing my kids' little faces could make me forget all about it."

"They're magical that way," I say.

"Did your uncle have any children?"

"No."

"Well, some people prefer it that way, I guess . . ."

"Yeah," I say, putting my phone back into my pocket.

"You want a beer?" she asks.

"Sure." Munoz thrusts two fingers into the air, and the bartender acknowledges her with a thumbs-up. "I need to find out what happened to him," I say.

"We never know what people are dealing with inside there," she says, touching her head. "Life gets to be too much sometimes. People check out."

"No," I say, trying to find the right words. "I saw something at the farm."

"What?" Time hangs heavier than I intend. "Enough with the suspense, Finn. Spit it out."

"When I found Hill, there was someone else out there . . . watching me."

"You mean, like, a neighbor?"

"I don't think so," I say. "It was like they knew Hill was in the barn and were waiting for me to find him."

"In the barn hanging, you mean?"

"I mean, yes, but he didn't hang himself," I say. "He wouldn't do that."

"Well, Finn, if he didn't commit suicide, then what happened to him?"

"I think he was killed." The words sound crazier than when they were thoughts boggling in my head. "I know what you're going to say . . ."

"Homicide by forced hanging?" Munoz asks. "That's what you've been thinking about?"

"It's possible."

"Anything's possible, but why?"

A blonde woman approaches the table holding a beer stein in each hand. She sets them on two cocktail napkins. "Enjoy," she says, leaving before we can offer a thank-you or a tip.

"What if I told you Cassandra Boyle didn't have anything to do with Riley's death?"

Munoz grabs the stein's handle and takes a long sip of the cold beer. A third of the beer is gone when she plops the mug on the table. "I don't know, Finn. I guess I'd need to hear a good reason you'd think that."

"The night Riley was shot, I followed the shooter into the parking lot. The person fired at me. I took cover behind some parked cars. Then, when it was clear, I saw the shooter flee on a motorcycle." Munoz glares but continues to listen. "Today, when I approached the biker on Hill's land, they were on a motorcycle, like the one Riley's shooter rode. The way they handled the bike, everything. It was the same rider. I know in my—"

"Your gut?" Munoz says, her sarcasm second only to her aggravation.

"Yes," I say. "I believe we're dealing with the same individual."

"So you saw two people on similar motorcycles, and you think what? A murder plot that targets who, exactly—Hill and Riley?"

"I don't know," I say, rubbing the back of my head. "I don't see all the pieces yet."

"And why the hell are you telling me this now? Didn't you say you didn't see the shooter up close? Now you're saying you took gunfire and let them get away?"

"I didn't let them get away."

"Did you return fire?"

"It wasn't safe to do so."

"That might have been the only chance we had to apprehend Riley's killer. You realize that?"

"I'm not a cop, Sally!"

"No kidding—hard to imagine you were ever one." I can hear the hurt in Munoz's voice and the ire in mine. "But now that Hill's dead, you've got all the details? How convenient. What else aren't you telling me?"

"That's it," I say.

"OK," Munoz says, leaning against the table. "You know what, Finn?" She stands up with her beer in hand, then pours it into my lap. "Go to hell."

"Ah, shit," I say, leaping out of the seat. Munoz storms toward the exit. "Munoz, wait!" I grab the two cocktail napkins and try to wipe my pants clean but give up when I feel the beer seeping into my boxers.

Outside, I'm met by patrons smoking cigarettes and waiting in a line walled by a velvet rope. An overweight bouncer checks IDs with a flashlight the size of a dry-erase marker. He startles, nearly jumping off his stool when I pass, and as if to reclaim his manhood, he shouts, "Hey, dickhead! Don't be running through here!" A trio of slick-looking people seizes the opportunity to point and snicker at my wet crotch. I ignore them and keep after Munoz, who's a few feet past the doorman and not slowing down, forcing me to do double time to keep pace beside her. "Look, Munoz, just hear me out?"

"What for? So you can keep lying to me?"

"I know you're angry. I should have told you."

Munoz halts, and I can finally slow down, feeling ridiculous with the wet cocktail napkins in my hand. I shove them in my pocket. "Why didn't you?" she asks.

"I wish I could . . ."

"But you can't?"

"No, I can't."

"I don't get you, Finn," she says. "What the hell's going on?"

"I just need you to trust me."

"Trust you?"

"Yes, we can do this together," I say, knowing her cooperation may be our only shot at solving both murders. "Ask yourself, have I ever steered us wrong?" Munoz scowls. "Any investigation we worked, we closed together because you trusted me, and I trusted you. All I'm asking is for you to trust me again."

Munoz looks up to the sky. The pallid moon gives her skin a ghostly glow, and I wonder if anything I've said tonight has mattered. "Fine," she says, lowering her head with a cutting eye roll. "Keep talking."

"Hill told me at Riley's memorial that they worked together out of Southwest."

"I see," she says. "In what capacity?"

"Hill didn't say, exactly." I remember to wipe my wet pants with the napkins again after two women in party dresses walk past, laughing as they zero in on my crotch.

"I'll pull any cases they may have worked together."

"Copy."

"But it was like twenty years ago." She pauses, then drums her fingers on her cast. "I'll have to go through records . . ."

"That a problem?"

"Got written up," she says. "They'll be monitoring me until my disciplinary hearing."

"Written up?" I ask. "For what?"

"Cassandra Boyle claimed I've been harassing her," she says. "Told IAB about our visit. Funny thing is, she didn't mention you."

"Why would she? We told her I wasn't a cop."

Munoz taps her boot on the grimy sidewalk. "Yeah, but it's funny, right?"

I don't know why Cassandra didn't mention me, but I suspect it has to do with our impromptu chat. Was it her way of thanking me for freeing her girls from Garvey and Yoshida? She knows I'm the one who's been burning dirty cops. That information is currency in her world, or there's another reason that I haven't considered . . .

"It's Cassandra Boyle," I say. "Only she knows why. So you think you can get the records?"

"I've got a guy in the department who owes me a favor," she says. "I'll tell him to be discreet." Munoz removes her car keys from her pocket. The Crown Vic is parked on the street, crammed between a cargo van that looks like it hasn't moved in weeks and a dumpster filled with construction waste. "I'll contact my records guy tonight. See if I can get access in the morning." She unlocks the car with her remote key and starts walking toward the driver's-side door.

"Munoz?"

"Yeah?"

"Cross-reference anything you find on either of them with the name Mateo."

"Mateo . . . Why's that?"

"I saw 'Mateo' written in Hill's note. So far, it's the only clue we've got." For a moment, it looks like Munoz might smile. Does she feel it, too? The rush of working together again, the familiar distinctness of forming suppositions, lobbing theories, extracting verity from hunches. Her mouth remains zipped, so I blurt out, "We're going to find out why this happened to them and who's responsible."

"Finn," Munoz says, looking slightly more convinced than she did a few moments ago, "I need that to be true." She gets into the car, starts it, and works the long sedan out of its parking spot before driving down the trash-littered street.

———

I pull into the driveway at 10:15 p.m. and go inside the townhouse. The light above the stove is on in the kitchen.

A note on the refrigerator reads:

Meatloaf is in the oven. Salad is in the fridge.

Looks like Sarada planned a special evening. It's good she went to bed. Hill is heavy on my mind, and I'm not the best company.

She's set the table with the *good* china—teal porcelain plates, holiday silverware, and stemless wineglasses. In the center of the table, cream flowers and baby's breath are arranged in a burnished vase. A candlewick is charred. Wax has hardened down bucolic wooden sticks that I vaguely remember Sarada purchasing in Asia.

I hear soft footfalls behind me and turn to see Sarada in nightclothes and slippers. "I thought you were asleep," I say.

"Couldn't sleep."

"Food smells good."

"Tasted good, too," she says, stepping into the kitchen. "You going to eat?"

"It's a little late . . . not much of an appetite."

"All right." She takes the meatloaf from the oven and sets it on the stove. "I was hoping we could talk tonight."

"Sorry about that," I say. "Got hung up with work."

"Smells like you've been investigating bars."

"I had a few with Munoz."

"You bathe in it?"

"What'd you want to talk about?" I ask, too tired to bicker.

"It's about France . . ."

"Shit, France," I say. The trip slipped my mind. I can't leave with Hill's murder looming large. Not only would it draw suspicion, but I'm the best shot at finding who killed him.

"Yes, Trevor," she says. "Are you coming with me or not?"

There's no way to break it to her without causing a fight or hurting her feelings. "I don't think I should," I say.

Sarada lowers her head. "All right . . . Care to tell me why?"

As close as I am to her, I've never felt further away. I should tell her about Uncle Hill, but if she knew I was mourning him, she'd cancel the trip and stay behind, upending all the time and effort it took for her to get accepted into the École de Pâtisserie de France.

"Things are a little hectic right now, that's all. I'm not saying I don't want to join you."

"I don't ask for much, Trevor, but this . . ." Sarada looks as if I've unearthed a well of sadness. "I was counting on you."

"I'm sorry . . ."

"If it's not work, then it's your father, and now . . ."

"A baby," I say. "Is that what this is about?"

"You tell me," she says, hands on her hips. "Are you wanting to stay in LA for them?"

"Not necessarily . . ." I can't even think about seeing Simone until I solve Hill's murder, but Sarada needs more reason than a hectic schedule. "I mean, sure, Simone is part of it, but can you blame me?"

"No, I don't blame you, Trevor . . . She's your daughter. But you can't expect infinite sympathy for the hot mess of a life you used to live. This is *our* life now. We made plans long before Tori and Simone popped up. Shouldn't you honor those commitments?"

"It's six months, Sarada. What's so wrong with me coming a month or two after you're there?"

"Because two months will turn to four, then five . . . and you'll look up, and I'll be home."

"There's no compromising with you, is there?"

"You don't get it," she says. "This trip wasn't only about me learning to bake stupid pastries. It was about us."

"Us?"

"Haven't you noticed? We're not doing so good."

"Since when?"

"Trevor, you work all the time," she says. "I barely see you. Even when you're here, you're not present. You're not *with* me."

"So France was couples therapy?"

"I wanted it to be an opportunity to reconnect," she says. "To get back to what we were."

"And what was that?"

"We used to talk about everything," she says with downcast eyes.

"I feel like you want me to choose between Simone and you."

"I'm not asking that. All I want is to matter again."

"You do," I say. "Simone and Tori haven't changed anything."

"You're right, Trevor. You stopped noticing me long before they arrived."

"That isn't true."

Sarada turns and starts walking back toward the stairs. "I'll refund your ticket."

"Sarada, wait . . ."

"I have to finish packing."

"So that's it?" I ask. "End of the conversation."

"Just put the food away if you're not going to eat it."

"Damn the food, Sarada! We aren't done talking!"

"There's nothing left to say," she says. "You need to figure out what you want, Trevor. Otherwise . . ."

"What's that supposed to mean?"

Sarada slips into the darkness of the stairwell, leaving me to wallow in the ocher glow of the stove light. I reach for the light switch on the hood and turn it off. The room goes black. I stand pitched in darkness, needing to scream but not making a sound. My phone rings. I pull it from my pocket—the screen's a glowing beacon. The caller ID reads "Brixton Hill."

Hill? But how?

Many horrors can befall a person in life, and I've had a front-row seat to more than I can stand, but this phone call from a dead man has turned my blood to ice. Electric current rips through my bones like a wild spur in the open rodeo circuit. My abdomen tightens, and my breathing turns to panting. I try to focus, to stay sharp, as I press the button to answer.

Phone to my ear, I ask, "Who is this?" I listen to breathing: controlled, almost soothing. "Tell me who you are."

"Stay away," a man says. "Stay away, or you'll die like the others."

"Who are you, dammit? Why'd you kill Hill?"

"Stay away. This is your only warning."

The call ends.

I'm suddenly drowning in a sea of trepidation. I'm confident I've spoken to the murderer of Detective Riley and Uncle Hill. The man was frighteningly relaxed, fearless. I consider the cunning ways Riley and Hill were killed. Their murders without parallels—a shooting, a hanging—days apart. Maybe to make the deaths look random?

Hill's phone was missing from the scene. I didn't think to even look for it. The last text I sent him was about dinner . . . I told him to expect me. The murderer must have known I was going to show up. He knew I'd find Hill's body.

I call Munoz. There's no answer.

I go upstairs to the study and lie on the couch. Sharing a bed with Sarada tonight means clinging to the edge of the mattress, her back to mine, not having the words to fix the mess I've made.

I place my phone on the arm of the couch in case Munoz calls me back. I close my eyes, wondering about the caller, trying to profile who he is. All I know is he's a man of above-average stature. Perhaps a professional motorcyclist, former racer? He's cautious; he likely wore gloves in Hill's home. But how did he get him to compose that "suicide note" and hang himself? A gun to his head or a knife to his throat?

I play back the call in my head, focusing my attention on the man's speech. His diction revealed nothing. I didn't detect an accent, either, but that doesn't mean he didn't have one.

My eyes get heavy. I close them and pray for a restful couple of hours.

—

My phone rings. I reach in its direction, taking hold of it before it falls from the arm of the couch. I bring the phone to my ear. "Finnegan," I say, alert but fatigued, sounding like I'm speaking through a meat grinder. "Munoz, that you?"

"Yes," she says. "I called in that favor. Got access to the records."

"You did?" I ask, sitting up on the couch. "Wait. What time is it?"

"Four thirty in the morning."

I knuckle the sleep from my eyes. "What you got?"

"A rap sheet for Mateo Ruiz. Also goes by Teo and King T."

"Gang affiliated?"

"Looks like he got out of the life in 1990 after the gang injunctions hit."

"Notable arrests?"

"Check fraud, bunch of misdemeanors, and murder in 1998."

"Who'd he kill?"

"LAPD Officer Jeremy Green."

"No shit? He killed a cop?"

"He was a third-striker," she says. "Charged with aggravated manslaughter and second-degree murder. Given twenty-five to life. No chance of parole."

"And Hill worked it? Who was his partner?"

"Doesn't say."

"Did you manage to get a copy of the arrest report?"

"Yeah," she says with less enthusiasm.

"What is it?"

"The whole thing has been redacted. All I've got is your guy Hill as the arresting officer, Mateo, and dead Officer Green."

"Cause of death?"

"That's the thing," she says. "There's no ME report, either."

"Weird," I say. "Where should we meet?"

"Cosmos in Silver Lake. Know it?"

"Yeah—leaving now."

———

I slide into a red booth across from Munoz. The seat is slightly damp. Maybe something was spilled and left behind by a customer, or the rag used to wipe down the booths was soggy. At this hour, there's no point in complaining. The waitresses, cooks, insomniacs, street dwellers, dopers, and those fresh off graveyard shifts—everyone's scraping by.

Munoz drinks from a mug of thick black coffee, a bitter-smelling concoction that looks worse than what used to pass as brew at Pacific Division. I can tell she's wired, with her dilated pupils and eyes encapsulated by redness, saddled with bags. She hasn't been here long. It might be her second cup, but I wouldn't be surprised if it were her fourth.

"You hungry?" she asks. "I ordered the shrimp plate."

"Seafood at a twenty-four-hour diner?"

"Why not?"

"One thing is for sure, Munoz—you're not short of courage."

"Watch them be delicious," she says. "You'll be ordering a plate, too."

"Doubt it," I say. "So sounds like we've come up empty?"

"Not a damn thing in this report seems worthwhile," Munoz says, sliding the case file over to me. "Someone went through the trouble of black-barring the whole investigation."

"What about Riley? His name come up anywhere?"

"Not once," she says. "But I think I know someone who might be able to help us fill in the blanks."

"Who's that?"

"Riley kept in touch with his lieutenant from Southwest. Might be good to talk to him, see if he remembers anything about the case."

"I got a call tonight," I say, still on edge from earlier. "It was the man we're looking for."

Munoz nearly spits out her coffee. "What? But how?"

"He used Hill's phone."

"And what did he say?"

"Told me to stay out of his way, or I'd be next."

"Well, damn," she says. "Not sure I've ever had a culprit call me."

"Could mean we're close if we can put the pieces together."

"You think he'll call again?" she asks. "Could try and run a trace."

"Not this guy . . . He's likely destroyed Hill's cell."

The waitress, an older woman in a blue-and-white uniform, arrives tableside with Munoz's breaded shrimp and crinkle-cut fries. She sets the plate down, along with a large bowl of chunky tartar sauce. The sauce is called for, judging by the shrimp's rubbery consistency and heavy breading. "Anything else, dear?" the waitress asks.

"No, I'm fine," Munoz says.

"And how about you, sweetie?" The waitress smiles at me. Her magenta lipstick is layered thick and smudged on her teeth. "What can I get you?"

"Water's fine."

"Ice?"

"Sure."

"One ice water coming up." As she walks away, I focus on the elephant veins that riddle her thin legs and the gum-soled retro-white Reeboks, the same kind my mother wore.

Munoz bites into the shrimp with a crunch. Maybe her meal is what should be ordered at Cosmos? It's audacious to serve six frozen shrimp and charge eleven dollars, but it's also audacious that Cosmos still exists. Like the Surfside Motel, the establishment is trapped in the past, and entering through its doors means being pulled into a time warp where the decor and people have languished.

"So who's the lieutenant?" I ask.

"Bill Kutcher. Retired. Lives in Monterey Hills."

"You got his contact info?"

"I do," she says. "Guy's a reserve officer. Used to help out at the police museum but stopped two years ago. Think he had some health issues."

Munoz chomps a few fries. "How is it?" I ask.

She chews hard, swallows, and washes it all down with coffee. "Not bad. Have some."

"I'm good."

"I'm not going to eat all this," she says, dipping another shrimp into the bowl of tartar sauce. "Go ahead."

I try to remember my last meal. The only thing I can recall eating is the protein bar and sandwich. Munoz goes to the restroom, and I shove a handful of fries into my mouth. I wipe the grease from my hands before texting Sarada, letting her know I left and not to worry. I'm not surprised when she doesn't respond. It's early, she's angry, and I've earned the silent treatment.

Ten minutes later, Munoz returns, looking unsettled. The shrimp doused in tartar sauce seems the likely trigger, but it could be all the coffee.

The sun has risen. More cars are populating the streets. Traffic will thicken soon, and what should be a thirty-minute drive will become an hour-long one. I'm eager to speak to Bill Kutcher and see what he remembers.

"You OK?" I ask.

"Let's get out of here," she says, lips shellacked white with tartar sauce residue. She pulls money from her pocket and lays a few bills on the table.

I slide out of the booth and follow her outside. We walk to the parking lot, where I've backed the Falcon into a corner spot near the diner's entrance.

"When we get to Kutcher's, just be cool," she says. "No mentioning his kids or anything off the cuff like that. I'm primary, and you're my shadow."

"Yeah," I say. "Got it."

"I'm serious, Finn. This interview is different. Guy used to be a cop. If he catches on, it's my ass."

"I said I got it, Munoz." She rolls her eyes like an ornery teenager. "You going to dial or what?"

Munoz works her thumbs on her phone's screen, then puts it to her ear. "May I speak to Bill Kutcher?" She drives her boot's heel into the concrete and straightens up. "Mr. Kutcher, this is Detective Sally Munoz, LAPD Robbery-Homicide Division. I'm hoping you can help me with an investigation. Do you have time to speak with me this morning?" A crabby voice blares on the other end. Kutcher's a loud-mouth, the way many older coppers are. It's been said that when a cop retires from the LAPD, their hearing is one of the first things to go. I used to see retirees, some no older than sixty, wearing hearing aids around the division, sorely out of place but still trying to command authority. They spoke decibels louder than necessary, telling war stories to officers with time to kill.

Munoz is doing more listening than talking. Then, as if seizing a break in a torrential downpour, she loudly interjects, "Copy, sir. Eight o'clock." She ends the call, puts the phone back into her pocket, and looks at me. "Let's get to it."

———

Monterey Hills is one of the few neighborhoods in Los Angeles that feels like it doesn't belong. There's a remoteness to it. As we drive up Via Marisol, the long ascending street feels like the path to Olympus, like we're on our way to break bread with the gods. Munoz makes a right turn onto Via Colina. The Crown Vic trudges up another hill. In the distance, I see townhomes and condos built on grassy peaks overlooking downtown LA. Munoz takes the street to the top, where it dead-ends at a brick wall.

"One way in, one way out," I say. "I'm guessing Kutcher's place is that one?" I point to the last townhouse in the row, closest to the wall. Munoz makes a three-point turn and parks across the street, facing downhill.

"I'm going to get you something." She gets out, opens the trunk, and takes something from inside. She tosses a navy windbreaker across her seat and into my lap. "You probably should wear that," she says. "And if you're carrying a piece, leave it in the glove box."

I turn the jacket over and see POLICE written in white block letters on the back. "You're not serious?"

"These old-timers are nostalgic," she says. "Don't say you're a cop and we're good to go."

"But it's implied. That's the same thing."

I have to keep reminding myself that Munoz has changed. It's one thing to omit that I'm not law enforcement to Cassandra. It's another for me to dress and front like I am to Kutcher, but if he gives us a lead to work, the payoff could outweigh the risk.

I put my revolver in the glove box, slip the jacket on, and get out of the car. Munoz leads us toward Kutcher's townhouse, an almond-colored trilevel with brown trim. The architecture is dated, circa the '70s, maybe earlier. The stucco and wooden slates on the roof could use updating, but the property's nowhere near as poorly maintained as Pop's condo building.

I follow Munoz to the top of the stairs, bracing my hip against the railing. I wait for her to ring the doorbell. It isn't a high-risk call. Kutcher isn't a suspect or a known criminal. He's most likely a pedantic man who I hope has a good memory, but training demands that every door knock be treated with care: wide stance, gun leg forward, standing clear of the threshold. Munoz looks over her shoulder to, I presume, note my position. She seems assured when she sees me covering her.

The door opens. A gray-haired white man stands dressed in a plaid button-down and brown pants. His shirt is tucked in, the arms starched and creased, and his loafers are caked with a white residue, as if he'd been polishing the old leather but couldn't buff it to a shine. He's dressed like he's headed to church or a town hall meeting, but I get the distinct feeling this is his everyday attire.

"Jesus, would you look at you two," he says, shrewdly noting Munoz's cast. "I sure hope you aren't LAPD's crème de la crème, or the department is worse off than I thought."

"Excuse me?" Munoz says. Maybe it's been some time since she's had to contend with a good old boy, but I'm schooled in all manner of asshole.

"You're the one who called?" he asks, inspecting Munoz from head to toe.

"I am," she says. "Are you Mr. Kutcher?"

"In the flesh."

"OK."

"Well, don't dawdle. Come in." He backs away from the door, allowing Munoz and me to enter. The entryway is marbled, a light stone with speckled veins that branch into unpredictable patterns. To the left of the entryway is the living room. If we were in the 1980s, it'd be considered tastefully decorated. The coffee table looks heavy, oak or mahogany, surrounded by a dark leather couch and two green accent chairs with curving backs. "Go ahead and take a seat," Kutcher says, walking into the living room. The walls have taken on a yellow hue, and the air has the ripe smell of old tobacco. Kutcher is a smoker, and if I were to remove the stodgy pictures of sailboats and lighthouses from the walls, I'm sure I'd find the original paint color shades lighter.

Munoz sits in one of the accent chairs, facing the door, and I sit in the other. Kutcher plops down on the couch. He opens a wooden box sitting on the coffee table next to prescription pill bottles. "So what can I help you with?" he asks, removing a cigar and cutter.

"I'm hoping you can tell me about Detective Martin Riley," Munoz says.

"Right, right." Kutcher chops the cigar's tip and puts it in his mouth, wrapping his lips around the brown paper. "Poor guy," he says. "That's what I was always afraid of. Staying on the job too long and then some shit stain punches my ticket."

"You think Riley stayed on too long?"

"It's Munoz, right?"

"Detective Munoz."

"Riley was a smart guy. He was decorated, well respected." He strikes a match and brings it to the cigar's end. "It's about going out on your own accord." He sucks until the cigar's cherry glows and thick white smoke seeps from the corners of his mouth. "He was too old to be working narcotics, anyway. Finding a cushy desk job until retirement would have been the move." He takes a steady drag from the cigar and puffs smoke in Munoz's direction. "I'll never understand why he stayed on . . ."

"Maybe he thought he could be useful," Munoz says, fanning the smoke with her palm. "Some officers learned a lot from him."

"It's an addiction," he says. "Running, gunning, and when you're gone, the city doesn't miss you. Not even for a second."

"We'd like to know if he worked any cases with Brixton Hill."

Kutcher rolls the smoke under his tongue. "Brick?"

"Who?"

"That's what we used to call him," he says. "Brixton 'Brick' Hill. I can't recall them working any cases together. It was a long time ago."

"What about Mateo Ruiz? Remember anything about him?"

"King T," he says, taking another puff of the cigar. "A real piece of work. What about him?"

"My understanding is Hill arrested Mateo for injuries he caused to Officer Jeremy Green?"

The smoke finds its way near Kutcher's eyes, and he squints until it blows clear. "Injuries?"

"Yes," Munoz says.

"He crushed Green's head on the curb." Kutcher stares into the cloud of smoke. "That's one I'll never forget. Green and his partner stopped Mateo for driving with a brake light out. Mateo took offense, got out of the car. There's an altercation, and Green ends up getting his head bashed in. Poor rookie died right there."

"He died at the scene?" she asks.

Kutcher nods. "Shitty way to go."

"Do you remember who Green's partner was?"

"Sorry," Kutcher says, his back arched. "As I said, this was a long time ago." He ashes the cigar into a porcelain tray shaped like a detective's badge. "I transferred out a few days after Green was killed. The whole department was beaten up about it. Still one of the saddest funerals I've ever been to. Felt bad for his wife and daughter. The girl had to be about four, sitting in front of that casket, crying her eyes out. That's hell on a kid . . ."

"What about Riley?" Munoz asks.

"Never got domesticated and was all the better for it. I always told him to travel solo. No wife. No kids. Makes you a better cop."

"Sounds like sage advice," she says.

I look to Munoz, unsure where her questions are headed.

Munoz leans forward, her left eyebrow cocked. "It's just that I didn't see you at Riley's service."

"Because I wasn't there," Kutcher says, looking at her the way chauvinistic men do when they think a woman is challenging them. "See, Munoz—"

"It's Detective," she says, almost ready to pounce.

"Riley knew how I felt about him. He was like a son to me."

Back off, Munoz. Our eyes meet, and as if she were a mind reader, she says, "You're right. Isn't my place."

"Might be time for your partner to switch to decaf." Kutcher winks at me. I'm quiet, per Munoz's gag order. "Your partner a mute or something?" he asks her with a half smile.

"He's under the weather. Doesn't want to spread what he's got."

"What's it, a tickle in your throat?" he asks. "Try a shot of bourbon. Clears it right up."

"I think I heard that somewhere," I say, realizing not talking is making things more awkward than they need to be.

"Nice to know you can speak." Kutcher laughs. Munoz mopes. "I was figuring that Munoz here wore the pants in the relationship."

"Excuse me," she says, getting up. "I think we're done here." I follow her lead, standing ready.

"Cool your heels a second," he says, the cigar's cherry dimming in the ashtray. "I want to show you something . . . a piece of LAPD history."

"We don't have time."

"It'll just take a minute." He stands and walks to the stairs leading to the upper level. "Trust me, you'll want to tell your whole division about it once you see it." He starts up the steps, leaving me and Munoz to look on.

"We really don't have the time!" Munoz shouts.

"That's the problem with you young coppers," Kutcher says, looking back. "You've got no regard for history. Quit your squawking and come get educated."

"After you," I say to Munoz, who begrudgingly follows Kutcher upstairs. I stay close behind, wondering if this visit can get any worse. When we reach the top floor, I count two bedrooms. One looks to be a den furnished with a television on a wicker stand in front of an orange sofa. Kutcher opens the double doors to the bedroom suite and walks in.

Munoz, who's sandwiched between Kutcher and me, turns and mouths the words, *"What the hell?"* I shrug, knowing this entire episode could have been avoided had Munoz kept to a solid line of questioning.

The bedroom is musty, seasoned with time. On cue, Munoz and I stop outside the doorway as Kutcher pulls back a dreary curtain, revealing a sliding glass door leading to a balcony. Sunlight illuminates white motes of dust hovering around us, begging to be breathed in. The stench of mold is outdone by only the filthiness. "I don't come in here much," Kutcher says, idling in the foulness like a surveyor touring a garbage heap. "I sleep in my den."

"No kidding," Munoz mumbles. "You want to tell us why we're in your bedroom?"

"Hold your horses." Kutcher moves a stained recliner away from a wall, revealing a small door. "She's a feisty one," he says to me, still on the quest for common ground. When I don't concur, he cuts his eyes in displeasure and turns back to Munoz. "I bet you're a wolf in the interrogation box."

"Let's just hurry things up." She's losing the little patience she had before coming into this man's room. I give Kutcher three minutes before Munoz curses him out and leaves. "What the hell are we supposed to be looking at?"

"It's a panic room," he says. "Put here by the man himself . . ."

"I don't follow."

"Me either," I add.

"The chief . . . *my* chief. Daryl Gates." Kutcher opens the small door to what resembles a cubby. "He built it: reinforced steel, shelves for rations, and enough firearms and ammo to start a revolution."

"This was Gates's place?" I ask.

"Bought it from him when he moved to Dana Point. Go ahead, look inside."

"I'm good," Munoz says.

"How about you, quiet man? Marvel at the ingenuity of the LAPD's finest police chief."

"I'll take your word for it."

"Oh, what the hell is wrong with you two?" he asks, gritting his teeth. "This is hallowed ground. Since when did the department start breeding codfish?"

"Codfish?" Munoz says.

"Don't go getting all sensitive," Kutcher says. "It's got nothing to do with you being a woman."

Though I'd like to think Munoz wouldn't clobber a retired officer, I don't want to test the waters. "All right," I say. "I'll look." I step closer to the hole in the wall, crouch down, and look inside. "Nothing but cobwebs."

"Use your flashlight," he orders.

Munoz pulls a small flashlight from a holster on her belt and hands it to me. I turn it on and point into the darkness. The space resembles a metal igloo, vaulted and large enough to fit Gates and maybe another person. An outlet and loose cables run across the grimy floor. There are two canteens, a book of matches, and metal drums, the type to hold ammunition. All the stuff is stacked against the walls covered in dust and cobwebs. I move to get up, and two large rodents cross the light beam and dart in the shadows. I quickly recoil onto my haunches, stand, and back away from the hovel.

"You've got movement in there," I say. "Mice, maybe?"

"Know what he lined it with?" Kutcher asks, his blue eyes wild with zeal. "Lead!" he exclaims, skirting my comment about the rodents. "After those vermin burned and looted in the name of ole Rodney King, he never took any chances."

"Thanks for the history lesson," Munoz says. "We're leaving."

"Yeah, yeah," Kutcher snaps. "The city doesn't pay you to shoot the shit all day. Given the homicide rate, it makes me wonder if you're working at all." His tone measures between sarcastic and obnoxious. Munoz wastes no time leaving the room. I can hear her stomp down the stairs before I'm able to get free of Kutcher, who's blathering about how tough policing was in the '80s and '90s compared to now.

I catch up to her downstairs. "Let's go," she says, keys in hand.

"I'll get the door," Kutcher says, working his way down the last few steps.

"Don't worry about it." Munoz opens the door and storms out. I manage to shut it behind me. We clear the stairs and walk back across the street to the Crown Vic. Before getting in, Munoz looks toward Kutcher's townhouse. He stands at his front door, watching. "El cabrón," she says.

I get in the car and check my phone. Two missed calls from a number I don't recognize. No voice mail. There's no text from Sarada, but there's one from Tori with happy-face emojis and a photo of Simone eating something green and pureed. I take off the police jacket and throw it in the back seat. "What the hell was that back there?"

"Gates's fanboy . . . some lonely nut," she says. "A waste of time."

"That's what you saw?"

"My vision's twenty-twenty, last I checked," she says, putting the key into the ignition. "He's probably been waiting years to show someone that rat's den."

"You're off your game."

"Say what?"

"Riley's memorial? What does it matter if the guy went or not?"

"It matters," she says. "What type of person doesn't pay respect to a friend?"

"Does it look like Kutcher gets out much? There could be a bunch of reasons he didn't show."

"Well, I think he's lying." Munoz turns the ignition with force, and the car starts. She reaches down into the catchall tray, grabs chopsticks in a paper sleeve, slips them out, and snaps the wooden sticks in two. She works a stick down into the crease of her cast, where the skin must be damp and itchy. I should tell her the cast has taken on an odor, but she may take offense, and I don't want to add to the animosity, since we're stuck together for the time being.

"You're right," I say. "But he isn't lying about being Riley's friend. He knows why that report was redacted."

"How'd you figure that?"

"That's why he sent us on that excursion to Gates's panic room. He didn't want to answer for it."

"So what do you want to do?" she asks. "Knock on his door again? Listen to his bullshit stories of when the good old boys ran things?"

"I've got another idea," I say. "We better eat and gas up. It's a long drive."

CHAPTER TEN

The California Men's Colony sounds upper crust, like an all-boys club for the coastal elites, not the state penitentiary in San Luis Obispo. It took Munoz nearly an hour to locate Mateo in the Department of Corrections and Rehabilitations database. She had to search by name, and there were about fifty Mateo Ruizes. Still, there was only one with the alias King T. The drive to the facility was three hours of coastline, two-lane highways, and Munoz humming along to an adult contemporary radio station. I should have slept or at least rested my eyes, but I couldn't stop thinking about the fight with Sarada and wondering if we'll mend what's broken.

Security protocols for entering any state prison are standardized. A correctional officer with facial hair beyond stubble but not quite a beard tells Munoz to go into a room and place her firearm in a locker. When she returns, we're instructed to empty our pockets, put our belongings in a plastic bowl, and pass through a metal detector. Next, we sign a log, providing our names, arrival time, and purpose for visiting.

"I was told we could speak with the warden regarding an inmate, Mateo Ruiz," Munoz says to a broad-shouldered correctional officer sitting behind a glass partition.

He nods approvingly, then picks up the phone and dials. "Yes, sir," he says blankly into the receiver before hanging up. "Warden St. James will be down. You can have a seat." He points toward several blue chairs bolted to the floor and lined against the wall.

Munoz declines to sit, opting to pace the lobby. I stand as well. This isn't the type of place a person wants to get comfortable. The lieutenant governor once said, "Prison is the most humane solution for the state's worst offenders." He was caught on a hot mic offhandedly adding, "A firing squad is what we need." The backlash was severe, but I know he only expressed what many in the criminal justice system believe: some are beyond redemption.

Warden St. James enters from a heavy door that looks like it requires substantial effort to open. He's a small man, a few meals short of feeble, and wears a drab gray suit, a white-collared shirt, and a striped red tie. "Detective Munoz?" he asks.

"Yes," Munoz says. "This is my associate, Mr. Finnegan."

The warden reminds me of my grade-school principal, Mr. Teague, a mild-mannered man who dressed and carried himself more like a Mormon than a hard-assed disciplinarian, complete with a warm smile and pleasant eyes and a penchant for telling troubled kids they'd be behind bars or dead by eighteen if they didn't wise up.

"Nice to meet you both," he says, extending his hand for us to shake. Munoz hastily obliges, rushing through the pleasantries. "On the phone, you said this visit was urgent?"

"We'd like to speak to Mateo Ruiz regarding an investigation," she says.

"I see." The warden looks to the correctional officer behind the glass and motions for him to open the door. "About inmate Ruiz, there's been a development. Let's take a walk?"

"All right," Munoz says, trailing the warden through the door by which he came. The waxed linoleum squeaks and glistens under the hot fluorescent lights as we walk down a long, narrow corridor. Prisons are labyrinths designed for sections to be cordoned off in the event of escape or uprising. The tight corridors accommodate only a few individuals at a time, and most would need to be walking single file. During a prison break, inmates competing to get out in a mass exodus would find themselves hopelessly pinned, like insects in a tube.

"Two weeks ago, Mr. Ruiz suffered a stroke and fell into a coma," the warden says. "He passed away days ago."

"Why wasn't that noted in the database?" Munoz asks. "Better yet, why didn't you tell me that on the phone?"

"Inmate records aren't updated as efficiently as we'd like," he says with the perfunctory concern I'd expect from a bureaucrat. "I thought speaking in person would be best . . . Perhaps I could provide you with some information?"

"You said Ruiz was in a coma for two weeks?" I ask.

"Yes," he says. "Since our facility couldn't provide long-term support for his condition, we advised his family that he'd need to be transferred to a secured health-care facility in Stockton that was better equipped."

"The Graveyard," I say, repeating the moniker most associated with the Stockton facility. "I thought that place was going to be shut down?"

"I assure you, it's a fine facility. Mr. Ruiz could have gotten help there."

"So why wasn't he transferred?"

"His attorney declined and instructed us to remove him from life support."

"Did his attorney give a reason?"

"No," he says. "And we don't make a habit of questioning the family's wishes. If the proper documentation is provided, we honor any decision."

"Have you cleaned out his cell yet?" I ask.

"Yes," he says. "I have his belongings in my office. I was waiting for word from his attorney on where to ship them."

"Maybe his family would like his things sent to them?"

"Well, Mr. Finnegan, in this situation, his family and legal representation are the same."

Munoz looks puzzled, an expression that I'm certain reflects my own. "Care to elaborate?" she asks.

"We should take this conversation to my office." He turns a corner. We're a few paces behind as he approaches a door with a brass plaque that reads DONALD ST. JAMES, WARDEN. He unlocks the door with a key tethered to his belt. The key draws back to his waist, retracted by the spooling string, and he welcomes us in. "Have a seat," he says, taking his position behind a long wooden desk. Munoz and I sit in two chairs facing the warden.

I look around the room. Framed degrees on the walls: MA in media studies from USC, a juris doctorate from Stanford, an MA in theology from Fuller Seminary. Two bookcases are packed with legal encyclopedias. There's also a collage of photos of Warden St. James standing with inmates in the mess hall, in the yard, and out in front of the prison, celebrating their release with loved ones. "How long have you been a warden?" I ask.

"Twelve years," he says. "Ten here at CMC and two at a prison in Arizona."

"Your taking photos with inmates seems a bit out of the norm. People don't raise issues with it?"

"What people might that be, Mr. Finnegan?"

"Victims and their families."

"My job is rehabilitation, not punishment. The inmates you see on the wall are success stories. Many of them served their time, paid their debt to society."

"Success stories?" Munoz balks. "You have a lot of faith in these men, given your recidivism rate."

"Sometimes faith is all these men require."

"What about Mateo Ruiz?" I ask. "Did you have faith in him?"

The warden opens his desk drawer and pulls out an eight-by-ten photo of him standing with Mateo, a young man in a military uniform with a prickly expression, and an olive-skinned woman, her shiny jet-black curls below her shoulders. "I rarely speak about my relationships with inmates, but you should know that my faith in Mateo never wavered. Many of the men who come to this facility—I can see who they are, what they've done, and the things they've been through right off the bat, and I can see the path that led them to commit crimes. These men are often victims long before becoming offenders."

"You saw Mateo as a victim?" Munoz asks.

"Perhaps not in the beginning, but I soon learned he was different. He had a gentleness that was at odds with who they said he was. I never once saw or heard of him exhibiting violence on any scale. In fact, he's the reason we have the community garden." The warden gets up, walks over to a banker's box labeled M. Ruiz, and removes a stack of photos. "See, Mateo was in the business of growing things, not destroying them." He spreads the photos on the desk for Munoz and me to see: tulips, daisies, carrots, cabbages, greens, and violets are displayed along with a smiling Mateo. "He made people's lives better and into something bearable, which is no easy feat in this place."

Munoz looks and then quickly dismisses the images of the garden, as if acknowledging Mateo's gardening constitutes a sin. "If you're so proud of him, why isn't Mateo's photo hanging with the others?" she asks.

"I took it down," he says solemnly. "Couldn't bear to look at it."

Munoz snatches a pencil from a cup on the warden's desk and begins digging into the space between her cast and skin. "It's great you're chummy with the inmates, but they don't come here because they're winning model-citizen awards," she says. "Mateo Ruiz murdered a cop."

"Yes," he says. "I'm aware of that."

"Yet here you are suggesting that because he liked watering daisies, he was a changed man?"

"I'm not suggesting that at all," he says. "I'm telling you that Mateo never changed. After being transferred from San Quentin, he came to us. Most men arrive broken or revert to their most debased natures, but not Mateo."

"Let me guess—he found religion?" Munoz asks.

"I suspect he had faith . . ."

"Faith," she repeats with a taunting grin. "Faith in what exactly?"

"I recognize that some may not understand this, but perhaps Mateo was put in this prison to do good."

"By something divine?" I ask.

"If you believe in that sort of thing, yes."

"Sure, he was a saint," Munoz says mockingly. He might as well have told her Mateo rode a unicorn to Jupiter. "You might have a whole prison full of saints here."

"Warden, I don't doubt you believe that," I say. "But it's hard to think Mateo came out of San Quentin unscathed."

"He was the strongest person I've known." He stares at Munoz, his eyes growing militant. Maybe he's awaiting another snide remark or rebuttal or hoping for an apology. Or maybe he just wants some respect for his dead friend. "Mateo passed his strength on to his children," he says. "They never stopped fighting to get him home."

"Are these his children here?" I ask, pointing to the soldier and woman in the photo.

"His daughter, Yolanda, and his son, Hector."

"Yolanda's his attorney?"

"That's right."

"Last name?"

"Yolanda Chavez."

"And his son?" Munoz asks. "What's his story?"

"Don't know. It was the first and only time I met Hector." Warden St. James stares at the picture fondly. He pinches the sides of the photograph as if a great wind threatens to blow it from his grasp. "I believe it was Father's Day. Might have been two years ago, maybe three."

Munoz gives a satisfied grunt, like she's just finished a scrumptious meal, and rises from her chair. She drops the pencil she used to dig into her cast back into the cup. "Thanks for your time, Warden," she says. "Might want to get that database updated . . . save people the trouble."

"One more thing," I say when Munoz is nearly out the door.

"Yes, Mr. Finnegan?"

"Do you think Mateo was guilty?"

The warden gives a hard sigh, as if it's a question he's grappled with often. "Most claim their innocence. Mateo never did. He didn't have to," he says. "In my heart, I know he didn't kill that police officer, not intentionally, anyway." He stands and runs his hands down the lapels of his suit, a delicate act of composure. "Mateo was a victim of the three-strikes law, as were many. But the suggestion he's a *cop killer* . . . I only ask, what man commits that kind of crime with his children watching from the back seat of his car?"

"We'll see ourselves out," Munoz says abruptly, prompting me to vacate the room.

———

Outside the warden's office, Munoz fumbles with her cell phone. "The reception is shit in this place," she says, swaying the phone high above her head, trying to find a signal. "Must be a dead zone."

"His kids were in the car, Munoz."

"So?" she says, glaring at her phone.

"Midday. Kids in the car. The guy attacks a police officer over a brake light?"

"Three strikes, remember? Maybe he had dope in the car or a gun. You know how it is—just the thought of life back inside, and these guys flip. Of course, we'd know if it weren't for the blackout job on the report." Munoz holds her phone slightly skewed. "Two bars . . . what do you have?"

I check my phone as well. More missed calls from numbers I don't recognize and a text message from Bergman that reads:

FBI's here.

Said they tried to call you, but you aren't answering.

What's going on?

The feds were quicker than I expected, sniffing around the law firm, hungry for a statement about Hill's death, no doubt. Even if I did know what truly happened to Hill, I wouldn't tell them. It's the type of theory that sounds far-fetched and sure to put suspicion on me.

Hill was hanged by a man in black who rides a motorcycle like a hellion.

I don't text Bergman back. The feds could be hovering over his shoulder, watching for my response.

"Finn, you got anything?"

"What?"

"A signal . . . bars?"

"Oh," I say. "Down to one."

Munoz puts her phone back in her pocket. "Let's get out of here. This place is depressing."

My mind drifts to the warden's sentiment: *Someone has to have faith in these men.* He may be more idealistic than I ever was, even as a rookie, but I share his belief in faith. Sometimes it's the only thing we have to hold on to.

———

The brakes grind hard, as if they're bound to lock. I open my eyes just as the Crown Vic screeches along the curb and stops, sending Munoz's jumbo-size cup of coffee splashing onto the console. "What happened?" I yank the seat's lever, bringing it out of recline. I glance out the window. It looks like we're back in LA. How long have I been asleep? "Why are we stopping?"

"I'll handle it." Munoz is focused on the red-and-blue lights in the rearview. A black-and-white is behind us—LAPD.

"Were you speeding or something?" I look at the clock on the dash. "You got us back here in two hours?"

"I had the lights going," she says.

"We're not going to a call, Munoz . . ."

She turns off the engine and rolls down her window. The dark halos around her eyes have grown prominent, and her skin has lost its warmth. She looks dehydrated, exhausted.

"Where are we?" I ask, looking out the window at an empty street. Kids stand in an overgrown lot turned soccer field, observing the traffic stop. Walls and fences are graffitied. It looks like we're stopped on a service road that runs along the 110.

"We're near Dodger Stadium," she says moments before an officer approaches her window. The other officer remains at the Crown Vic's rear. "Stay quiet, Finn." Munoz's nervousness seems out of place, since detectives habitually receive passes for speeding and other traffic violations while on duty. Then again, I'm in the car. PI credentials and being recognized might lead to an unpleasant exchange.

"Good afternoon," the officer says as Munoz hands over her police ID. The officer is a black man with a mustache that looks like a caterpillar perched on his upper lip and died. He holds the ID below his chin. "Detective Munoz?"

"Officer"—Munoz strains to see his name tag—"Milton."

"You working?" The ID is between Milton's dark-brown fingers like a playing card.

"Always."

"Let me rephrase," he says, unamused by Munoz's attempt to be witty. "Are you on a shift?"

"Yes."

Milton's partner, a younger redheaded man, approaches my door.

"Who's your passenger?" Milton asks.

"My CI." Munoz holds her hand out, expecting the return of her ID.

"You usually let informants ride in the front seat like that?"

"Sometimes," she says. "Is there a reason you stopped us, Officer? It's just that we've got a meeting."

Milton's partner leans down, looking at me through the glass like a child fascinated by sea life in an aquarium. He motions for me to lower my window. I do, slowly. "My partner will keep you company," Milton says. "Sit tight." He heads back to the black-and-white.

The redheaded officer stays low to the cabin and lays his arm on top of the car's hood. "So, you're a narc?" he asks, his attention on Munoz, speaking as if I don't exist. Dried jelly, or what could be ketchup, is smirched on his bottom lip, and he smells of chicken grease. "You like it?"

"Most days."

"Is this one of 'em?"

"That remains to be seen," she says. "I think you got something . . ." Munoz rubs her thumb against her mouth, drawing attention to the residue from the officer's meal. He whips his tongue across his lower lip.

"I get it?" he asks.

Munoz sneers at his freckled face. "Sure," she says nonchalantly. "I didn't catch your name."

"Oh, it's Connors," he says, perking up.

"Can you see what the holdup is, Connors? We got places to be."

"Officer Milton is just thorough, Detective. It shouldn't be much longer."

Something's off. Encounters like this don't typically last more than a few minutes.

"How long have you been on, Connors?" Munoz shifts in her seat. Her legs and back might be troubling her. She's driven all day.

"Two years," he says with the pride of an officer who's made it through the probationary period and still loves the job.

"You any good?"

Connors straightens up, tucks his thumbs into his Sam Browne. "Sure . . . I think so." He pauses. "I mean, yes, Detective. I'm squared away."

"Funny," Munoz says snidely. "You haven't once checked your surroundings since we've been talking." Connors's pridefulness burns away like mist at first light. The truth suddenly burdens his face: an officer should keep their head on a swivel—always. "Ambushes are the most common way patrol officers die out here. Your partner could be back there with a hole in his head, and you're over here in our shit. It only takes a second." She snaps her fingers. "And everything can change. Do you know that?"

"I do," he says, hanging his head sheepishly.

"What?" I'm certain Munoz heard him. "Speak up!"

"Yes. I know that, Detective."

"Good for you. Now back away from my fucking car." Connors slowly steps back, holding his position a couple of feet from my door. Munoz notes my disquieted disposition. "What? The kid needed to hear it . . ."

Moving beyond Connors's hazing and glaring lack of situational awareness, I ask, "What do you think Milton's doing? Feels weird, him back there. Doesn't it?"

Munoz looks in the rearview again, watching closely, appearing to clock Milton's movements. "He's coming back," she says.

"About time."

Milton returns to Munoz's window. "Detective," he says, "I have orders to escort you to headquarters."

"Excuse me?" she asks in a pitchy voice. "What orders?"

"I'll need you to follow my unit."

"I don't get to know why?"

"Do you understand the order I've given you?" Munoz's thumb beats the steering wheel. "Did you hear me, Detective?"

I watch her closely, her gaze no longer on Milton. She's focused on the road ahead. "What the hell, Munoz?" I say softly. "Answer him."

"Detective Munoz, I need an acknowledgment," Milton says.

She remains silent and keeps thumbing the wheel.

"I need to know you comply," Milton says, harsher, with more bass in his voice. He reminds me of my drill instructor in the academy before we'd be disciplined with twenty push-ups, sit-ups, and jumping jacks. "Detective, answer me!" Milton squirms, his hand on the car door, looking ready to snatch Munoz out of the driver's seat.

"Copy, sir," Munoz says, coming out of her reverie. "I'll be right behind you."

"All right, then." Milton nods to Connors, and together they return to their shop. Strangely, I don't feel relieved. I know Munoz. I know she's on the precipice of idiocy.

I lean in close. "You're going to follow them, right?" Munoz turns the key in the ignition. Some people become dumb animals in moments like this, giving in to their first thoughts, never wading through the possible consequences.

Milton pulls from behind us. Driving past, Connors flips Munoz the bird. The unit positions itself in front of the Crown Vic. I ask again, speaking more slowly, emphasizing each word. "Munoz . . . you're going to follow them, right?"

"Put your seat belt on," she says, her voice flat. I hadn't realized it was unbuckled. "Hold on." Munoz shifts into reverse, stabs the gas pedal, and sends the car shooting backward.

I'm glued to the seat. "Do you know what you're doing?" I struggle to buckle the seat belt. Munoz brakes hard, sending me forward. I brace myself, pressing against the dash. The smell of burned oil and brake dust seeps into the cabin. Tires squeal. The car stops at an empty intersection. She shifts into drive and jerks the wheel left, then we speed down a narrow street headed away from Dodger Stadium. Munoz doesn't slow down until we're blocks from where we left Milton and Connors.

After a series of dizzying turns, I ascertain we're traveling to a specific destination. I listen for sirens, the indication of pursuit, but hear nothing. The radio crackles—I didn't realize Munoz turned on the rover. It's dispatch.

Detective Munoz, you are instructed to return—

Munoz switches off the line.

Who is this woman? She isn't *my* Munoz. I explore the possibilities: a brain tumor, a chemical imbalance, an evil twin.

"Let me out," I say.

"I can't do that."

"Dammit, Munoz. Pull the car over!"

"You don't understand, Finn . . . They suspended me."

"What?"

"This morning."

"So you run during a traffic stop? What the hell are you thinking?"

"It doesn't matter," she says. "They're going to learn the truth . . ."

"What are you talking about?"

"Riley and I, we did things . . . things I'm not proud of." She turns right and down a street, passing an older woman peddling elote from a pushcart. Cars, some with racing stripes and spoilers, others lowered an inch to the ground, have back windows turned to tombstones. White lettering has been placed on the tinted glass along with illustrated faces, soaring doves, and long-stemmed roses painted with the simplicity of clip art. I see birth and death dates and messages like "Gone Too Soon" and "Our Sweet Angel."

As we continue down the block, the markings become more familiar. A bleached-brick eatery boasting a six-dollar machaca burrito lunch special with chips and Coke is defaced with placas: graffitied warnings to rival gangs.

A grassy median separates flowing traffic and serves as a greenway. A man sits on a plastic crate under a large green sign that reads HISTORIC HIGHLAND PARK. He's blending and serving frutas frescas to children.

Munoz knows these streets.

The Crown Vic moves at a moderate speed. She's no longer in a rush, acting as if she didn't ignore an officer's commands minutes ago. Munoz may outrank Milton, but the conducting officer holds perpetual authority at a traffic stop.

We enter through an open gate and drive down a gravel road belonging to what looks to be an abandoned autobody shop. Munoz parks outside a garage adjacent to a small building. Broken cars maligned by age and consumed by rust sit tarnished along a barbwire fence. Judging by their condition, they haven't been moved in years.

"What is this place?" I ask, noticing weeds sprouting like husks from the hood of a Lincoln Continental where an engine once was.

"What's it look like?" Munoz turns the key. The engine sputters, then quits.

"I want a straight answer." I grip Munoz's arm above the elbow. "What are we doing here?" Impulse is taking over. I shouldn't have touched her, but I can't let her get out of this car without telling me what's going on.

"Let go of my arm," she says, pulling away. There's danger in her eyes, and I'm suddenly reminded of her fight in the Swashbuckler and how she sent the fat man to the floor.

"OK," I say. "I'm sorry."

"Don't ever touch me like that again." She unfastens her seat belt and inches away from me, moving closer to the door.

"I'm only trying to make sense of things. All this because you were suspended?"

"No, Finn."

"Then what?"

"I took the money," she says. "Riley and I had been investigating Cassandra Boyle's operation for months. The way cash was flowing through those dispensaries . . ."

She had told me their investigation was fresh, only three weeks old. I already know what comes next, but I'm still not prepared to hear it.

"It was Riley's idea," she continues. "Cassandra already had him in her pocket. She gave us a cut to look the other way when she started pushing pills and heroin through the dispensaries."

"That night in Venice, you were collecting?"

"We had agreed on 15 percent, then Riley started taking a little more. He took 30 that night and knocked out two dispensary staff when they tried to stop him."

"But why take money in the first place? Gambling? Debts? What did you get involved in?"

Munoz looks out the window at the rows of vehicles, a cemetery of steel and glass. "It's easy to sit there," she says, "judging me."

"I'm not."

"You are, Trevor, I know you," she says. "I know how you think. And right now, you think whoever sent you to Venice that night to surveil me and Riley was right."

"Munoz . . ."

"There's no point in lying anymore. I know what you do. I've always known." She tearfully takes my hand. "I'm not angry," she says. "I guess it was only a matter of time before I'd end up on your list, but I'm not like the others. You have to know that."

"Tell me what happened, Munoz."

"Attorney's fees, court dates, supervised visits . . . two hundred dollars to file this appeal, another three hundred for that," she says, exasperated, hands open, palms in front of her. "I only wanted to be with my children. It's not fair. I've been a good mother, sacrificed so much only to end up here. It was supposed to be enough money to hire a better attorney, someone who could fight for me."

"How much did you take, Munoz?"

She tugs at her shirt, brings it to her face, and wipes her tears. "Thousands," she says, her shirt bearing wet stains like inkblots. "Enough to pay off my shitty attorney and hire an entire team to defend me."

"C'mon, Munoz," I say, rubbing my temples. "Get dispatch on the radio."

"What? You want to give up?"

"This isn't going to end the way you think it is."

"You're wrong, Finn. I can fix this." She snatches the key from the ignition. "I'll show you." She opens her door and steps onto the gravel. I get out, wondering if Munoz has truly lost her mind or if this is just a temporary break from reality. "It's an old safe house. The department decommissioned it eight years ago. No one knew about it, except for Riley."

I had heard rumors that safe houses still existed. Many were slated to be demolished like LAPD's old headquarters, Parker Center. But some buildings were spared due to budget cuts and shifting priorities. Money once earmarked for their sunsetting was then allocated to other initiatives. People soon forgot about the random structures around the city that were once used to house witnesses and facilitate sting operations.

A sign on the door reads Lo sentimos, estamos cerrados. Munoz removes a brass padlock and chain from the door's handle and unlocks the dead bolt. "I'll need to get some tools," she says. We enter the building, which confirms what I expected. The dilapidated exterior is a clever ruse. There's a surveillance bay with multiple monitors from when functioning cameras helped secure the perimeter. A long table, TV, sink, and small fridge make the space habitable, along with an array of chairs and cabinets. Munoz walks over to a metal storage tower purchased from a hardware or garden supply store. She opens it, digs around, and produces pliers and a screwdriver. "What are you going to do with those?" I ask.

"LAPD installed new transponders. An upgrade over the older ones—less temperamental with a greater range."

"Sally, you can't . . ." I say.

"I have to," she says. "Otherwise, they'll find us again."

"How deep are you trying to dig this hole? Take a minute and think this through." Munoz heads outside. I follow her, trying to find the right words that'll make her abandon her course of action. "This is only going to make things worse. Can't you see that?"

"I don't expect you to understand," she says. "If I was the one with my brains splattered on the boardwalk, I know Riley would do anything to make sure whoever did it got what was coming to them."

"This isn't about revenge," I say. "Hill wouldn't have wanted that."

"Never stopped you before."

I'm regretting the late nights spent in bars drunk, spilling truths to Munoz that I should have kept to myself.

Munoz opens the trunk and reaches in with the screwdriver. "The housing can be a bitch to remove," she says, working behind the taillight. "But once it's off, disconnecting the transponder's a cinch." She struggles to unscrew the housing with her left hand. "Got it," she says, holding the metal covering. She pulls the pliers from her back pocket, reaches into the trunk, and with a few snips brings out the transponder—a small black device with a bud antenna and red LED.

"What are you going to do with it?" I ask.

She carries the transponder inside. I follow behind her like a pitiful mutt and watch her take a hammer to the device, splitting it open. She brushes pieces of the transponder into a bucket.

"You're out of control—"

"If you don't have the heart for it anymore, then fine," she says. "All I ask is one last thing . . . We interview Yolanda together."

"What?"

"This is our only chance," she says. "I know it. Yolanda could be the key to knowing who killed Riley."

"And what if she isn't? Only another dead end?"

"If it's a bust, it's a bust," she says. "But you'll take point, control the interview. I'll follow your lead. This could be our shot, Finn. The break we've been waiting for." Munoz grips the edge of the table and leans in. "What if Riley and Hill were the beginning? More cops might be targeted, and we need to warn them."

"The FBI is looking into Hill's death, which means they're looking into me. I don't know how long I can keep them at bay, especially with you fleeing traffic stops."

"If we do this," she says, "if we solve this thing, the feds and LAPD will have to make concessions. Extenuating circumstances, right?"

"Not quite," I say. "You took the money beforehand."

"I was undercover, remember? It was all part of getting Cassandra."

"But you didn't get Cassandra," I say. I'm reminded of Boston, how easy it was for her to rationalize killing Brandon Soledad and Ruben Montgomery. "Even if we find out who murdered Riley and Hill, you'll still have to answer for what you did with the money."

"Look, Finn, I just need to know if you're with me."

Munoz is crooked. I can't save her. She's going to burn her world to a cinder. I should walk away, but I can't—not yet. What if she's right and Yolanda can lead us to Hill's killer before more cops die? That's all that matters now. I find who hanged Hill, turn the culprit over to the authorities, and my uncle gets the justice he deserves. Munoz can sort her own shit out.

"I'll squeeze Yolanda," I say. "If nothing worthwhile comes out, I'm done."

"Fine," she says. "Clean break."

"What makes you so sure Yolanda will meet with us today, anyway?"

"I called her while you were knocked out in the Vic," she says, leaving me to wonder what else she managed to do while I was sleeping on the job. When we worked together, I always drove, rarely felt tired. But this arrangement, sitting in the passenger seat staring at vehicles' back ends, put me out like a light. "Yolanda sounded relieved, almost like she was expecting my call."

"Where's the meeting?"

"Five miles from here." Munoz begins texting on a phone I don't recognize. It's small and flips open, outdated by ten years. She notices me looking. "Gas station burner, came with a shitty cup of mild roast."

"What happened to your department line?"

"It's somewhere on the 101," she says, awaiting Yolanda's reply. The phone chimes. "Yolanda's good to meet now."

"You tossed the LAPD's phone?"

"Nothing I can do about it now," she says. "Want a beer or something?" Munoz walks to the fridge and opens it, revealing random condiments along with half a loaf of bread and a shelf stocked with beer.

"No, I don't want a beer, Sally," I say. "I want you to start acting like a cop."

"That's funny coming from you," she says, removing a longneck. Munoz struggles to twist off the cap, resorting to using her teeth, and drinks the beer fast. When the bottle is empty, she chucks it into the garbage. "Burn all the cops you want, but you can't buy your soul back, Finnegan."

Munoz marches out of the building. What if I've made a pact with someone more dangerous than the killer we're chasing? Munoz is a train off the tracks with a fire raging in the cabin, barreling toward a cliff, and she's anchored me to the engine.

"Finn!" she yells, already at the driver's side of the car. "Let's move!"

"Yeah . . . coming," I say, already doubting my resolve.

———

"Look at it," Yolanda says. There's a gaping hole in her business's storefront window patched with plastic sheeting and electrical tape. "Second time this month." She's shorter than I expected. I mistakenly judged her height from the warden's photo, or she was wearing heels that day. "I called you all weeks ago. You've got a real problem with customer service down there." Both Munoz and I have heard the phrase before, usually during community-relations training: *Members of the public should be treated as customers, with patience and empathy.* "The officer who answered my report was rude," Yolanda adds. "Do you know what he said to me?" She doesn't miss a beat. "Get security cameras." Her eyes bulge in an exaggerated way. "We're a nonprofit, for goodness' sake. We work on donations."

"Any idea who's behind the vandalism?" I ask.

"Your guess is as good as mine," she says. "But the last time it happened, *Go Home BAD Hombres* was spray-painted on the side of the building. I guess I should be relieved this time it was just a rock?"

I can tell the wording on the glass once read Yolanda's Immigration Services before the rock removed most of the letters in *Services*. The building was already unsightly, the color of pumpkin, an eyesore that can be seen blocks away. But with Yolanda standing in front of it, it's growing on me. Her black turtleneck sweater and flowing skirt with a brown, red, and yellow print complement the orange exterior. "I'm sorry about your window," I say. "Bars could help deter this kind of thing."

"Bars? My family's been in this neighborhood for over thirty years." Her declaration carries both pride and pain. "This building was one of the first shoe stores for miles. It's never had bars, a gate, or a fence. Nothing. People respect what we do. We're a service to the community." Munoz moves closer to Yolanda, an understanding in her eyes that I've seen before. It's the way my mother used to look at me. Well acquainted with my heartache, powerless to fix it. "They have no right doing this," Yolanda says, staring into the window's crater.

"Do you think we can talk inside?" I ask.

"Don't you want to take pictures of the damage?"

"We're not here about the window, ma'am," Munoz says. "It concerns your father, Mateo Ruiz."

"My father?"

"Yes," I say.

"He's dead," she says coolly. "What's there to talk about?"

"You were his attorney, correct?"

"Not by choice," she says, attention still on the broken window. "I practice immigration law, not criminal. But no one we could afford wanted to represent my father."

"I understand that you were a passenger in the car on the day your father was arrested?"

"I saw the whole thing," she says. "My brother, too. But doesn't LAPD know all this? You're the ones who arrested and charged him."

"There've been some new developments."

"Now that he's dead?" She's curt, with reason to be. Police often have a knack for showing up decades after some botched investigation, looking to make things right. "Don't tell me that now you think he's innocent?"

"It really is best that we speak inside," I say.

Yolanda reluctantly leads us through the building's doors. The bones are still a shoe store, maybe some mom-and-pop shop that couldn't survive the big-box chains. There's a checkout counter repurposed as a workspace, and from the looks of it, the building had closed-circuit cameras near the doors. There could be more, and if the wiring is good, Yolanda could install cameras with motion sensors at entry points, maybe outside, too. Floor lamps are scattered, erected wherever there's an outlet. Gray-walled cubicles that offer little privacy are padded with turquoise foam, likely to dampen sound, and are packed with card tables and metal folding chairs. I'd expect to see these furnishings in thrift stores or in church basements, not in a law office.

Anything that looks valuable—lockable file cabinets, desktop computers, bulky printers, a fax machine—is chained and anchored to the floor, the only measure of security I see. "We can talk in here," Yolanda says. She opens the door to a cramped, cream-painted room lit by incandescent tubes affixed to the ceiling. "Not much space . . . used to be a storage closet." Dignity chases away a look of embarrassment that briefly washes over her face. "But it's what we've got, and we make it work."

There's barely enough space for the three of us to stand comfortably. A young girl wearing a blue-and-white dress, something akin to a school uniform, sits at a foldable table, shading a man's face with colored pencils. It's more of a caricature than a lifelike rendering, but I recognize Mateo: the curvature of his cheekbones, the thicket of eyebrows, the overstated eyes, and the black, oval-shaped pupils.

"Maria," Yolanda says. The girl looks up, her drawing nearing completion. "Meja, can you go color out front so Mama can talk in private?"

Munoz walks over to Maria and bends down so that she's at eye level. "What are you drawing?" she asks, with a degree of tenderness I've never seen her show until today.

"It's a get-well card for my abuelo." There's a precociousness to how the girl speaks, an alarming worry in her words. I've heard this strain in grown folks, those ravaged by stress and suffering. "Mama says he's sick."

"I'm sorry to hear that," Munoz says. Maria gets up, tucks her coloring pad under her right arm. She places three pencils—brown, yellow, black, all dull and splintered—into a clear plastic pencil box containing other colors.

"It's all right," Maria says. "He's strong—he'll be OK." A ghostly gale moves through the room, bending the hairs along my arm. "Bye." The girl smiles, taking small, plodding steps toward the door. Her departure seems to affect the room's aura, turning it soupy and cadaverous.

Once she's disappeared into the hallway, Yolanda closes the door gently. "I haven't told her that he's dead," she says. "Haven't found the right time."

"There's never a right time," I say.

"She doesn't know why he was in prison. Only that the LAPD put him there and we've been trying to get him out." Yolanda tightly grabs the bend of her arm and rocks nervously. "She loves him because she's never had him. Maybe I filled her head with too much hope . . . telling her he'd be free one day?"

"Children are resilient," Munoz says.

"Survivors," Yolanda adds. Her words pierce like a blade's tip. "I remember everything about that day and the days that came after. The years, too. The empty chair at the dinner table. Missed holidays and birthdays . . . my quinceañera. But I feel worse for Maria. She never really got to know him."

"Can you walk us through that day?" I ask.

Yolanda shudders. Just thinking about her father's arrest seems to upset her, even years later. "LAPD pulled us over. They said it was the taillight. My father complied; he kept both hands on the wheel while they ran his plates. Green returned to the car, yanked the door open, and pulled my father out. Threw him over the hood. My brother and

I didn't know what was going on. We started screaming, begging them to stop."

"Them?" I ask.

"Green had a partner," she says.

"Tell me about the partner: Man or woman?" I glance at Munoz, writing in her field notebook. "What was his partner doing while all this was happening?"

Yolanda wanders to the seat Maria left empty and sits. "A man," she says. "He wasn't doing anything but watching."

"Then what happened?"

"Green cuffed my father, lifted him from the hood, and fell backward."

"Green fell?"

"He just dropped."

"He wasn't struck . . . maybe accidentally by your father's head? Or maybe tripped?"

"No," she says. "As I said, my father complied. That cop fell on his own, like he'd had a seizure or something."

"A seizure? Why'd you think that?"

"His eyes were rolled up in his head," she says, spinning her fingers upward. "And he bent over how a tree would after its trunk's been cut—fast and hard. But I saw it in his eyes . . . emptiness."

"And then your father was arrested?"

"Charged with battery on a peace officer," she says. "The murder charges came later. I mean, Green's partner tried to resuscitate him. That man pounded on his chest for what seemed like forever. After some time, he stopped, and I knew . . ." She looks meek, helpless, maybe a trace of how she was that day. "Nothing would be the same for our family." Tension builds in her hands. Her fingers stiffen, then retract into a clenched fist. "Twenty-six years he was behind bars. Thinking of what he went through in there makes me sick to my stomach, but knowing it was no fault of his own is what makes me crazy."

"Was there anything in the car?" I ask. "A weapon, drugs?"

"Papa was clean," she says. "He had gotten out of the life, moved on. He wasn't going back to prison."

"After your father's arrest, did anyone speak to you about what you saw?"

"You mean to take our statements?"

"Yes."

"A detective did, briefly."

"You remember the detective's name?"

"Hill, I think," she says. "But the other officers called him Rocky or Brick or something like that. He talked to my brother and me. Asked us what we saw, and we told him. Green passed out or something, smacked his head on the curb. And that was it. We never talked to another cop or the prosecutors. The public defender didn't even want to hear from us."

I glance over to Munoz. She's flipped to another page in her notebook. "And your brother, Hector—older or younger?"

"Younger by two years."

"Does he know about your father?"

"I called him," she says. "Told him Papa was dead . . . I know he was upset, but he didn't cry. He never does."

"Is he local? We'd like to speak with him."

"Sorry," she says. "Even if he was around, he's supposed to be shipping out soon."

"Shipping out?"

"He's a sergeant in the army."

"When did you speak with him last?"

"A few days ago," she says. "I can't be sure exactly when. It's been a lot to manage."

"And you're certain he was shipping out?"

"That's what he said, but for all I know, he could've already left."

"Do you have his last known address?"

"Wish I did," she says, looking at her watch. "Hector barely keeps a working number. I do remember he was staying with an old girlfriend in Tarzana, but that was maybe a year ago." She looks at her watch again. "I'm sorry to cut this short. I need to get my daughter to a dance class."

"I understand," I say. "Before you go—"

"Yes?"

"The warden mentioned you haven't collected your father's things," I say. "The prison will only hold an inmate's belongings for so long. It'd be a shame for them to be thrown out."

"I appreciate your concern, Detective . . . ?"

"It's Finnegan. Just Finnegan."

"OK," she says. "Finnegan and Munoz—thank you." She picks up her purse from the table. The clasp comes undone, and its contents spill out. I see the handle of a small-caliber firearm. Without a second of panic, she slides the weapon back into her purse along with a few pieces of chewing gum and lipstick. "I have a permit," she says. "The paperwork's in order if you want to take a look."

Munoz seizes the opportunity. "Actually, maybe we should—"

"I'm sure it's in order," I say. "We'll be leaving now."

Munoz rolls her eyes at me and mumbles, "I'm the cop here, remember?"

We follow Yolanda out of the office toward the exit, passing Maria as she puts the finishing touches on her grandfather's portrait. It's a smiling Mateo fitted in prison-issued clothing: a light-blue shirt, dark pants, and white slip-on shoes. Red flowers surround him with white clouds above. Made of bold yellow and orange, the sun burns brightly. Is Yolanda right to let Maria make a get-well card for a dead man?

"You have my number," Yolanda says, holding the door open for us. "Call me when you're ready to clear my father's name."

Munoz and I walk across the street in silence. Once at the Crown Vic, she says, "That gun could have been dirty."

"Doubt it," I say. "Besides, it doesn't match the caliber of what killed Riley."

"So you believe her?"

"I don't know . . . could be some truth to it." I open the door, sit in the passenger seat. Munoz gets in. I watch her fingers slide across the blistered steering wheel. She stares intently at the vandalized storefront of Yolanda's make-do law firm. "What are you thinking?"

"I know who can help us locate Hector," she says.

"Who?"

"If Hector's serving overseas, Rodrigo will know how to get in touch with him."

"Your husband? You sure you want to do that?"

"What other choice do we have? If Hector can corroborate Yolanda's story, maybe he can fill in the gaps, too? We know Hill was there, but Yolanda said nothing about Riley."

"I feel like we're chasing our tails out here, getting tunnel vision . . ."

"We both know something about this Mateo Ruiz business doesn't feel right. Let's keep digging."

"You think Rodrigo will help you?"

"It'll cost me, but yes, he'll help."

"And if he can't?"

"Come up with plan B," she says with the resolution of a sailor lost at sea. "With your help or not, I have to know who killed Riley and why. I've already come this far . . ."

"All right," I say. "But take a few hours. Go home. Rest. Get the knives out of your eyes."

"I can't go home." She digs the chopstick into her cast, its odor sharper, accentuated by Munoz's days-long funk. "My sergeant probably has uniforms waiting there."

"So what are you going to do?"

"Find a motel, call Rodrigo," she says, browbeaten by the day. I know my pity for her has reached new heights when I envision her holed up in a motel room, drunk, begging for her estranged husband's help. Her plan, and that's putting it kindly, is far-fetched, even more so if Munoz and Rodrigo despise each other as much as she says. But like Maria creating a card for her dead grandfather, sometimes letting somebody cling to hope is the kindest thing we can do.

———

It's after six p.m. when Munoz drops me back at Cosmos to retrieve my car. Before getting out of the Crown Vic, I take my snubnose from the glove box. The Falcon's driver's-side window has been broken. The car's radio has been ripped from the dash, along with my police scanner. Feathers and bird droppings speckle the floor. Some delinquent poured strawberry milkshake into the passenger seat. "Dammit," I say. "Just perfect."

Sometimes I hate my city.

"Shit, Finn. I should have told you this neighborhood is hot with break-ins." Munoz peeks inside the car. "At least it's pigeon shit."

"As opposed to what?"

"Human."

I open the trunk to see if anything else has been taken. Everything looks intact. Since the trunk can only be unlocked from the outside, the thieves would've needed a crowbar to pry it open—clearly not worth the effort.

"Call me as soon as you've got a channel to reach Hector," I say.

"Where are you going to be?" Munoz asks.

"My father's place." I remove a plastic garbage bag from the trunk, scoop as much of the congealed pink liquid and glass into it as possible, and throw the bag in a nearby dumpster.

"Here," Munoz says, handing me her flashlight. "Knock the rest of the glass out with the end." I do as she says, sending the large shards to the ground with the flashlight's handle. "You gotta get that fixed."

"No kidding."

"We're going to crack this thing, Finn," she says, getting into the Crown Vic, looking at me with sympathy, the way she did Maria. "Keep your phone on."

———

I drop by the townhouse to get cleaned up. I sit in the driveway, hoping Sarada isn't home and thinking of what to say if she is. I'm running out of words that won't cause an argument.

I go into the garage and open the storage cabinet Sarada has assigned for cleaning supplies that she says are too toxic to keep in the house. I remove a can of upholstery cleaner, a brush, and a rag. I scrub the bird droppings from the seats and floor, letting the foaming cleaner set in the fabric, then vigorously brush until the excrement is gone.

Afterward, I take an old blanket, something we used to pack breakables during our move from Hancock Park, and cover the passenger seat. It'll do until I can get the car detailed after repairing the window.

The townhouse is dark. Sarada isn't home. If it weren't for the small decorative lamp turned on in the dining room, I couldn't see my way. I keep the lamp on a timer. It comes on at seven p.m. because it's never pleasant or safe coming home to darkness.

I go upstairs and into our bedroom. Piles of Sarada's clothes are folded on the bed. On the floor, her suitcase is partially packed.

I shower and get dressed: jeans, a sweatshirt, and a knit cap. Before leaving, I eat some of last night's meatloaf and consider taking a bottle of brandy with me over to Pop's. As much as the liquor is needed tonight, I leave it in the cabinet. Though it would be a soothing balm for Pop's grief—mine, too—I can't supply him with booze. Especially not after he almost shot me.

I open the front door. "Mr. Finnegan?" a dark-suited man asks, walking up the driveway.

Another man, heavier but equally authoritative, asks, "You have a minute?"

I presume they've emerged from the silver sedan parked on the street. "Who are you?" I ask, standing in the doorway, apprehensive.

"FBI—Special Agent Cunningham," he says, then points to the heavyset man. "This is Special Agent Beltran." They flash their badges, without the intent of me reading them.

"OK."

"Can we come in and speak with you?"

"What for?"

"My understanding is you found Brixton Hill?"

"I'll come out," I say, walking onto the porch. "Yes, I did."

"Do you mind taking us through how you discovered him?" Agent Beltran opens a black leather-bound book, his pen ready.

"I told the local PD everything I know."

"We understand that, but we've taken over the investigation."

"Investigation?" The neighbor's light shines through the window. She peeps through her curtain, retreating when our eyes meet. "This isn't the best time," I say. "I've got someplace to be."

Cunningham smiles through his displeasure. "What type of work do you do for Mr. Bergman?"

"Excuse me?"

"We've gone by Mr. Bergman's law firm on numerous occasions and have yet to see you there," he says. "It's curious, that's all."

"Next time you're there, ask him."

"To be frank, he's been about as helpful as you . . . which is to say, not helpful at all."

"I think you're wasting your time."

Cunningham takes a few steps toward me. "You used to be a police detective, correct?" I nod, knowing he's dug into my past. "If someone were behaving as you are, would you think them suspicious?"

"Depends," I say.

"On what exactly?"

"If I show up to their home unannounced or if I properly schedule a meeting with them."

"I see . . . A scheduled meeting?"

"That's right," I say. "Call the firm and have the receptionist set it up."

"I'll do that," he says, as if the thought never crossed his mind. "Did Hill tell you what he was working on?"

"Why would he?"

"Oh, I don't know . . . Maybe you'd be interested?" he says. "He was looking into Amanda 'Boston' Walsh and seemed to believe she was in Los Angeles. If Hill was right, her presence could pose a danger to you and your family."

"As you can see, not much happens around here. The only thing stirring tonight is you and the wind."

"You don't need me to tell you, but take appropriate measures . . . just in case."

"Noted," I say, leaving the porch and heading for the Falcon. "The receptionist's name is Kimber. She'll set you up with a time this week."

"How about you take my card in case your schedule changes and we can chat sooner?" I pause and Cunningham hands me a business card with two phone numbers, a landline and a cell, and an email address. "I look forward to our conversation."

I leave the agents to confer as they walk back to their sedan.

———

When I arrive at Pop's, it's 8:30 p.m. I walk the stairs to his unit. The TV echoes down the hallway. Normally, I'd tell Pop to turn it down, but he isn't alone tonight. The same broadcast permeates loudly through his neighbors' doors. I listen closely. It isn't the prime-time news, a football game, or cultish reality television—it's election night in America, and Pop is sure to be in rare form.

I knock on the door. "Pop, it's Trevor." He opens it enough to peek at me. "You going to let me in?"

"Didn't see your duffel this morning," he says, moving aside so I can enter. "Figured you worked things out with Good Genes." The condo is messy, as usual. Beer bottles and burger wrappers are everywhere. Fuel for his high blood pressure. Drugstore vodka sits on the kitchen counter.

"I'm back home . . . sort of," I say. "How's it looking?"

I peer at the TV screen.

"We're in for it now," he says, walking into the kitchen to pour another drink. "I knew it'd go this way, just hoped it wouldn't."

I guess Sarada was right to be worried, I think.

"It's still close, Pop," I say, joining him in the kitchen.

Pop twists the cap off the vodka bottle. "Close, my ass." He drops an ice cube into a tumbler and fills it with the clear spirit. "That man is going to be president." He holds the drink before his face, the cube bobbing about like a tiny fractured glacier. "It's the zero hour," he says. "This whole damn country's on borrowed time." Then he knocks the drink back. I can almost hear his throat burn like muriatic acid stripping a coat of paint.

"I'm sure people will survive," I say. "We've had worse."

"Survive?" he asks. "Aren't you tired of surviving? We've been surviving since day one."

"You sound like Sarada."

"Well, she has sense," he says. "Talks a little too much but has sense." Pop's assessment of most women is that they talk too much, making them less attractive and deserving of the label "irritating feminists." When I told Pop that Mom was a feminist, he first called me a liar, then said if it were true, she was corrupted by talk shows and *Essence* magazine. "I sure hope your ass voted," he adds, breathing through the liquor's burn.

"Mailed it early . . ."

"I stood in line for four hours today," he says. "Wanted to be sure my vote counted."

I didn't think Pop could go without a drink for more than two hours, so standing that long is either a testament to his will or his fear for where the country may be headed. "But if you didn't come here to watch the election, I guess you're here to talk about the other night?" Pop examines the ice in the glass; a small bit of vodka is left in the bottom. He pours more until the ice is just broken slivers floating at the top. "You know I wasn't going to shoot you," he says. "Just lost my head for a minute."

"That ever happen before?" I ask. "You believing Mom's still alive?"

Pop nods reluctantly. "Just know, I'm dealing with it," he says. "And it's not for you to worry about."

"Dealing with it?" I ask, wanting to press further but knowing it's the wrong time.

"Yes," he says with finality. "Dealing with it. Now let's get back to this." He begins walking toward the couch, his eyes focused on the TV. "History's being made tonight."

"Isn't every election historic?"

"Not like this," he says. "Tonight's a test to see how far this country's come."

It's the first time Pop's admitted he has a drinking problem, though I don't know what he means when he says he's dealing with it. For him, it could mean decreasing his intake from twelve beers a day to ten. Under different circumstances, I'd try to talk him into seeking treatment for his addiction, but tonight my father's drunkenness takes a back seat.

"Pop," I say, trying to get the words out without choking. "Uncle Hill is dead."

He drinks the vodka quickly, then shakes the empty glass. "Guess it's too much to ask for good news," he says, chin raised to me. I might as well be an unwelcome solicitor who dropped in to ruin his night further. "But we Finnegans only court disaster, don't we?"

"I'm sorry, Pop."

"What are you sorry about? You're not the one who killed him."

"What makes you think someone killed him?"

Pop returns to the kitchen and pours more vodka. He works the liquor around in his mouth, as if to savor it. Then he returns to form, slamming the drink back with force. "Nothing . . . You tell me what happened."

"I don't exactly know," I say. "Might've done it to himself." Though I know Hill was killed, I can't prove it, and my father is the last person I want to share conjecture with.

"Bullshit," he says. "That man didn't have it in him."

"Either way, it's not sitting right," I say. "Be straight with me. Did someone want Uncle Hill dead? Some beef from his LAPD days?"

Pop wipes vodka residue from his upper lip, cups his jaw, and strokes his fingers along his coarse skin. "He's a cop," he says. "Could be a million reasons why someone would want him dead."

"This isn't the time for that blue-wall bullshit, Pop."

"Watch your tone!"

"You're hiding something, and whatever it is might help me find out what really happened to Uncle Hill."

"Look, I'm not thinking straight. I'd only be talking out my ass."

"You're thinking fine." An unintended consequence of being a drunk: Pop spins into the past. Glassy-eyed memories turned to parables. Stories of incidents, investigations, things that went south—maybe tonight I'll hear why someone would want to kill his former friend and partner.

The lights go out, along with the TV and microwave clock.

"Not again," Pop says. "This damn building's falling apart."

"Where's the fuse box?" I ask. "I'll check it out."

"No," he says. "I'll do it."

"Pop, you've been drinking. Might not be the best idea messing around with electricity."

"Send in a damn search party if I'm not back in ten." He takes a flashlight from a kitchen drawer and turns it on. The beam is weak. He can see one foot, maybe two feet, in front of him. Pop snatches a set of keys off the coffee table and walks into the hallway, headed downstairs.

I stand in the doorway, anticipating Pop calling for me to help. Upset neighbors in nearby apartments yell and gripe, confirming the power is out for the entire building. A few doors open. I can't see anyone clearly but can smell cooking, pepperoni pizza, wine, and beer. I envision their bewildered faces peering out. "Is anyone checking the fuse box?" a woman asks. Her tone suggests saltiness. Is it spurred by the election results or the loss of power? Likely both.

"Someone's on it," I call out to the voice. "He'll be right back."

"And who are you?"

"Trevor."

"You live here?"

"Visiting my father . . . unit 216."

"Oh," she says before slamming the door, affirming what I've long believed. Pop couldn't rub two neighbors together to get one who cares. If he were to die in his condo and I didn't find him, no one would. It would take the vaporous stink of his decomposing corpse for anyone to take notice.

It feels like I've waited long enough. Pop still isn't back, and I can no longer see the faint glow of his feeble flashlight. "Pop, just flip the switch!" No response. Maybe he's forgotten where the fuse box is.

I return to the kitchen, thinking he may have an extra flashlight in the same drawer. It's packed with miscellaneous items, and in the dark I can't be sure of what I'm grabbing. I suspend my search when I hear footsteps near the door. "You see what the problem is?" I ask in the darkness. Pop is close. I can smell him, tainted by the hum of vodka. "Just give me the flashlight. I'll take a look." I move closer to the door, anticipating that the flashlight has died or the fuse box wouldn't open. But something isn't right. It feels like my dad's loitering in the doorway. "Pop, what are you doing?"

Something hits my chest. It feels like a palm strike. I tumble backward, tripping over a stack of newspapers. I reclaim my balance and pivot on my heel in the direction of whoever struck me. "Who's there?" I ask, my fists up in a fighting stance.

The flashlight comes on. Pop is standing in front of me. The back of his neck is clutched by a gloved hand belonging to a tall figure in a dark leather jacket and motorcycle helmet. "Sit down." I know the voice—it's him, the biker. *But how'd he find me?*

"What do you want?" I ask.

"Sit down," he says. "I won't say it again." I walk to the couch and sit. My thoughts are tangled. I try to focus. *What are my tactical options?* I left my snubnose in the Falcon's trunk, believing that not having guns around my father made for safer visits. The biker shuts the door and continues holding Pop by the neck. "If you don't listen to me, I'll kill you both."

"Kill us?" Pop says. "You ain't got to kill nobody. You want money? I'll give you money."

"Money?" the biker asks. His laugh is muffled through the helmet.

He's not here to rob anyone. He's come for me. I brought this on us.

"Got a couple hundred in cash in my bedroom," Pop says. His bedroom is an armory. There's no telling what firepower he's got in there.

If he can get his hands on a piece, we might stand a chance. "You can take the cash and go. We won't follow you."

"Shut up!" The biker pushes Pop onto the couch next to me. "Don't move from there."

"Just tell us what you want," I say, feeling something bulky under the cushion. *The gun?* It's the piece Pop pulled on me in his drunken confusion. I need to get my hands on . . .

The biker reaches behind his back and pulls out a pistol—a Glock, maybe a Sig? There's a suppressor attached to the barrel. He balances the weapon, elbow pinned to his ribs. Gun pointed at Pop. The flashlight is in my eyes but dim enough for me to concentrate on the intruder, watching his movements. "Shaun Finnegan," he says calmly, speaking Pop's name like some officiant. "You are Shaun Finnegan, aren't you?" Pop offers nothing. "I know you are." He aims the gun at my father. "Mateo deserved better." He fires twice. Pop screams in pain, falling onto the arm of the couch.

"Pop!" I rip the gun from under the cushion, aim, and fire—three flashes in the dark. The biker drops. The flashlight rolls across the floor. I jump up from the couch to assess him. He isn't moving. I reach for the flashlight, point the beam. Blood runs from the biker's chest, coating the jacket in red. I kick him hard; he doesn't move. I reach down, push up the tinted visor, and cast light over the man's face. He's a white man, a crucifix tattooed on his cheek. Scars resembling gator skin cover his forehead. Something about him is familiar, but I can't place him.

I turn to Pop, run the light over him, searching for the entry wounds. Slugs are buried in his arm. "Pop, can you hear me?" He mumbles incoherently. I remove my belt and wrap it around his arm as a tourniquet. I take my phone from my pocket and dial 911. "My father's been shot," I say. "Yes, he's conscious." I confirm the address. "Hurry."

"Is it bad?" Pop whispers.

"I've seen worse," I say, pulling the belt tighter until blood spurts from the cavities. "The ambulance is on the way. We have to slow the bleeding."

"You get that sonofabitch?" he asks. "He good and dead?"

I look at the biker's lifeless body. "Yeah, Pop . . . he's gone."

CHAPTER ELEVEN

"He's stable," the doctor says, approaching me from the end of the hall. He's a short, brown-skinned man whose walk is a choppy shuffle across the waxed floor. "I'm Dr. Patel."

"Trevor Finnegan," I say. "Is he going to be all right?"

"He lost a good amount of blood." He's relaxed, arms by his sides, body language that reads as concern, not alarm. "We have him sedated, and we'll continue to monitor his vitals."

"And his arm?"

"He'll have pain," he says. "We'll need to manage that while it heals. There may also be a limited range of motion. Of course, we'll recommend physical therapy. If he adheres to our recommendations, a full recovery is possible. However, there are other concerns."

"Like what?"

"We ran some blood tests." He gestures like he's presenting findings in a board meeting. Seeming to notice me staring, he slips his hands into his white coat. "Your father's liver shows signs of cirrhosis." And there it is, slight creasing in his brow—alarm. "We can give him medications to help slow the progression, but the pills will only do so much. He needs a drastic lifestyle change."

"He needs to stop drinking," I say. The affirmation is a warning signal that pulses in my head every time I watch Pop drink.

"Yes, his alcohol consumption has taken a toll."

"And if he doesn't stop?"

"It could be fatal."

"That man's been a drunk since Clinton was in office," I say. "Stopping might not be an option at this point."

"He can change," he says, sincere, hopeful even, but he doesn't truly know Shaun Finnegan. "We have programs for older adults. They've been very successful."

"I'll talk to him," I say, fearing our future conversation will end with Pop cursing me out.

"Talking is the first step." Dr. Patel pats my shoulder. "Please let me know if I can help." Maybe he can see it? The hurt I carry—it's what the photography student saw in the park. I must wear it like a shroud. "I'll have one of the nurses call you when your father wakes."

"Thank you, Dr. Patel."

"It will get better, Mr. Finnegan." I force a smile, partly thinking Dr. Patel is a fantasist but also praying that he's right.

———

The Crown Vic is parked next to the Falcon. Munoz gets out of the car wearing the same clothes as when I last saw her. She's drinking coffee again, looking haggard. "You give your statement already?" she asks. The acrid coffee on her breath does little to mask the tequila.

"Back at the scene," I say.

"What the hell happened?"

"Guy cut the power. Came in and held us at gunpoint. Pop took two slugs in the arm."

"Shit," she says. "You two got lucky tonight."

"I should've dropped him before he got a shot off. Wasn't fast enough."

"And Biker Boy?"

"Glendale PD is working to ID him."

She guzzles the coffee. "You think he followed you?"

"No . . . he wasn't there for me," I say, working the pieces around in my head. "Riley, Hill, and now Pop. They all must've been there when Mateo was arrested. Someone must be targeting officers at the scene."

"That could be twenty cops for all we know."

"Could be," I say. "Or there's more that connects them."

"Dammit," she says, hurling the cup into an island of bushes that divides parking rows. "I'm tired of being in the dark."

"Look, whoever's behind this might've been at the scene when Mateo was arrested."

"You mean, like, an onlooker?" she asks. "Somebody who saw everything?"

"Or at least with access to the unredacted report."

"So anyone named in that report could be next," she says, still riding her rage.

"And there's the man I shot," I say. "He could be responsible for both killings, which means if someone hired him, they might not know he's dead."

"Hired him?" she asks. "Like Mateo's children?"

"It's where motive falls," I say, considering they may have conspired together. "Yolanda and Hector believe their father died an innocent man after spending two decades behind bars; they're rightly pissed."

"So, retribution . . ." Munoz ruminates on the theory. "Then Yolanda's playing us."

"Any word on Hector?"

"Rodrigo's still working on it," she says. "I just wish we could get our hands on the original reports."

A thought burrows its way to the forefront of my brain as if by a divine hand. *Why did I not consider this before?* Hill's file cabinet—a reservoir of records chronicling past investigations, a testimony to how he spent his time on earth, seeking justice for those unduly taken, like him. "I think I know where the police report could be."

"Where?"

"Chino," I say. "Hill's ranch."

"We're going to Chino, then," Munoz says, thirsting to get behind the wheel. "It's midnight. Traffic should be light."

"Better to follow me," I say, cautious of her mental state and blood alcohol level. "Try to stay close. Call if I lose you."

"Don't worry about me," she says, not with bravado but with a dim awareness, like she's still trying to prove something, but not to me. "I'll keep up."

I get into the Falcon, signal to Munoz with a high sign to follow, and exit the parking lot onto Brand Avenue. I drive toward the 134 east, headed to the 210.

Munoz follows the Falcon closely, as instructed. When a minivan cuts her off and then travels under the speed limit, she rides its bumper until it departs the lane, returning to her place behind the Falcon.

We reach Chino shortly after 1:30 a.m. Streetlights are placed sporadically along the pitch-black road. It's a darkness I'll never get used to. I flick on my high beams and slowly drive the private road, not disturbing the dust too much. The granules still blow through the broken window, settling against my skin.

I park outside the barn. The Crown Vic comes to a stop next to the Falcon. "Talk about the sticks . . ." Munoz says, after getting out of the car.

"We have to make this fast," I say, opening the Falcon's trunk, taking out my flashlight.

"You get no argument from me." She sniffs the air. "Is that methane? People really live out here?"

"It's Southern California," I say. "People live wherever they can."

Munoz reaches under the Crown Vic's passenger seat and pulls out her department-issued Maglite. We walk to the rear of the house.

"Guess they didn't buy it was a suicide, either," I say, yanking the yellow police tape that crisscrosses the back door. A large white label seals the threshold with black-and-red lettering—a warning that entering the structure is a federal crime and violators will be prosecuted. I turn the door's handle and push, breaking the seal.

"Never broke into a crime scene before," Munoz says, exhilaration showing in her bounce. We step into the dingy kitchen, which smells of spoiled food. The bowl of corn is just as Hill left it. Munoz finds a switch on the wall. "Power's cut," she says after flicking it twice.

"They've wrapped up the scene," I say, noticing the fingerprint dust on the counter. No wonder the feds are hounding me. They're suspicious, and logical reasoning makes me a person of interest, though I'm without a motive.

"Where to?" Munoz asks.

"Upstairs." We climb the creaking steps to the study. Things are undisturbed, just as I left them. "The file cabinet is over there," I say, pointing to the metal behemoth against the wall.

"How many files does that thing hold?"

"A lot . . . We should get started." I open the file cabinet with Hill's key and remove brown folders, manila envelopes, and loose pages. Munoz reaches in, takes a handful, and starts building a stack on the floor. She sits down as a child would, legs crossed, sifting through the old cases.

———

Our flashlights burn for hours as we carry on in silence, save for the occasional whistle of delight when Munoz thinks she's found something pertinent, followed by a lament of defeat when she realizes it's meaningless.

Four hours in and the search feels bleak. The night gives way to dawn. The emergent sun offers a reprieve for my flashlight's disappearing beam. Munoz's batteries died an hour ago, and she's been working by her cell phone's light. "I'm crashing, can't see straight," she says, files scattered around her. "Would it have killed him to organize this stuff?" I cringe. Munoz's foot-in-the-mouth disease has progressed beyond a cure. "Sorry," she says.

"Keep looking. There has to be something here."

Munoz's phone rings, playing a raunchy song I've heard on the radio—part club banger, part action plan for getting back at an ex. "Shit," she says, hunting for her cell. "Damn, the phone was right here." Annoyed, she shoves a stack of files to the side, uncovering her phone inches from where she's working. "Munoz," she answers.

A man speaks raucously on the other end. He might as well be on speaker. "What took you so long?" he asks.

"I had to look for my phone," she says. "Just tell me what you found."

"First, I need to hear it . . . our agreement still holds?"

Munoz turns from me, a futile attempt at privacy. I continue to look through files, eavesdropping as best I can. "I'll sign whatever you need me to. Now tell me." She cocks her hip, and her neck cradles the phone. "Dead?" There's a long pause. "All right," she says and ends the call.

"What is it?"

"That was Rodrigo," she says. "He pulled Hector's file. He never returned to Fort Irwin after leave. He was reported deceased six months ago. Stabbed outside a bar."

"Yolanda lied," I say.

"Well, she definitely hasn't talked to her brother recently, unless her phone plan's a Ouija board."

"She needs to be brought in," I say. "Make the call."

"If I involve the department now, she could be in the wind by the time they're brought up to speed," she says. "And we run the risk of another murderer becoming a fugitive."

"As much as I don't want a repeat of Amanda Walsh, I'm out of my depth here, Sally . . ."

"I have to bring her in," she says. "It's the only chance I've got to explain myself." Munoz is still hopeful for the department's understanding, believing one hand washes the other. But I know the LAPD. She can deliver Yolanda's confession on a silver platter, and it isn't going to change the outcome. Anyone who besmirches the department isn't spared reprisal, especially in this climate.

"So you're convinced Yolanda set all this into motion?" I ask.

"Well, yeah," she says. "You said it yourself—retaliation."

"And the guy I shot?"

"A nobody, probably some hired gun."

"I don't know," I say. "Something still feels off. Yolanda commissions the murder of a cop because she *thinks* they framed her father? She was a kid looking over a back seat. Even if she's convinced she didn't see Mateo hit Green, it doesn't mean it didn't happen."

"What's your point?"

"Yolanda isn't stupid," I say. "She has a daughter to care for. She wouldn't have risked throwing her life away by hiring some homicidal biker unless . . ."

"Unless what?"

"Something . . ." I say, digging through the files again. "Something she didn't see but suspected."

"Come on, Finn. We're wasting time," Munoz says. "I say we go hook Yolanda up."

"Just give me a second." I continue to dig, opening more files. I slide papers in and out of the brown folders until I find them. "I got it!"

"You serious?"

It's the police report, unredacted, stained with coffee. I read the summary of events: It began with a routine traffic stop. Officers responded to the nonoperational brake light. Officer Jeremy Green took point. His training officer, Shaun Finnegan, my father, commissioned the search of the vehicle. "Known drug dealer" is noted as probable cause for the search. An altercation occurred between the suspect, Mateo Ruiz, and Officer Jeremy Green. Green collapsed in distress while attempting to arrest the suspect. Lead investigators Detectives Brixton Hill and Martin Riley were first on the scene.

"What is it?" Munoz asks.

"Hang on." I pull out the medical examiner's report. "Cardiac arrest."

"Green had a bad ticker?"

I sigh, feeling the same heaviness I experienced when I discovered Hill swinging in the barn. "Alcohol, cocaine, marijuana—he was doped up. It's what caused the heart attack."

"Yolanda was right," she says. "It might have looked like a seizure, but it was a drug overdose."

"That's what the department was hiding," I say. "Green's tox screen."

"They sent an innocent man to prison over some stoner rookie?"

"What was that Kutcher said? Green had a wife and kid, right?"

"Yeah, a daughter, I think."

"Green died on the job because of the drugs. If LAPD had disclosed that, his family wouldn't have gotten a cent. No survivor benefits, no claim to his pension."

"He violated his oath," Munoz says. "Someone was looking out for him."

"Not someone," I say. "Hill."

"You think he would have done that?"

"He kept the original report, didn't he?" I slip the pages back into the folder. Everything is illuminated. "He made a choice . . . ruin one family to spare another."

"But what reason would he have? You think he was that tight with Green?"

"I don't know why he did it, but my father might." I set Green's file aside. We dump the other files back into the cabinet. I lock the cabinet, and we leave out the back door. I carry the folder to the car and put it in the glove box.

I speed down the private road with no regard for the dust that collects in the cabin. Munoz follows me to the 91. My thoughts are on our destination—Yolanda's storefront firm.

———

I park across the street. Exhaust puffs from the tailpipe of a maroon minivan parked close to the entrance of Yolanda's firm. Its windows are tinted. The aftermarket wheels look newer than the vehicle. It's a family car with street flair. Sometimes cars have a strange way of resembling their owners, so I'm not surprised to see Yolanda exit from her building and walk toward the minivan carrying a black trash bag. She opens the hatch and tosses the bag into the rear. Munoz gets out of the Crown Vic parked behind me. She knocks on the passenger-side window. I motion for her to get in. "What do you think she's doing?" she asks.

"No telling."

"Should we move on her?"

"Hold tight," I say, watching Yolanda close the hatch and go back into the storefront. "I think her daughter might be in the back."

"Might be best to press her inside," she says.

Yolanda returns to the minivan with another black trash bag. She puts it with the other in the rear, closes the hatch, and moves toward the driver's-side door. "Come on," I say, getting out of the Falcon. We run across the street. I've spent too much time in the car, not stretching as I should. My right knee pops and tingles. By the time I reach Yolanda's door, my entire leg is throbbing. "Yolanda!" I shout.

"What is it, now?" she asks, holding the driver's-side door open. "I have to get my daughter to school."

"I didn't realize your office opened this early."

"I live upstairs," she says, pointing to the four-pane windows above the firm. "What is it you need?"

"It's about Hector," Munoz says.

"You found him?" Yolanda lets the door shut, then steps closer to Munoz. "Please tell me you found him."

"No," she says. "We didn't find your brother . . . but I think you know that already."

"What are you talking about?"

"He's dead," Munoz says. "Been that way for months."

"What? No . . . How?"

"Cut the act, Yolanda." Munoz's hand glides to her gun's holster like butter on hot cast iron. "I'm going to ask that you come with me."

"Excuse me?" The tension in Yolanda's hands has returned. Is this the countenance of a killer? Her eyes are red, nostrils flaring. "I'm not going anywhere with you!"

There's a twitch in my shoulder; it'll soon become a tremor. I get this way before it happens. Either Munoz or Yolanda is about to do something stupid, and someone might end up dead. "Everybody take it easy," I say. "Yolanda, Detective Munoz only wants to talk."

"There's nothing to talk about. If you were going to arrest me, you'd have done it by now." Yolanda's right. Munoz doesn't have a warrant. No grounds for an arrest. Suspicion isn't enough.

"The bags," Munoz says, moving to the hatch and opening it.

"You can't do that!" Yolanda runs to the rear of her minivan, where Munoz has ripped open the trash bags, exposing cash and jewelry.

"What the hell is this?" Munoz asks.

"That's my property."

"A man's watch . . . rings, money?" Munoz continues to comb through the bags. "These aren't yours. Who do they belong to?"

"They're gifts," she says.

"From clients?" Munoz asks. "Are you taking people's shit in exchange for legal services?"

"Could be stolen," I say.

"They aren't stolen," Yolanda says. "I told you, they're gifts—you have no right to do this!"

"Maybe a tip about an attorney accepting stolen goods as payment for legal services gives me the right?"

"No, please," Yolanda says. "They'll close me down."

I walk to the storefront's door and look inside. The cubicles are against a wall. The desks and chairs have been removed, along with the electronics. "You going somewhere?"

"What is it, Finn?" Munoz asks.

"Everything's cleared out," I say.

"You're running?" Munoz pushes Yolanda against the side of the minivan and forces her hands behind her back. "I'm arresting you."

"For what?"

"Receiving stolen goods." She applies the cuffs and takes hold of Yolanda's shoulder.

"Stolen goods?" she says. "Bullshit. You're crooked like the rest of them."

The minivan's rear sliding door opens. "Let my mommy go!" I look to see Maria moving around the vehicle, her mother's pocket pistol in her hand. "Let her go, now!"

"Maria, baby, put the gun down," Yolanda says.

Munoz's good arm is working to control Yolanda. She's got no chance of a quick draw. By the time Munoz's weapon is online and she's clear to shoot, Maria could have several holes in the both of us. "What's the plan, Finn?" she asks.

"Maria," I say, "I'm going to need you to put the gun down." Someone's taught the girl how to hold the firearm, both hands gripped firm, eyes focused on her target.

"Just leave us alone," she says. "Mommy didn't do anything wrong."

"We can't do that, Maria. Your mom hurt people."

"You're lying."

"I'm not . . ."

"Don't believe them, baby!" Yolanda cries out. "All they do is lie."

"You're a bad man," Maria says. "You want to take her away like you did my abuelo."

"Your mom's done things," I say, keeping my hands where she can see them. "Things that she's got to answer for. I know why she did them, but it doesn't make it right." My snubnose is holstered on my hip, but I don't consider it a viable option. Even if I had a clean shot of Maria, I wouldn't take it. "Please, Maria . . . I'm telling you the truth. One of the men your mother hurt was my father."

"Your papa?"

"Yes," I say. "He's in the hospital."

"Your father was one of them?" Yolanda asks.

"No," I say. "He was not one of *them*—"

"He was dirty," she says, rolling her neck like she's poised to spew venom. "Just like the others. I hope he dies!"

"And what will happen to your daughter?" I ask. "If she pulls that trigger, her life is over. Her world will be behind bars, just like your father's was—just like yours will be." Yolanda's eyes well with tears. "Look at Maria. She still has a chance. Spare her the pain."

"Mommy?" Maria asks, the fear in her voice unmistakable.

"Please, Yolanda," I say. "Your daughter deserves better, just like Mateo."

Yolanda's mascara is running. Two black lines score her cheeks. "OK," she says. "Baby, listen to me . . . are you listening?"

"Yes, Mommy."

"I want you to put the gun on the ground and back away from it."

"But, Mommy . . ."

"Do it, baby. Do it now."

"OK." Maria slowly lowers the gun, placing it between us. She backs away, taking slow, short steps until she's three feet from the pistol.

"Now stay there. OK, baby?"

"OK," Maria says.

"Can you get it, Finn?" Munoz asks.

"Yeah," I say, approaching the weapon, taking it by the grip. "It's secure." I remove the bullets, clear the chamber, and put the gun in my pocket. "Maria, I'm going to need you not to move. Can you do that for me?"

"Yes," she says, standing on the sidewalk. "I'm scared."

Munoz has Maria's mother detained at the minivan's rear. "Everything is fine, baby," Yolanda says. "Let's play that game from school. The one where you close your eyes and count."

"OK."

"Can you count backward nice and slow?"

"OK," Maria says, closing her eyes. "From what number, Mommy?"

"How about one hundred? Can you do that?"

"Yes," the girl says and begins to count.

I turn to Yolanda. "Who did you hire?" I can see the motorcyclist's face in my mind but still can't place him. "Who is he?" I ask. "Give me a name."

"I don't know."

"Don't play with me," I say. "I want the name!"

Munoz yanks down on the cuffs and shoves Yolanda forward. She draws a loud yelp. "Tell us," she says.

Maria stops counting. "Mommy, what's going on?"

"Keep counting, baby," Yolanda says, and after a moment, the girl returns to the game.

"Who killed Riley?" Munoz asks.

"I don't know," she says. "I wasn't the one who hired him."

"Then who did?"

Maria reaches eighty, then begins to taper off. "Still counting, baby?" Yolanda asks. "Make sure it's loud enough for Mommy to hear, OK?"

"Yes, Mommy." Maria counts louder. "Seventy-nine!"

"The name," I whisper to Yolanda. "Tell me."

"St. James . . . Donald St. James."

"The warden?"

"He said he knew a professional who would do it for cheap. He wouldn't care who the targets were."

My heart's in my throat. The warden? "What does he have to do with any of this?"

"St. James came to me," she says. "He asked if I wanted to make things right by my father."

"You call this making things right?" Munoz asks.

"Oh, who the hell do you think you are? You're the loco ones. Look what you did to my father, to our family. If you think those badges mean you don't have to answer to someone . . ."

"Someone, yes, but it ain't you," Munoz says.

"How much did you pay St. James?" I ask.

"Ten thousand. He said it would be clean."

"Clean?"

"Their deaths weren't supposed to draw suspicion."

"Jesus," Munoz says. "They were cops!"

"So what?" Yolanda pulls away, spinning her head to look at Munoz. "Every time I close my eyes, all I can think about is my father and those machines, pumping his lungs full of air, keeping him alive. He was never supposed to be there, don't you understand? He should have been home with his family, not dying alone in some infirmary."

Munoz looks away for a moment as if to gather her thoughts. "And my partner shouldn't have had his brains blown out on the boardwalk."

"Well . . ." Yolanda says. "At least you were there when he took his last breath."

"It's time to call it in," I say, knowing we've gotten what we need from Yolanda. "Maria goes in the back seat with her mother." The girl has finally stopped counting and walks around to the minivan's rear. She watches her mother weep.

"Mommy?" she asks, seeing Yolanda cuffed. "No, Mommy!" She begins to cry. I take her by the hand and walk her across the street as Munoz escorts her mother to the Crown Vic.

"Watch your head," Munoz says before placing Yolanda in the back of the Crown Vic. I put Maria in the back with her mother.

Munoz takes a blue evidence bag from her trunk and hands it to me. "Drop the gun and rounds in here," she says. I put Yolanda's pistol and bullets into the bag.

"It's time," I say, handing Munoz the bag.

"I know." She turns the radio back on and speaks into the receiver: "Requesting a supervisor and additional units to 422 Ash Street." The dispatch operator confirms, and Munoz signs off. She looks to me, gnawing the inside of her cheek. "It's over for me, isn't it?"

"You know a good attorney?"

"Not really," she says.

"Try David Bergman."

"You think he'd help me?"

"Depends," I say. "The money you and Riley took, you spend it?"

"Some."

"How much?"

"Five grand on lawyers," she says. "It's what Riley had in his jacket on the boardwalk. The rest is put away for my kids."

"Turn the money over to the LAPD."

"But I'd be admitting guilt," she says. "They'd put me away for sure."

"You're not a criminal. It was a mistake—"

"And what if it wasn't?"

"I know you, Sally. It was never about the money." I can hear sirens in the distance. It won't be long before they arrive. "I should go."

"Might be the last time I see you for a while," she says. I recognize the agony on her face. I've felt it, too. It wasn't long ago that I was at a similar crossroads. I embrace her, believing if I let go, she may vanish into a justice system that's terrifying for anyone, but especially for disgraced cops.

Muffled sobs and dampened breathing warm my chest. "It's going to be OK," I say, remembering our first assignment: a string of liquor store robberies in Mar Vista. And I'll never forget how Munoz gloated after outperforming me on the firing range. "Loser buys the first round of beers," she'd say, and I did so gladly because I was proud to call her partner. One day I'll understand why she threw her career away, but for now, maybe it's better that I don't.

We break, and I leave Munoz standing next to the Crown Vic, minutes from having to answer for all she's done. I get into the Falcon and check the fuel gauge. I've got enough to get to San Luis Obispo. I take one last look at Munoz before leaving. I've been lying to myself, not wanting to see what was always there, and it isn't Munoz who changed—it's me.

Before hitting the 5 north, I call FBI Agent Cunningham. "There's something you need to see," I say. "Meet me at the Men's Colony in San Luis Obispo."

"The prison?" Cunningham asks.

"There's a man there I believe to be responsible for killing Agent Hill and LAPD Detective Martin Riley . . ."

"You've got evidence?"

"I've got a confession," I say. "Detective Riley's and Agent Hill's homicides and the attempted murder of my father were carried out by the same man."

"Your father was attacked? When?"

"Last night. I believe Warden Donald St. James hired a professional." I can hear Cunningham taking notes, his pen flying across the paper.

"Where's this *professional* now?"

"He's dead—I shot him. Glendale PD can fill you in on the details."

"OK," he says. "We'll be there."

I hang up and merge onto the 5.

CHAPTER TWELVE

"Mr. Finnegan," the warden says as I enter the room. He stands up from behind his desk, dressed in a white collared shirt and a faded gray cardigan. It's the kind of sweater I'd lounge in around the house but wouldn't dare wear to work, especially if I were a warden. "What prompted your return?"

"It's about Mateo Ruiz," I say. "I came to tell you that you were right."

"Right about what?" he asks, sitting down.

I walk over to a window that overlooks the parking lot. Below, I can see Agents Cunningham and Beltran parked in their sedan. "Mateo Ruiz was innocent," I say, walking from the window over to St. James. "We recovered evidence that suggests the officer he was sentenced for killing died of other causes, nothing Mr. Ruiz did."

"My God," he says. "What does this mean?"

"Expect a federal investigation . . . lawsuits."

"No," he says. "What does it mean for Mateo? His name will need to be cleared."

"Given the evidence, I'm sure the state will vacate his conviction."

"And people will know he was an innocent man, right?"

"People will know the truth."

The warden buries his face in his hands. "It's an answered prayer," he says. "If only Mateo were alive to see it . . . Does Yolanda know?"

I walk over to the warden's wall of photos, scanning the many faces. "She does," I say, "but there's something else."

"What is it?" he asks, then adds, "I should call her. She'll want to talk."

"That might be difficult." My attention is on a particular face. "Can you tell me about this man?" I point to a tall, well-built white man in a tank top standing next to the warden. I notice a tattoo on his arm—one I've seen before on members of the Aryan Lowriders.

"Who is that?" he asks, boldly feigning a struggle to see the figure in the photo. He gives up, then starts moving documents and envelopes around his desk. "One second, just need to find my glasses."

"Your pocket," I say.

"My pocket?" He brings his hand to his shirt pocket and removes the wire frames. "I lose them more than I wear them," he says, getting up and joining me near his inmate Hall of Fame. "Now, who are you referring to?" He squints at the photo. "Yes, that's Clyde Coley. One of our success stories."

"How so?"

"Mr. Coley was extremely disturbed when he came to us," St. James says. "Drug abuse. Violent history. A lifetime of criminal offenses . . ."

"And where is he now?"

"Living a fruitful life, I hope. When he was released, he had a job waiting for him at a motorcycle repair shop in Buena Park," he says. "Considered himself an enthusiast. He could talk for hours about 'hogs,' as he liked to call them."

"Clyde Coley?"

"That's right. Is there some kind of interest in Mr. Coley? I don't see what he has to do with Mr. Ruiz."

"Clyde Coley is dead."

"What?"

"I shot him," I say. "Regrettably, not before he shot my father."

"I don't understand," St. James says, backing away from me.

"I think you do," I say. "You hired Clyde to kill Detective Riley, Agent Hill, and my father. Yolanda told us everything."

"That's false," he says. "I had nothing to do with any murder."

"It's over, Warden," I say. "She's giving the FBI everything."

"No, Yolanda wouldn't do that," he says, backing into the edge of his desk, then working his way around it. "You're lying."

"Keep your hands where I can see them."

He eyes a desk drawer with intent. Before he moves to open it, I reach over the desk, grab hold of his sweater, and yank him across, knocking over his cup of pens and sending his computer monitor to the floor.

"My father could have died," I say, balling my fist, suspending it over St. James, fighting the urge to bash him.

"Please, don't!" His voice is shrill, palms over his face. "I'm sorry . . . I'm so sorry."

"Why did you hire Clyde to kill them?" St. James looks too afraid to speak. All that comes from his mouth is a low croaking sound followed by a gurgle.

"I . . . can't . . . breathe . . ." He squeezes out the words. I realize my other hand is wrapped around his throat.

"Shit." I let him go. His head bangs against the floor, and he rolls over on his side. I see something folded in his shirt pocket. "What's that?"

"Please, leave it!" he moans.

I snatch the folded paper and open it up.

"It's all I have now . . ." He coughs, still recovering from his neck being wrung.

It's a photo of him with Yolanda and Maria. The edges are jaggedly torn where Mateo once appeared. "What did you think? If you killed for her that she'd love you?"

"What do you know about love?" He struggles to his feet. "I see what you are," he says. "No different than the men rotting in here. You've got blood on your hands."

"I guess we both do," I say, walking over to the desk and looking inside the drawer that St. James was determined to open. There's a switchblade and a Bible. I put the knife in my pocket. "It was all lies, wasn't it?" I ask. "The business about these men being able to change for the better?"

St. James's legs buckle. Incapable of standing, he returns to the floor. "Go to hell," he says as I walk out of the office.

Outside, Agents Cunningham and Beltran approach from the end of the hallway with two other agents. "He's all yours," I say. I lift my shirt, exposing a bud-shaped microphone and thin wire taped to my chest. I remove the recorder from my pocket, rip the wire from my skin, and hand the device to Cunningham. "You got what you need?"

"We'll make it work," he says, signaling for Beltran and the other agents to enter the office.

"You might want to hold on to this," I say, handing him the switchblade.

Cunningham chuckles. "The warden is full of surprises," he says. "We'll bag it. Oh, and about Hill, we pulled his financials."

"OK?"

"He'd been donating to Yolanda's law firm under a pseudonym since 2000. Nearly a hundred thousand in total. Even had more money earmarked for her in his will, poor bastard."

"Doesn't change anything," I say. "He let a man die in a cage when he knew he was innocent, and we might never know why."

"Could be it's not meant for us to know," Cunningham says. "Some things are best taken to the grave."

"My mother used to say that graveyards are libraries of secrets."

"Even if you knew, what difference would it make?"

"Maybe I could forgive him," I say, feeling shame for speaking ill of a dead man but also for admiring Hill, knowing how he wasn't impervious to duplicity. "What'll happen to his farm?"

"It's paid off," he says. "But since he didn't have any family, the property will go into probate, including the horse."

"And his body?"

"Sent to a cemetery in Palestine, Texas."

I pretend to be apathetic with a shrug. "Good luck with everything, Cunningham."

There's shouting, then the breaking of glass. "What the hell?" Cunningham goes into the warden's office. I enter a few seconds after to find a broken window, glass on the floor, and no warden. The two agents and Beltran stare down at the parking lot from the demolished frame. "Beltran, what the hell happened?" Cunningham asks.

"He just slipped away from us," he says, bewildered and panting. "Couldn't get a handle on him."

"Ah, shit." Cunningham rushes to the window. "Call an ambulance."

"On it." Beltran pulls his phone from his suit pocket and thumbs the screen. He moves away from the window, leaving room for me to take in the view. St. James's body is twisted limbs amid a large pool of blood. He looks to have struck a vehicle, then bounced onto the pavement.

In what feels like minutes, correctional officers and FBI agents fill the room. The chatter grows so loud that I can barely hear my phone's ring. I step out, finding space in the hallway to take the call.

"Hello?"

"Mr. Finnegan?"

"Yes."

"I'm calling from Glendale Valley Hospital," she says. "It's your father—"

A small nurse with a thunderous step slows her brisk stride and directs me to my father's room. Through the door's observation window, I see Sarada sitting across from Pop, holding his hand. It's a sight I'm unprepared for. Sarada tolerates my father, but they've never so much as hugged.

I open the door, uncertain what news awaits me on the other side. "Trevor," Sarada says. "You're here?"

"The hospital called."

"They called the house, too," she says, her flour-dusted T-shirt bearing the Spinners logo, an apple-red top twisting into a blur. "I just got home from the bakery, and it was ringing off the hook. I didn't want him to be alone."

"Thank you." I feel detached, the words transactional. "Is everything OK, Pop?"

"Me?" he says. "I'm fine. But you two might need to talk."

"Can we go outside?" Sarada asks.

"OK." She brushes past me. I quiver like we haven't touched in ages. I follow her into the hallway to a small space near the drinking fountain across from Pop's room. "Is he really all right?" I ask.

"He's fine," she says. "If it weren't for being shot, I'd say he's doing better than the last I saw him."

"How's that?" I ask.

"He apologized."

"For what?"

"Everything, I think . . . how he's treated me over the years."

"We are talking about *my* father, right?"

"Yes, Trevor. So is there a reason you didn't tell me about last night?"

"I wanted to—I should have," I say. "Things have been—"

"You killed somebody," Sarada whispers, leaning in as a man passes in blue scrubs. "Why wouldn't you call me? I should have been the first person you called."

"I was trying to keep you away from all of this."

"Trevor, I'm not glass," she says. "I won't break. It's time you start talking to me."

"Last night, a man came after my father," I say, gripping the nape of my neck. "He tried to kill him. And had I not been there, he probably would have succeeded."

"Why would someone want to kill your father?"

"Something to do with an old case he and Uncle Hill worked on."

"The FBI agent?" she asks. A loud beep echoes like an alarm. We both look to my father's room and are relieved when three nurses rush past his door, headed for the end of the hall.

"Hill wasn't as lucky as we were . . ."

Sarada grips her purse's strap. I can tell she's processing the news. She never met Hill but knew how important he was to me. Part of me still doesn't believe he's gone, despite seeing him hanging from a noose in the barn.

She hugs me, and I want to fall apart. "Trevor, I'm so sorry . . . I knew you were dealing with something, but all this?"

"I didn't want to worry you," I say. "I was afraid if you knew, you wouldn't go to France."

"You're right," she says, pulling away. "I can't leave you. Not now."

"You have to go."

"Why?" she asks. "I can just reapply next year—"

"Not an option, Sarada."

"You lost your friend and almost your father," she says. "You can't manage this alone." She takes my hand. "It isn't healthy, Trevor. Let me help."

"Maybe I'm what's unhealthy . . ."

"What?"

"This thing . . . it's like a fog I can't get out from under. Ever since the Brandon Soledad case, it's like I'm cursed."

"Cursed?" she asks.

"It's the only way I can explain it," I say. "I'm a lightning rod for heartache."

"Which is why you need me . . ."

"I don't think you understand." I slip my hand from hers, letting it fall along my side. "All of this is my albatross—I'm not finished paying for the past."

"That's what you think? All this is punishment?"

"As you said, there's always going to be *something*."

"Trevor, you know I didn't mean this . . ." she says with gravity. "You don't deserve to hurt."

"No, but you were right," I say. "It's always going to be something with me. We Finnegans court disaster."

"This isn't you talking," she says, brushing her hand along my cheek. I close my eyes, giving in to her touch. "You don't believe that. You're upset."

An acute fear rises in me, taunting me, telling me I'm no better than Boston. She ruined Cynthia's life, and perhaps I'm bound to ruin Sarada's. "You want to help me? Leave. Be great in France."

Sarada shakes her head as her sympathy turns to frustration. "Why are you pushing me away?"

"That's not what's happening. I'm trying to save you from this, and I need time to get things under control."

"Alone?" she asks.

"Well, yes," I say. "Alone, just for a bit."

"For six months?" she asks, beginning to cry. "I'll be worried sick about you."

"I'll come when I can," I say. "Give me a month or two. I promise. Nothing will keep me from getting on that plane."

"You shouldn't make promises you can't keep," she says, taking a tissue from her purse, wiping her tears.

"Trust me," I say. "I'm going to work it out. We'll get back on track." She steps in and hugs me again, tightly. We kiss, and our love feels hopeful, a relationship that may be worth salvaging.

"I love you, Trevor."

"I love you, too," I say. "Once I finish up with Pop, I'll be home in time to take you to the airport."

"You should stay here with your father. I can take an Uber or something."

"No," I say. "I want to be there to see you off."

"Trevor . . . it's really OK. You have enough to worry about."

"Please, babe. I need to see you off."

Sarada searches my face. She sighs gently. "Flight's at seven thirty," she says, "so we'll need to be on the freeway by five. If four thirty rolls around and you're not home, I'll get a ride. All right?"

"Deal," I say, looking at my watch. It's two o'clock. There's enough time to visit with Pop and get Sarada to the airport without her having to rush for her gate.

She kisses me again, then departs down the hallway through the double doors, her purse across her body, rocking on her hip.

I go into Pop's room. He's sitting up in the bed looking stiff, heavy as concrete. There's an IV drip in his arm and a brown blanket stretched over his chest. "Damn thing," he says, trying to work the TV remote. "They told me they've got cable."

"I'm sure they do," I say.

"Well, I ain't been in a hospital since your ass was laid up in one." He mashes buttons to no avail. "Ah, give me a break . . ." When the TV doesn't turn on, he flings the remote with what little force he can muster to the foot of the bed. "As much as they charge to be in here, you'd think the TV would work."

"It's not the Waldorf, Pop."

"Always the smart aleck," he says, lint caught in his gray scruff. "You work stuff out with Ms. Lady?"

"It's a start." Pop fights to clear his throat, triggering a raspy cough and wheezing that worsens the longer he carries on. "Do you need something?" He shakes his head, dismissing me, then takes a cup of water from the end table and drinks. When his fit is over, I ask, "Were there fragments?"

"It was clean," he says, his throat sounding coarse. "Bullet exited out the back, above my elbow. The other shot grazed my shoulder." He pulls the blanket down, showing a crater in his arm plugged with gauze and sealed with a clear bandage. "Good thing his aim was shit. Doctors are monitoring for blood clots."

It's hard to look at my father. The bullets consumed muscle and burned away tissue. His arm wasn't in the best shape to begin with, mostly flab, but with this devastation, it may be a useless appendage for some time. "How long do you have to be here?" I ask.

"For a while," he says. "They want to run more tests."

"What kinds of tests?"

"See how things are working upstairs. They think the alcohol's caused some issues in my brain." Pop fidgets with the pulse monitor on his finger.

"And you agreed to this?"

"Asked for a full workup," he says.

"What happened to 'nothing's wrong with me'?"

Somberness sweeps across his face. I presume he's thinking about Hill or how close he came to dying. "Your mother," he says. "She talked some sense into me."

"Mom?" I'm taken aback, his words unnerving. "What the hell are you saying, Pop?"

"I saw her."

"Like you were hallucinating?"

"When I was under," he says. "She came to me. Told me things."

"She told you things?" I debate pushing the call button for the nurse. *Are delusions a side effect of blood clots?*

"She said if I don't get myself together, I'm gonna die," he says, the soberest I've seen him in years.

"It was the drugs, Pop," I say. "What they pump you full of, people kill for on the street." Even if I believed in spirits, it's hard to imagine Mom would appear caring toward Pop.

"It wasn't the drugs!" he snaps. In his eyes, there's something new. Harrowing. "I saw your mother as I see you now," he says. "And I promised her I'd do better."

"So you're going to stop drinking?"

"I've got to," he says. I want to believe him, but I know my father. He's a supine man, a liar, a philanderer, an addict. To change means rearranging his molecules, rewiring his brain, rinsing himself clean. "Your mother said to tell you the truth about Hill."

"What truth?"

Pop haws like he's trying to recall the dream, then says, "That nothing endures."

"Can you be more cryptic, Pop?"

"Will you listen, dammit?" He continues. "When you were about ten, your mama went out of town. Your aunties came up from Texas to watch you. You remember that?"

"Kinda."

"We told you she was visiting an old friend in Santa Barbara. She stayed gone for a week. When she came back, she was different. Something had changed, but I didn't ask. Too much of a coward in that way, and life went on."

"What's this got to do with Uncle Hill?"

"Hill told me a month before he made detective that he and your mama spent a night together. Here she was, dead and buried, and he confesses that shit to me."

"You're lying."

"I'm telling you the truth, son . . ."

"This is low, even for you."

"It's why we fell out," he says. "And it's why I didn't help him when he asked."

"Help him do what?"

"Get Mateo Ruiz out of prison. It wasn't his idea to bury that report. A white boy like Jeremy Green had friends in high places."

"The department knew Green was using?"

"Green worked personal security part-time. Mostly for celebrities and VIP types," he says. "Got to the point he was hanging with them off hours, too. Partying. Bragging about the women he had on the side. That's when I saw the change . . . boy couldn't focus. Lashed out. Got rough with suspects for no reason."

"What'd you do?"

"Tried to talk to him. Told him to get his shit together, but he was past saving," he says. "I hoped he'd get transferred after his probation or just quit."

"He could have gotten you killed, Pop," I say. "He was a liability and you let him roam the streets?"

"My hands were tied," he says. "And after he died, they weren't about to let his family go without. The DA said the coroner's report was inconclusive. Nothing about the drugs was mentioned, and the brass leaned on Hill to say Ruiz attacked Green. It was all lies, but it would've been our asses if we had come forward and said Ruiz never touched him."

"You could have told the feds," I say. "An anonymous tip . . . something?"

"And if they came nosing around, what do you think they'd dig up? Every one of us at that crime scene would have been investigated. Every case we ever worked, scrutinized. Who knows the number of criminals that would have had grounds for release?"

"And you never thought to help Ruiz, even after you retired?"

"So much time had passed, but I knew whatever came of it would fall on Hill."

"You were protecting him?"

"No," he says. "I did it for you."

"What?"

"I knew you spent time at his place. It was hard to admit, but I saw how he stepped in after the drinking took hold. Probably was more of a father to you than I had been in a long time . . . I couldn't take that away from you. I'm sorry, son . . ."

"*Sorry?* That's all you can say?"

"I'm trying my best," he says. "I want to do right."

A wave of fury consumes my body. "Goodbye, Pop."

I head toward the door, unable to stand the sight of my father any longer. I want to doubt Pop's confession as windblown rumor and watercooler hearsay, but truth has a way of speaking to my conscience like a bloody riot in my gut. My mother was seldom gone, and the times she did leave, my world was quiet and still. I ached for her, and somehow, I knew her leaving was because of my father.

"She forgives me, you know?" Pop yells. I stop short of the door to face him. He shifts in the bed, straining to turn his neck my way. "Despite everything, she forgives me." A tear rolls down his cheek. My father doesn't cry, ever. "I hope one day you can forgive me, too." He's become a vague sketch, a shadowy outline. I don't recognize him. "Take it from me, Trevor. Do whatever you can to keep that woman. You hear me? Don't lose her like I lost your mother."

In the hallway, I hear the curative tone of Pop's surgeon, Dr. Patel. He's standing near the nurses' station. I walk with purpose to meet him, disregarding decorum by standing slightly too close. It doesn't take long for him to turn around, surrendering to that primal sense of having someone at your six like an itch demanding to be scratched. "May I help you?" he asks, backing up to reclaim some personal space.

"You remember me? My father's Shaun Finnegan."

"Yes, Mr. Finnegan. Is everything all right?"

"What did you give him?"

"Excuse me?"

"The painkillers," I say. "What do you have him on?"

"He was given hydrocodone shortly after his surgery," Dr. Patel says, bringing the chart to his chest. "But the only medication he's allowed us to administer is naproxen."

"Drugstore pills?"

"His milligrams are slightly higher than what's sold over the counter, but yes . . ."

"That can't be," I say. "He's confused. Delusional."

"I assure you, Mr. Finnegan, your father was adamant that we not give him opioids."

"But he's talking nonsense," I say. "Nothing makes sense."

"I don't understand." Dr. Patel cocks his head slightly. "We're following his wishes."

"It's withdrawal, right? From the booze."

"I've seen no reason to doubt his faculties," he says. "But he has requested we run tests to better gauge the impact his drinking has had on his mental capacity."

"He told me," I say with skepticism.

"Good." Dr. Patel's expression brightens as I relax. "I've also recommended a treatment facility."

"Rehab?"

"An exceptional program in Palm Springs."

"My father hates the desert."

"Well, he seemed very interested. Even had a nurse call to be sure they accepted his insurance." Dr. Patel pats my shoulder again. Does he conclude most of his conversations this way, or am I in dire need of comforting? "He's in good hands, Mr. Finnegan. Not to worry." An airy voice calls Dr. Patel away.

I stand in the hallway with splintered thoughts: indignation, sorrow, confusion . . . *Uncle Hill and my mother?* I tell myself that if it's true, it won't change how I see her. She was a good woman, loved me dearly. But she suffered through a dismal marriage, and if a night with Hill was a reprieve, can I fault her?

My phone rings. It's Bergman.

"Finnegan," I answer.

"Trevor," he says, hardly audible.

"Bergman? Speak up. I can barely hear you."

"There's a situation." He clears his throat. "I need you at the office."

"It'll have to wait." There's silence and then a ruffling. "Bergman, are you there?"

"I need you to come by now," he says.

"Is this about Sally Munoz? Did she call you?" More silence, then mumbles. "Did you hear me, Bergman?"

"Yes," he says. "Sally Munoz called . . . It's best discussed in person."

"Ah, Bergman. I really don't have the time today."

"Thirty minutes," he says, still speaking low. "All I need is thirty minutes."

I haven't heard from Munoz, so I've been thinking the worst. But if she's managed to convince Bergman to help her, she might have a shot. He could use my summary of events to lay the groundwork for her defense.

"Trevor?"

"I'm here," I say. "Thirty minutes . . . that's it."

"Thank you, Trevor," he says. "Thank you for everything." He ends the call, and I head toward the double doors.

———

Paranoid about being late to the airport, I drive the carpool lane, watching for CHP and anyone with authority to pull me over. When I reach Bergman's office, I enter the garage and park next to Kimber's two-seater.

Rusty's gathering his lunch bag and thermos when I enter the lobby. Menthols are tucked into his uniform jacket pocket. "Mr. Finnegan," he says. "Haven't seen you around. How have you been?"

"Making do," I say. "You off?"

"Bergman cut my hours. No more overnight shifts."

"Why?"

"Didn't give a reason," he says. "Tried to talk him into at least letting me stay on until eight tonight, but he wasn't having it."

"Bad move."

"Tell me about it." Rusty steps out from behind the desk and walks toward the exit. "Have a good night, Mr. Finnegan."

"You too," I say as Rusty leaves the building under an imperial violet sky.

I ride the elevator to the sixth floor, get out, and walk the hallway to the firm, prepared to tell Bergman how asinine it is not to have overnight security, but I concede it's best to criticize him later, when I'm not rushed for time. The door's unlocked, which is strange for after hours. I go in, expecting to see Kimber at the front desk, but her chair is empty. There's a ring of condensation around her cola can; it's been sitting for some time.

Maybe she's grabbing dinner or talking to Myra on the phone somewhere? Has she worked things out with her? I can never give relationship advice, but Sarada and I have managed to keep the blood pumping, despite all that's conspiring to destroy us. Perhaps that's my testimony? In the face of despair, I keep fighting for us . . . keep driving toward happiness.

Light spills into the hallway from Bergman's office. The door's ajar. "All right, Bergman," I say. "It's been a helluva day, so get to it." I move to open the door when I smell it—blood. I chew the air, taste its tang—potent and porous. It's a naked world on the other side, a hellish sight. Bergman's gagged, palms on his desk. Hovering over him is a shadowy figure in an oversize coat and hat holding a pistol flush to Bergman's temple. It's hard to tell in this light, but it looks like the person I saw sweeping out front the other day, the one who made Rusty nervous. Bergman's nose is crooked. A hunk of bone has breached the skin. His eyes are swollen to slits.

The figure turns on the desk lamp, and I see . . . Amanda Walsh.

"Don't move," she says.

"All right," I say, keeping my hands visible. She rips the gag from Bergman's mouth. A sack of bloodied teeth falls to his desk, chased by a cry of terror.

"I'm sorry, Trevor," he says. "Forgive me."

Pop.

The bullet enters his skull, snapping his head left. Blood and a custard-like substance pour from his ear as his left eye avalanches from its socket. "She died today," Boston says as a swirling fume escapes the gun's barrel.

I'm held in stasis, can't move. There's ringing in my ears. The gunshot seems to have shaken the walls, filling them with smoke and brimstone. "You killed him!" I cry out, my heart raked through smoldering embers. "Why?"

Boston points the gun at me, holding its duct-taped grip as police are trained: two-handed, isosceles stance.

"I watched them carry her body from our home," she says atop a mountain of wrath. "I huddled at a bus stop watching as they carted her off like she was nothing."

"You think Cynthia would have wanted this?"

"I should have been there—"

"And Brandon Soledad should be alive," I say. "What about him?"

"Don't say his name!" She grips the back of her neck and squeezes like she's juicing an orange. "You'll never understand what it's like," she says. "You've never lived a life worth losing that you'd do everything to keep."

"This was your plan?" I ask. "Masquerade around the office as a gardener, and then what?"

"I needed to get close to you," she says. "I was right there, could've killed you then if I wanted. You never saw me . . . When people think you're worthless, they don't bother looking hard."

"You're worth three hots and a cot," I say. "Even that's pushing it."

"Save the tough talk, Finn. We both know you're fooling yourself." She removes her cap. I'm able to see her clearly: haunting eyes, pulled-in lips, skin greased with sediment. Amanda "Boston" Walsh has stalked my dreams for two years, and here she stands, stiffer, leaner, no less threatening. "You aren't in control, Finn. You never were." Her finger's on the trigger. "I wanted you to know how it felt to lose someone. To be there the minute before it happens, unable to do anything but watch." I've experienced this pain twice over, thinking of my mother dying of cancer, and the moment she left me. Boston reaches into her coat pocket and removes a bottle of lighter fluid and sets it on the desk, avoiding Bergman's blood. "We're part of it now, just a thread in LA's tapestry of horrors. We'll be studied. Books will be written—"

"What you're proposing is suicide . . . We'd never make it out." My phone rings, lighting up my pocket.

"Give it to me," she demands, aiming the gun at my chest.

I slowly take the phone from my pocket and hand it to her. I'm able to see the caller ID—it's Sarada. Boston throws the phone to the ground and stomps it with her heel until the screen cracks and goes dark. "Where's your piece?"

"I'm unarmed," I say.

She walks behind me, jams the gun into my spine, and runs her hand about my waist, groin, and legs. She takes out my wallet and studies my driver's license. "Not a bad neighborhood," she says, noting my address. "I see where your settlement money went." She flips to a picture of Sarada—my favorite picture. Taken one morning in the sunroom. She stands wrapped in a throw, touching the steamed glass. The cold morning light is on her face. "So you took my advice, got someone worth coming home to?"

"I tried," I say. "Not sure if she knows how hard."

"Forever the pessimist . . ."

"What's with the stalling, Boston? We both know neither of us is walking out of here."

"Speak for yourself." She squeezes the lighter fluid onto the floor, the desk, Bergman, and my feet. "Maybe afterward, I'll swing by your place, sample life in Sierra Madre."

A woman's maddening cry startles me from behind. "Trevor!"

I turn to see Kimber standing in the doorway. "Go," I say. "Clear the building!" Boston fires in Kimber's direction. The bullets strike the door, bursting the wood and nearly striking Kimber as she flees. I take hold of the gun's barrel, pointing it up to the ceiling. My knee explodes into Boston's stomach. Her grip loosens. I push her back with the ball of my foot. She releases the gun and crashes into the desk, knocking the lamp over.

"On your stomach," I say. "Don't move."

"Good for you, Finn," she says, struggling to catch her breath. "I misjudged you."

There's a crackle and the smell of burning carpet and wood. I look to the lamp, where a small fire builds, consuming the shade and inching up the side of the desk. The flames creep closer to Boston, following the path of the accelerant. "Get up, or you'll burn," I say, watching as the flames clamber onto her boots.

"This is how it was supposed to be," she says, motionless, staring into the fire. A rolling flame moves around my feet, forcing me backward.

"Don't be stupid!" I say, reaching out my hand. "Come on." The fire rises, climbing the walls toward the ceiling. Thick smoke begins to overtake the room. I cover my mouth and crouch lower to the floor.

"Come on, Boston!" Flames race up her legs, and she kicks madly. Her hair catches, then her neck and face.

"Get up!" I yell.

Screams follow. Bellows of terror. Flesh sears and blackens until she's unrecognizable. Then, as if to summon her last grain of strength, she cries out, "Cynthia!" In moments, she's consumed.

The fire rages, threatening to box me in. I breathe in soot and ash. Drenched in sweat and coughing hard, I race out of the room to the stairway. The smoke alarms blare with pulsing light. I open the door, taking long strides and skipping steps until I reach the fifth floor, then the fourth, third, and second. I'm met in the lobby by three firefighters guiding tenants clamoring to exit.

"What floor did you come from?" a firefighter asks, carrying an axe and a flashlight.

"The sixth," I say, struggling to catch my breath. "Go to the sixth . . ."

"Do you know if anyone else is there?" I begin to cough; my chest is tight. "Sir, are you OK?"

"They're dead," I say, light-headed. The firefighter extends his arm, and I take hold.

"Who's dead?" he asks loudly through his face mask.

"Bergman . . . Boston . . ." I'm gasping for air, and my vision's blurred. "It was Amanda 'Boston' Walsh," I say before collapsing. "She killed him."

CHAPTER THIRTEEN

DECEMBER 2016

I've always loved the artwork that hangs in Dr. Juana Angell's office. Before our sessions, I look at my favorite painting, a large oil-painted canvas of Palawan, an island of the Philippines. It's an abstract work. Dr. Angell likes to say it's "a reimagining of a place . . . not how it is, but how the artist wishes it was." The waters are celestial; the sunset cascades purple, orange, and red; and the palm trees lean ever so slightly, as if swaying in a subtle breeze. Palawan is already beautiful, but the artist isn't interested in its beauty the way that most people are—it's about the soul of the place.

Dr. Angell sits in a red Victorian-style chair that looks like a prop for a TV or movie production, a period piece in which people speak properly with British accents. "So how are you sleeping?" she asks. The office smells of potpourri. It feels like a romance writer's study. Floor-to-ceiling bookcases, potted flowering plants, trinkets, decorative vases, and the art—beautiful lavish paintings of islands and beaches. "Trevor?"

"Yes," I say, jarred from a daze. "Sorry—"

"Your sleep. How has it been?"

"Not horrible, considering . . ."

"Well, the type of trauma you experienced will take time to manage." Dr. Angell adjusts her red cat-eye frames, which match her flowing dress.

"It's just that I'm still on high alert," I say. "Like I'm waiting for things to get bad again."

"It's a process, Trevor . . . That feeling is what trauma causes," she says. "When that feeling happens, remember your breathing exercises."

"I'll remember."

"I guess we'll continue our sessions when you return from France." Dr. Angell gets up and walks to the door.

I follow behind her, stopping to look back at my favorite painting. "You visit Palawan often?" I ask.

"Sadly, it's been decades," she says, looking at the painting dotingly, as she might an old friend. "I guess I'm afraid if I go back, it won't be as I remembered it, and somehow, the memories that live in my mind will disappear."

"I really hope memory doesn't work like that, Doctor."

"Oh, I'm sure it doesn't. But that's how fear works. Often it's irrational but powerful all the same." We share a smile, and she opens the door. "Be well, Trevor."

"Thank you, Doctor," I say before stepping into the lobby.

———

"So what happens now?" Tori asks, pushing Simone in her stroller as we walk the concrete path through the park. A boorish breeze stirs dead leaves into a frenzy and teases the hem of Tori's pleated skirt.

"Investigation's over," I say. "Boston's dead."

"And your friend, Bergman?"

Simone watches me from the stroller with a smile that seems at odds with my world. Is this how my parents felt, wondering how to preserve innocence in sordidness? "Kimber handled the funeral arrangements," I say. "He didn't have any family still living. Only a prepaid plot at Forest Lawn." Chilled by the crisp morning, I shove my hands in my pockets. "He's buried next to his parents."

"And how are you doing?" she asks, pushing the stroller under an evergreen. Other trees have lost their leaves, becoming playthings for children who climb limbs in defiance of their parents.

"Started jogging again," I say. "Still get a little winded, though."

"I guess that's to be expected, right?"

"Right," I say, recalling the doctor who told me that had I inhaled more smoke during the fire, I could have gone into cardiac arrest.

"Well, I'm glad you're doing better," she says. "This little one needs you to stick around . . . We both do."

Having lost my mother young, I know the vacancy it leaves. I never want that for Simone. "Sorry, I'm staring at her," I say, watching my wide-eyed daughter take in the world around her.

"Don't apologize," Tori says. "She's yours." But I know better. We no more own our children than we own our place in the world. "I'm worried, Finn . . ."

"What's wrong? Is it Simone?"

"No, she's fine, thank God," Tori says. "It's me. I've just been feeling anxious since the election."

"Right, the election."

"Do you think we're going to be all right?" she asks. "Things just seem different . . . people at each other's throats."

I replay the election night in my mind as if to summon flashes of a nightmare, but not the nightmare Tori's talking about. "It's only four years," I say. "We can survive four years, right?"

"I guess so," she says. "If I weren't breastfeeding, I would've made my home in a margarita pitcher that night." She laughs as if to vanquish her worry.

I imagine Simone in four years, having graduated from babble and broken sentences to opinions and sayings, asserting independence, learning things about the world. By then, will I be a better father, perhaps a husband to Sarada?

"We're loving the apartment, by the way." Tori's pitchy voice frees me from my fog. "Thanks again for the deposit."

"I need to take some time to see it. Maybe when I get back from France?"

"That would be nice," she says. "So you'll be gone a few months?"

"Yes," I say. An older black man, dark-skinned, dressed in a suede jacket and starch-stiffened khakis, passes by. He walks alongside a woman of analogous complexion and cascading salt-and-pepper dreadlocks trussed in a rainbow-colored scarf. As black men often do, he nods—a silent acknowledgment that says, "I see you, we're the same." The woman looks at Tori. Her eyes widen with dejection, then fall somber. She tugs on the man's arm, and they pick up their pace down the rolling path.

"That happens sometimes," Tori says, trying not to show injury. It's a look that yearns for a rationale, but some things are inconceivable for her. She'll never understand the energy that exists between black folks, the intangible connection that lies in our storied past. Some, like my father, will see Simone's existence as an affront to that history.

"Sometimes it's going to be hard," I say. "For you, but especially for Simone. She'll need to know who she is . . ."

Tori looks at me, my words weighing heavy on her face, and I realize she arrived at this conclusion long ago. "I know," she says. "Is it OK if I text you pics of Simone while you're away? She's changing every day, looking more like you."

"I'd like that very much." I crouch before Simone, lean in, and kiss her forehead. "I'll miss you," I say. She reaches for me and wraps her fingers around my thumb.

"Feels great, doesn't it?" Tori asks as I stroke Simone's tiny hand.

"It's magical," I say, not wanting to let go. If there were a way to bottle this moment, I would.

My cell vibrates, alerting me to a meeting. "I should go . . . need to see a friend before my flight."

"For sure," Tori says, ambivalent. I feel certain something else is happening under the surface. "We'll see you when you get back." I kiss Simone one last time. Tori looks on with a smile. I walk the path back to the Falcon, get in the car, and call Sarada. It's night in France, but not too late to hear her voice.

She answers: "Trevor?"

"Hey, babe," I say. "How are you?"

"Just about to sleep . . . You all packed?"

"Good to go," I say, looking at my suitcase in the back seat. "Meeting Pop's Realtor at five. Then it's off to LAX."

Before meeting with the Realtor, I plan to see Munoz. It's a weekly occurrence that Sarada doesn't know about because I'm afraid she wouldn't approve.

"All right," she says. "Straight to the airport."

"Straight to the airport," I repeat. "No stops."

"Can't wait to see you . . ."

"I'll call you before I board . . . I love you."

"I love you, too," she says before ending the call.

———

The prison's visitation room is decorated with tinsel and Santa Claus cutouts taped to the walls. An artificial tree is positioned in the center, surrounded by gift bags and wrapped boxes for children. It's the tenth annual toy drive at the California Institution for Women. Such a celebration should bring cheer, but the anguish on the inmates' faces is palpable.

"You think they'll come for Christmas?" I ask Munoz as she sips from a generic carton of milk. Her navy jumpsuit is as insipid as the utilitarian uniforms we wore in the police academy.

"I don't want them seeing me in here," she says, looking around at other inmates sitting across from loved ones and attorneys. "Not much reason for them to come anyway. I promised Rodrigo I'd stay out of their lives."

"You agreed to that?"

"That was part of the deal," she says. "I sign the divorce papers and keep away from the kids." She drops her elbows on the steel table. "In exchange, he gave me the information we needed on Hector."

"Sally . . . I don't know what to say."

"Your pity is the last thing I need right now."

"But they're your kids," I say. "He can't do that."

"It's done—no point in crying over spilled milk," she says.

"I'm sorry, Sally."

Munoz shrugs as if to shake off defeat. "Any new pictures? Let's see that angel." I remove my phone, search the photos, and show her a picture of Simone in a reindeer outfit looking unbothered on a mall Santa's lap. "Now, that's precious," she says.

I put the phone back in my pocket, wanting to say something that'll lift Munoz's spirits but knowing that words are moot, given the time she's facing. She looks to the room's rear, where Yolanda sits with a suited man. "I still can't believe they stuck you in here with her," I say.

"The judge's parting gift . . . the cherry on top of a fifteen-year sentence."

"Has she tried anything?" I ask.

"You mean to get at me?" Yolanda stares at Munoz and me with the same level of contempt that Boston held when the room was burning around us. "Not yet," Munoz says with a sigh, like a confrontation is imminent. She leans in, lowering her voice. "I'm not going to make it in here, Finn."

"It's two months until your next court date . . ."

"You know what I mean," she says, her hands fidgety. "I won't die in here. Do you understand that?"

"I'm working on it."

"I know, Finn," she says, looking to the clock mounted above the exit—it's a quarter to four p.m. "But I can't afford any of the attorneys you've sent my way."

"I'm going through Bergman's Rolodex. I'll find the right one."

Munoz tugs at the milk's cardboard flap until it slips from her hand and falls to the floor. "Shit," she says, scrambling to pick it up and keep milk from spilling. The commotion attracts the attention of a guard. The double-chinned man stares at her sternly, neck swelling like a bullfrog's. Munoz sets the carton on the table. I study the man. Malevolence emanates from him, causing Munoz to straighten her back like a schoolgirl fearing detention. "I'm going to make a deal," she says, cringing under the guard's gaze.

"What kind of deal?"

"I know who Cassandra's supplier is," she says. "It's what I've got on her, and the feds are willing to work with me."

Munoz lied about not knowing the supplier. She's been sitting on a gold mine of information. "Are you sure you want to do that?"

"What, inform on that bitch?" she asks. "What other choice do I have? I did what you said. Turned over the money, and I'm still facing fifteen. The DA wants to make an example of me."

"Cassandra's dangerous."

"Look around," she says. "Do you know what they do to ex-cops in here? And protection doesn't come cheap. I should have run like Boston."

"And be a fugitive, Sally? Come on . . ."

"Hell, she came close to getting away, didn't she?"

"Close only counts in horseshoes, remember?"

"Well, she had something to come back for. I don't."

"What about your kids?" I ask. "Cassandra's sure to have intel on them and your ex-husband."

"Federal witness protection for my family. And they'll set me up with a new identity once I'm out. If the case sticks and Cassandra does time, I can see daylight in a year or two."

"You know it's never that simple . . ."

"It beats rotting in here," she says.

"I'm just trying to look out for you."

"I've been thinking," she says. "When you get back from France, you shouldn't come to see me anymore."

"Why?"

"It's not good for you or me. Save your gas."

"Sally, don't be like that. I want to help."

"Help?" she asks. "I'm in prison. You get that? There's not a damn thing you can do by coming up here every week."

"Then tell me what I can do."

"Look, you've been good to me, but I got it from here."

"Let's wrap it up," the guard announces loudly. "Five more minutes."

"You should go," Munoz says.

"I have a few more attorney referrals for you," I say. "Can I at least send them your way?"

"Don't bother."

"You can still appeal. Don't give up, Sally."

"Easy for you to say. You're on the outside." Munoz stands up and waves to the guard. "I'm done!" The guard approaches, shackles her wrists, and latches his fat hand on to her arm. "I mean it, Finn. Don't come back."

The guard walks Munoz across the room, where she's taken into a hallway, a fluorescent conduit to a realm of suffering I'm fortunate not to know. I understand now that Munoz sacrificed everything for Riley. Not because she was in love with him but because she thought she owed him. She needed to prove herself a loyal partner, matching the destruction of any perverse love affair.

I look to Yolanda, who's still staring. I get up to leave, believing it's the last time I'll see my old partner.

———

Pop's condo's been cleared out. I put his personal effects in a storage facility down the street, along with his table and chairs, TV stand, dresser, and bed frame. The couch and coffee table were taken away by junk haulers after the Salvation Army didn't accept them.

"It'll have to come up," Marjorie says, staring at the oval bloodstain where Clyde Coley died. She's a tall brunette, spry with confidence, wearing a cheetah-print blouse.

"Yes," I say. "I'll have it taken care of."

"We'll need to disclose someone died here," she says, looking away from the bloodstain, clearly uncomfortable. I wonder if it's the first time in her Realtor career she's listed a home where a homicide occurred.

"I understand."

"May I ask what happened?"

"Home invasion."

"My goodness," she says. "I'd never expect that in this neighborhood."

"Will it affect the listing?"

She giggles kindly at my naive query. "Not in this market. Your father should expect at least one million, give or take. I must ask, though: Does he have anything against investors? Sometimes my clients prefer selling to a family rather than those looking to turn a quick profit."

"He's not the sentimental type."

"Well, I think you should prepare for quite a few high offers . . ."

I hear shuffling in the hall and notice an older woman with radiant brown skin and sunglasses standing in the doorway. She walks into the condo with purpose, and I presume she's an investor looking to snatch up the unit before it hits the market. "Excuse me?" she asks.

"The open house isn't for a week, ma'am," I say, giving her a once-over. She's well dressed: a chic blouse and blazer, tapered jeans, and pumps. "You'll have to hold your offer until then."

"I'm not here about any open house," she says. "I'm looking for the owner."

"The owner?"

"Shaun Finnegan."

"He isn't available. What's this pertaining?"

"I drove from Nevada to see him," she says. "I'd rather speak to him directly. Where might I find him?"

"That's not possible, ma'am. You're welcome to give me the message, and I can pass it along to him."

"All right." She removes her sunglasses, revealing cinnamon eyes. "It's about our son . . . He's missing."

I breathe in and slowly exhale—controlled, like Dr. Angell taught me. Thoughts burrow and weave through my mind, each competing to be heard. I struggle to keep them straight, but one phrase screeches loud and clear from the darkness.

We only court disaster.

About the Author

Photo © 2020 Stanley Wu

Aaron Philip Clark is the author of the novel *Under Color of Law* and a screenwriter from Los Angeles. In addition to his writing career, he has worked in the film industry, higher education, and law enforcement. Learn more at www.aaronphilipclark.com.